*Man
in Motion*

Man in Motion

Michael Mewshaw

RANDOM HOUSE   NEW YORK

To George P. Garrett,
Dr. Herbert Schaumann,
and my Mother

What we call the beginning is often the end
And to make an end is to make a beginning.
The end is where we start from. (. . . . .)

We shall not cease from exploration
And the end of all our exploring
Will be to arrive where we started
And know the place for the first time.

"Little Gidding"
T. S. ELIOT

*Man
in Motion*

Chapter 1

"Time, Mr. Murdock, that's . . ."

"Hawley."

"Pardon?"

"Mr. Hawley. My mother and I don't have the same last name."

"I see." Leaning back in the swivel chair, Dr. Wolter shifted his weight from one fleshy buttock to the other, and his un-buttoned hound's-tooth jacket parted to expose an ample belly. "She never told me that."

"How much longer will she have to stay?"

"That's hard to say."

"Later than Christmas?"

"Yes. She may be here until spring."

"Oh God."

"Time is the only cure. Time and attention."

"But I don't have that much time, Doctor."

With lazy grey eyes the doctor stared at Walker Hawley, who was straining to hold his rail-like body firm against the agitation of his bones. Tall and spare, the young man fidgeted as if his skeleton were slicing him in half. "You're not the one who has to stay," Dr. Wolter said at last.

There was a sigh. "I know."

"Although I suppose your mother would like you to." Somehow he made this sound like a question.

"I guess she would."

"As a matter of fact, she's often told me she doesn't want to leave Oak Knoll, because then you'll leave home again."

"Jesus Christ, I'm twenty-six, and . . ."

"Have you been away from home often?"

"When I was in the Army. Then college."

"After that?"

"Weekends. Vacations. Just . . . just trips."

"Your mother makes you sound like a perpetual motion machine. She says you've been in every state."

"That's not true. Never Hawaii."

"Alaska?"

"Yes."

"Sounds to me like you've run around quite a bit."

Walker's voice rose, "I didn't run. I," then, in the light of Dr. Wolter's dispassionate eyes, faltered, ". . . drove. Like I said, just trips."

"And now you plan to take another?"

"This time I'm not coming back." He stirred uneasily, as if afraid his shanks would cut through the upholstery.

"I see. And you want to know what I think?"

"Yes. Before I leave I want to know if it's all right."

Dr. Wolter's eyebrows jackknifed. "That's for you to decide, Mr. Hawley."

"I mean, will it hurt Mom? It's hard for me to tell. I don't even know what's wrong with her."

For a moment the doctor's eyes roved about the room. A small, cheerful cubicle. Walls buttercup-yellow. Green carpet. A couch, of course, but it looked as if no one had ever laid back his head there and let go. Probably they sat, like Walker, in this uncomfortable armchair, bent away from the greasy blueprint of unsteadier heads that had fallen and spilled the muddled matter of their minds..

"What's wrong with her?" Walker pressed.

"That's not easy to say."

"I'm not asking for a complete analysis. I just want to know how far gone she is."

The eyes swooped down from the ceiling. "She's not 'far gone.' Not at all. From what I've heard in the last two months, I don't think there's anything—given time—that we can't handle. True, she is a bit neurotic. Well, actually a little more than a bit, but that's not uncommon these days. She's had a hard life. She's tired and a little depressed."

4

"Yes, I know. But what can be done? And what exactly is the difference between being psychotic and simply neurotic?"

Dr. Wolter laughed. "I don't think I could *exactly* tell you. It's not a simple matter. But I know a definition that might help. Neurotics build castles in the air. And psychotics live in them."

The doctor laughed again, but Walker, still troubled, interrupted. "Where do the neurotics live?"

"What?"

"The neurotics. Where do they live?"

The doctor's eyes, now stern, seemed to be passing new judgment on him. "Are you serious, Mr. Hawley?"

"Yes."

"Hmm. I guess you could say the neurotic has no place to live in peace. He's in a state of permanent dislocation, one foot on earth, the other groping in the thinnest air. Does that make things clearer?"

"Unfortunately, yes."

Something creaked. The chair? Walker's slender frame? The doctor appeared to be nervous himself and stood up. "I'm glad you stopped by, Mr. Hawley. Having met you may help me with your mother."

"I hope so," he mumbled in a voice devoid of hope.

"Your mother tells me you're a writer."

Now Walker stood up. At six-three he was much taller than the doctor but at least twenty pounds trimmer. "An aspiring one."

"Published?"

"One short story."

"Wonderful. Where?"

"It was reprinted last year in an anthology called *Best Short Stories on Campus.*"

"I'll have to remember that."

They shook hands then and started for the door, where Dr. Wolter, after a moment's hesitation, gave him a feeble clap on the back and told him not to worry. Her condition wasn't serious. She simply needed rest. That was all. And it would take time. That was everything.

"Before you go, you will let me know, won't you? And, of course, your mother, too."

"Yes. I'm going over to see her now. I plan to leave the Monday after Thanksgiving."

"Is that so? Well, good luck. And just between the two of us, I think this might be good for her."

"And me."

The doctor nodded.

As Daddy Dick never tired of saying, Oak Knoll didn't look like a sanitarium, but rather a private estate, or a country club. Quiet, of course. Yet not that sad hush of hospitals. The dread of noise at deathbeds. Here the air crackled with tension, like the silence on a putting green. Strung tight between lingering hope and imminent despair.

The buildings were white, always freshly painted, and in the distance a split-rail fence surrounded the rolling hills. Beyond it stood a forest where now that the leaves had fallen, another fence, this one of chain link, eight feet high, could be seen through the naked branches. Over the rise a road led to Baltimore, and from there to Washington, Cottage City, and home.

The fields were brightly freckled with unraked leaves, and through them several dozen patients, dressed in blue and white striped robes, followed well-worn paths, strutting like automatons. Some walked in small groups or pairs, but most were alone, eyes down, hands clasped behind them, preoccupied with the metronomic motion of their legs. Others, sheathed in woolly blankets, faces tilted to the pale November sun, lay on lawn chairs next to the main building.

Only a mad nun, still in her habit but divested of rosary beads, which might have served as a noose, left the paths and fumbled among the fallen leaves, as if searching for gold, brown, and purple medallions with which to catechise her imaginary pupils, and teach them God's grandeur. It was rumored she'd been caught in the boys' lavatory of St. John's parochial school, rinsing the private particulars of a second-grader.

She waved to Walker, and he waved back, but his mind was far away. In part, of course, on Mom, but also on the short story, "Drowning Voices," he'd written two years ago. And on the ones he hadn't been able to write since. On the abortive sketches and descriptions in his notebook. On the openings, end-

6

ings, and middles which were still locked in his brain. With only a short story to his credit, he wasn't a writer at all. Just barely an aspiring one. And "Drowning Voices" seemed almost like a mistake, a cruel one at that, for it'd made him think a career in writing lay ahead. Yes, a mistake, an accident. A light that had blazed for an instant, then gone out, leaving him with a glimmering memory, and dissatisfaction with darkness. Now he no longer wondered whether he could do it again but, instead, how he'd done it in the first place.

He thought, also, of his name. Matthew Walker Hawley. Commonly mistaken for a Murdock. And he remembered a time nineteen years ago when on his first day of school he'd learned the difference.

On that summery September morning he woke at six, watched Daddy Dick shave, and went downstairs with him to breakfast. Together they sat at the kitchen table, while Mom cooked three eggs and six sausages for Daddy Dick, and one of each for Walker. Then, when he'd finished the sport page, Daddy Dick folded the *Washington Post* and gave Walker a rap on the head.

"So, you little bugger, you're starting school today. Trying to get ahead of your old man. Well, let me tell you something," he said, doling him another playful rap and pointing to the toe of his work shoe. "See this foot? Size twelve. You give any trouble to the Sisters, and you'll get a stiff boot in the ass. Understand?"

"Yessir."

But both of them were grinning, for Mom dished out all the needed punishment. And some that wasn't needed, too.

"Let him finish his breakfast," she said. "He'll be late, and so will you."

"Okay, Mina." He gave her cheek a kiss, Walker's arm a pinch, and lumbered out the back door.

"Try to come home sober, for once."

Bang! The screen door slammed, and the pickup truck spun gravel from the driveway against the house.

Walker finished his egg, gagged, washed away the gummy taste with a mouthful of milk, and went upstairs. But after brushing his teeth and putting on his school uniform—maroon gabardine trousers, a white shirt, its collar stiff and cold as a knife blade, and a tie which Daddy Dick had knotted the night before—he felt the yolk oozing its way back up. Dashing to the toilet, he vomited in the sink. He wasn't sick, just excited, and so, after he'd brushed his teeth a second time, he went to the door of Mom's bedroom and waited for her to finish dressing.

As always she was beautiful, short and slender, except in the belly where a baby had been growing for seven months. Before Christmas he'd have a brother or a sister. She was brushing her hair. It was auburn, she'd told him, and had a soft shine like the slip she was wearing. Suddenly she stopped and pressed both hands to her stomach.

"Come here, Walker. Put your hand on Mommy's belly."

Through the white nylon it was hard and slippery.

"Do you feel it?"

Troubled, he forced a tentative grin and shook his head.

"There! Now you feel it, don't you?"

Her stomach moved. A small tremor under his small fingers.

"It's the baby kicking."

"Yes," he said, still grinning. "It's like a little rabbit."

Before they left the house, Mom handed him a notebook with a picture of Hopalong Cassidy on the front, and a plastic case containing a pencil, a sharpener, and a ruler.

"I want you to be a good boy today," she said, straightening his tie. "Don't give the nuns any trouble. Remember what your father said."

Then, taking his hand, she led him to St. James School seven blocks away.

First-graders were sent with their parents to the cafeteria, a long, ill-lit room full of yellow formica tables that smelled faintly of sour milk. For a moment Walker felt he might throw up again, but drawing a deep breath, he swallowed, and tried to stand still while Mom talked with a nun.

"I'm Mina Murdock, and my boy, Walker, is in first grade this year."

"Isn't that wonderful? He'll be in Sister John Patrick's class." The nun smiled through rimless glasses which made her right eye appear larger and brighter than her left. "Mrs. Murdock, if you'll fill in these papers, he can go up to his room."

When Mom finished them, the nun said, "Now may I see Walker's birth and baptismal certificates?" And after a glance, started to mark the registration form, when suddenly her un-plucked brows knitted. "Excuse me, Mrs. Murdock, I believe there's been a mistake. You've written Matthew Walker Murdock, but on both certificates the last name is Hawley."

"What's wrong, Mom? Can't I get in?"

"Go over next to the wall. I have to talk to Sister." Her face was nearly the color of her hair.

"If you're his guardian, it's a simple matter to . . ."

"He's mine," she snapped.

"In that case, I . . ." Nervously the nun shuffled the papers, as if hoping to find in them an escape from her embarrassment. Walker, who'd gone only to the end of the table, heard her murmur, "If his name's Hawley, he'll have to be registered that way."

"The name's going to be changed to Murdock. This'll just confuse him."

"I'm sorry, but we're . . ."

"Mom, my name's Walker Murdock, isn't it?" he called.

"Did you hear me? I told you to go over to the wall, and I meant it."

"You can speak to Mother Superior or Father Relihan," said the nun, "but I don't think it'll help. It's a state law. A child must be enrolled according to the name on his birth certificate."

Letting the tablet and pencil case crash to the floor, Walker raced to his mother, and wrapping his arms around her thick waist, said, "It's okay. I don't want to go to school anyway. Let's go home."

She took him by the shoulders and pushed him away. "I'm not going to tell you again. Get over to the wall while I'm talking to Sister."

Standing against the wall, he could hear nothing, and because of his tears, see little, but he knew who he was. If nothing else, he knew his name. Why wouldn't they let him into school?

At last Mom came and silently led him upstairs to Room 15A. Empty-handed, having left the tablet and pencil case in the cafeteria, he followed.

That first day of class lasted two hours. Roll wasn't called, rules weren't enforced, and the first-graders were allowed to color and talk until Sister John Patrick told them they could go home. Even though still confused, Walker felt better now that things had worked out and he'd been let into school. When he found Mom waiting outside, he said, "I liked it."

"Good." Without looking at him, she took his hand, and as they walked home, began to speak with a brittle quickness, just as she did when she talked to grownups on the telephone. The words skated after each other, fast and dizzy as water bugs on a pond, but not one followed what had gone before. If this was an explanation, he couldn't understand it, and so interrupted the tireless chase of words to ask, "What do you mean?"

"Aren't you listening?" Her hand tightened. "I said your father's in San Francisco."

"But when did he go? I saw him this morning."

"Not him. Not Dick. I mean your *real* father. The one whose name is Hawley. That's your name, too."

Walker's eyes began to cloud. "If Dad . . . if Dick's not my father, aren't you my real mother?"

"I'm your mother." But from her weary and worried voice the tenderness had disappeared. "Your father and I got a divorce when you were a baby. That's what people do when they don't like each other any more. It's nothing to worry about. But you'll have to get used to people calling you Hawley."

"Hawley." He turned the word in his mind. "I don't like it."

"It's your name," she insisted, squeezing his fingers.

"But what about Murdock?"

With a jerk at his arm, she brought him to a stop and whirled him around. "I'm going to tell you one more time. Dick and I are trying to get your name changed to Murdock, but until then, you're going to be called Hawley. That doesn't sound too hard, does it?"

It didn't sound hard, but it sounded wrong, and each time he said it, his belly tightened. That night, looking into the bathroom mirror, he repeated it again and again, struggling to match the strange name with the familiar face. Even the next day, walking to school, he whispered to himself, "I'm Matthew Walker Hawley. My father's in San Francisco. His name is Hawley, too." But when the classroom door shut behind him, his mind went blank and he couldn't remember who he was. He

10

only knew he wasn't Walker Murdock. That's who he used to be. Now he was . . .

As Sister John Patrick called roll, each student answered, "Here." Kevin Kernan? Here. James Riordan? Here, Peter Libernini? Here. Chester Oshkowsky? Here. Idalo Amatucci? Here. Everyone here. No matter how strange their names, they knew them. Yet Walker couldn't remember.

"Has everyone been called?" Sister asked.

Walker raised his hand.

"What's your name, young man?"

"I . . . it used to be . . . I don't know."

The class laughed, and Jimmy Riordan, who lived next door to him, called out, "He knows. Everybody does. He's Walker Murdock."

"No, I'm not," said Walker tearfully. "That's who I used to be. Now I'm somebody else. My father lives in San Francisco."

"That's a lie," shouted Jimmy. "He lives on Whittier Street."

Sister John Patrick banged her desk with a ruler. "Class, quiet down immediately. And you, young man, tell me your name, or go to Mother Superior's office."

When Walker still couldn't answer, she glanced again at her roll book. "Are you Matthew Hawley?"

"Yes," he said, but the name released the tears he'd been fighting to hold back.

"Well, young man, we'll make sure you don't forget again." With a red felt-tipped pen she scribbled on a filing card, moved down the aisle on a swirling cloud of black petticoats, her rosary beads clicking against each desk, and pinned the square of cardboard to Walker's shirt pocket. "Matthew Walker Hawley is my name. If I can't remember it, I'm the one to blame."

Mom had tried, but never could keep her promise. Walker's name wasn't changed back, and he'd remained a Hawley among Murdocks because his father—the mysterious Matthew Hawley in San Francisco—threatened to cut off his support payments. Then soon afterward he received a letter from the strange man, along with a photograph of his new wife, Tanya, and of himself standing in a redwood grove.

In that snapshot Tanya looked tall, limber, and willow-waisted, but smiled only with her wide mouth, while on the surface of her faded eyes fear and uncertainty sought to hide behind long blond lashes. Although her breasts were full and her hips flared nicely in a pair of slacks, his father seemed to look at her with something like disdain. After six years of marriage they had no children. Yes, the Hawley eyes were a hard, cruel blue on this man, and drooping mustaches did nothing to soften the lines of his unkind smile. No doubt it was the contrast of those eyes—hard blue against soft grey—which led Walker to wish, even before he met them, that he were related to the woman, and not to the man.

For months after this he referred to his stepfather as Dick, but when Nancy was born, Mom asked Walker to start calling him Daddy again. After all, she reasoned, he was the only father he had ever known. But with an unexplained reluctance, which had nothing to do with the depth of his feeling for Dixon Murdock, Walker compromised and called him Daddy Dick. Later Nancy, and then his stepbrother, Ben, followed his example, and the slow hulking man became Daddy Dick to everyone, father to no one.

Walker had gone from the clinic to Levering Hall, the largest building in the compound, where the lobby was paneled in knotty pine and furnished with sturdy tables and chairs constructed by patients in the woodworking shop. On the walls were pictures, also done by patients, of ducks on ponds, geese on the wing, cows in cornfields, and schooners under full sail. High French windows led to a terrace, giving a view of the grounds, the mechanically strolling patients, and the mad nun.

In the bright, pleasant room, only the switchboard nurse looked out of place. Stout and well-muscled, she sat like a bulldog, watching everyone who came or went. On Walker's first visit she'd said loudly, "Sure, you can go upstairs and see her. We don't keep them in cages." With a curt nod to her he passed into the elevator.

Alone in the lift, he felt his heart sink as the tight blue box ascended with the sound of greased gears. It had been two weeks since his last visit, and Mom would be sure to mention this, or, worse yet, pointedly ignore it. Not the best day to tell her he was leaving. This time for good. Thanksgiving on the way, and Christmas an insistent specter at the horizon. He'd have to be careful not to rouse Mom, who when crossed was like a live wire, crackling, haphazard, full of hidden danger.

Out of the elevator and down the hall, his footsteps faltered. Up here things weren't so cheerful. The country club atmosphere, save for brass fire extinguishers mounted like tarnished trophies at either end of the corridor, was replaced by a pungent antiseptic which killed off any scent of turf or wood smoke Walker might have carried in on his clothes. The tile, too, seemed brittle, forbidding, its pattern an explosion of blacks, greys, and greens. Vomit-proof because it looked so much like vomit itself. Somewhere a door opened on the sound of a man's moronic laughter.

"You hold him, Lonny. I'll get a nurse. Don't let him swallow his tongue."

A woman with hair like a pad of Brillo passed him as he inched his way toward Mom's room. She would know. Some way she'd be able to tell he'd seen Grandmother Hawley. This was his last thought before he knocked.

"Come in."

For some reason he felt compelled to knock again.

"Who is it?"

"Walker."

"Come in." This time the voice was glacial.

Wearing bra, underpants, and slip she stood in front of the sink shaving her underarms. Her body was no mystery to Walker —she'd always been immodest—and so he noticed at once that she'd lost weight. The brassiere was wrinkled with emptiness. Her backbone ran like a notched stick beneath her pale skin. Under her eyes the deep rings ran wet with tears she couldn't hide. She looked older than he remembered, the short auburn hair now lost to lusterless streaked henna.

"I hope this visit doesn't interfere with your busy schedule." She went for the jugular vein.

"I don't have a schedule."

She brought the razor down hard on her left armpit, making a dry, grating sound. "No. You're a foot-loose bachelor, aren't you? Plenty of time and money to toss away while you're living in my house rent-free."

"Don't you use lather?" he couldn't help asking.

13

"I'm used to pain by now." Down came the razor again.

Let her shave without lather, he thought, as his eyes sought a safe place in this sad room with its single unmade bed and gun-metal bureau whose top had taken on the stark limits of her life. A snapshot of Nancy, Ben, and him at Nancy's wedding. Punch glasses raised high. Ben's eyes red and glaring from the flashbulb. The look of a cheerful werewolf. Next to the photo a hairbrush and comb, a carton of Pall Malls, a ballpoint pen, and a set of green chipped-glass rosary beads, blessed by the Pope, which Walker had bought for her in Montreal. On the night table her reading glasses marked a page in the latest issue of *Cosmopolitan*.

"Why did you come?" she asked, rinsing the razor.

"To see you. Why else?"

"Yeah. Why else?" In the mirror above the sink, she looked at him, her first-born and only blue-eyed, dark-haired son. He bore her maiden name and little else, save for his fair skin. "I don't suppose it occurred to you I'm here every day. Waiting. Alone."

Walker leaned against the door.

"Well, did it?"

"Did it what?" he asked wearily.

"Occur to you I was waiting for you?"

"For Christ's sake, I'm here. Will you put on some clothes and give me a minute's peace?"

At last her face went soft as putty, and she began to cry. "Oh, please, Walker, don't yell at me."

"I'm not yelling. I just don't want you to catch a cold on top of everything else."

She pulled on her robe, and sniffling into a Kleenex, sat at the edge of the bed. Walker took a chair facing her, and now that she was crying, felt almost comfortable. Her coolness had made them both uneasy, but with her wailing and him feeling rotten and guilty as hell, they were at last on familiar ground. The scene was timeless, changeless, and since he knew all its variations, it didn't surprise him to see her choke back the tears and murmur, "I'll be all right." Then, bravely forcing a smile, "No matter what, I'm glad you came."

"Did you know I was coming?" he asked.

"Yes. Daddy Dick called and told me. But I thought you'd be

here later. I wanted to fix myself up. How is he? Has he been taking care of himself?"

"He's fine."

"I know he's sick with worry. He can't understand I've had a little attack of the nerves. I need rest. That's all." She coughed up another sob, but caught herself before losing control. "And how's the house? Clean, I hope."

"I haven't noticed."

"If things get too dirty, you can always call on Nancy."

"Daddy Dick and I'll manage."

"Now, Walker," her voice quavered, "I don't want you and Nancy to fight while I'm here. Settle your differences for the time being."

"We don't have any differences," he said, then realized what a lie that was. "Have you been outside? It's beautiful up here. Like a country club," he parroted Daddy Dick.

"Yes, but it's lonely, and sometimes I get so depressed, I just sit and stare out the window. At night the nurse gives me a pill, but I don't sleep. I lay here for hours thinking back to when you and Nancy and Ben were little and we used to walk out to Fort McHenry to see the clock made of flowers. I even think about Matthew, and wonder what would have happened if we hadn't gotten a divorce." She shook her head. "He was such a . . . such a shit. I remember a time he sneaked back into town right before I married Daddy Dick, and said he wanted . . . a kiss for old time's sake and I let him . . ." Her shoulders slumped forward and she started to cry again. "Oh, Walker, I'm afraid I'll never get out of here."

Unable to hold out any longer, he went to her, and putting an arm around her, said, "Don't be silly. You'll be better in no time." But this was all he would allow himself.

She patted his hand and smiled—the change of expressions so sudden it jarred Walker. "You're right. I'm going to look on this as a long vacation."

Wary of her and of this rubber-faced facility of mood, he got up and went back to his chair. "Yes, the important thing is to get better."

"I'm trying, Walker. All the doctors and nurses will tell you that. I'm not going to let this thing whip me. I'll be home to put the turkey in the oven Christmas Eve. You can count on it."

"Now don't get your hopes up. I know you're trying, but it takes time."

"That's what Dr. Wolter says, but then he goes on and wastes half the day asking me about my dreams. How's that going to help my nerves? There's only one dream I remember anyhow. I've had it half a dozen times. It's about you, and you're dying, but I can't get to you in time, because Daddy Dick won't get up off his ass from in front of the TV and take me to you. That sounds like real life, doesn't it? Him dead drunk in front of the television, watching a football game? Well, doesn't it?"

"A lot of men like football."

"Yes, but they don't drink a case of beer every Saturday afternoon. You know, sometimes I think that's how I got sick. From all those times I saw him pass out, and the nights I worried that he'd burn the house down with his cigarettes, and the days I was stuck there with no way to get out. Sometimes I could sense it coming, and I knew I was going right out of my mind. But I guess it doesn't help to talk about it. Not with you. It's probably boring. Why don't you tell me about yourself? How's work?"

"Same as always. Eight straight hours of boredom and aching feet." He got up and walked to the window, leaning his hands on the ledge, as if ready to vault through the glass. The sun had fallen behind the hills, but in the orange off-light the patients still prowled the silent grounds.

"You've got nobody to blame but yourself. Jesus, Mary, and Joseph, the very idea of it! A college graduate working as a cashier in Saveway. Why I remember your Uncle Raymond saying . . ."

He let her talk, hoping she'd wear herself out before he told her why he'd come. First he had to work himself up to it, and struggle to hold back for a moment the cold monosyllables which would fall like drops of poison to her heart. He did care. It wouldn't be easy for him to leave. Although it should have been. But it was impossible to explain all this to Mom. Anything but stark, merciless, and irreducible facts would only lead them on a blind and bitter chase they'd often run before.

At last, still facing the windowpane, fearful of any abrupt movement, he said, "I know. You're right. And that's why I'm quitting."

"Quitting? What?" Already a trace of hysteria had tightened in her throat.

He turned to her. "Didn't you just say I could do better?"

"Yes, but . . . but quit your job, just like that? You ought to think it over."

"I have thought it over, Mom, for days. Weeks." Coming back to the chair, he took her hands, which were cold and tense as sparrow claws. Her lips had begun to quiver. "And I've decided I've got to do it. I've got to give myself a chance to . . ."

"Do what? What chance? Walker, what are you saying?"

He held the hands tighter, trying to warm them, but instead his fingers started to freeze. "I plan to quit my job and go out and live on the West Coast. It's something I . . ."

Angrily she pried loose her hands. "Shut up. I don't want to hear another word. Haven't you had enough vacations, and trips, and running around? You'd better grow up and get a brain in . . ."

"Mom, it's not a vacation. I'm going to San Francisco to work. I'm going for good. Don't you see I . . ."

"Didn't I tell you to stop?" She put a hand to her throat. "I can't breathe. I'm choking. Where's Dr. Wolter? Why isn't he here now? I told him this would happen. I told him as soon as I got out of Oak Knoll you'd leave again. But you, you don't even give me a chance to get out. You just leave."

"Mom, you've got Daddy Dick, and Nancy, and Ben. I'll write. You know I will. But I have to . . ."

"Who put you up to this? Matthew? Or Grandmother Hawley? Or Dede? Was it Dede? That little bitch! Don't lie to me! I hate lies."

"I'm not lying. Nobody put me up to it. I simply want to live in California."

"Why? What's wrong with Cottage City? Is it your writing? I let you fix the attic into a study. What more do you want?"

"It's not the writing. I just want to try something different. My God, I can't stay at home all my life."

"All your life? Who are you kidding? You're never home. You're free to come and go as you please. And no rent either. Show me another mother who'd . . ."

"Okay then, I want to go."

She cocked her head to one side. "What?"

"You said I'm free to come and go as I please, and I said I choose to go."

"You choose to go," she said, shaking her head. "You ungrateful, snot-nosed, wise-mouthed little pup. You choose! Who do you think you are to just choose? Look at me. Do you think I can choose?"

"Mom, I'm sorry you're here. I wish there were some way I could help. But there's not. It's a matter of time."

"Time my foot. It's you. You put me here, with all your leaving and dashing around in that damn little car of yours." She was off the bed now, hunched over him like a bird of prey.

Looking up into the dark fury of her eyes, he asked, "Wouldn't you like to see me doing what I want? Don't you want me to be happy?"

Her lips trembled, and she audibly swallowed. "Yes. You know I want you to be happy. Don't I always say that?" She flopped back on the bed. "But find a nice girl and marry. Stop running. And . . ." Voice quavering, she didn't sound convinced of her own words. Perhaps, like Walker, she knew that although as a rule she was happy when he was, if his happiness entailed leaving home, she preferred him to remain miserable in Cottage City. So the tears started once more. "I was crazy to think you'd stay and help. My mind's just not right. I'm on my last legs. Forty-nine, and already a grandmother. Put away, and forgotten now that Nancy's got a baby, and Ben's in the Army, and you're leaving the country."

"No, I'm going to California."

"Same thing," she murmured. "Sometimes I wonder why people bother to have kids. They just grow up and leave you. That's how they repay you. It happens every time, but no one learns. You're so smart, you tell me why people do that?"

"Maybe passion gets the best of them." He tried to joke her out of this malign mood.

"Very funny." Her eyes flashed anger. "Look, smart-ass, Daddy Dick and I did our best for you. Damn sight more than your own father's ever done, and . . ."

"It's got nothing to do with you or Daddy Dick. I simply want to go to San Francisco. It's beautiful. It's stimulating. It . . ."

18

"Stimulating! What you need is a boot in the ass. You've had it damned easy. Let me . . ."

Mercifully a buzzer sounded. Visiting hours were over.

"I've got to leave, but I'll be back," he said, and stood up.

"When are you leaving?" she asked in a voice suddenly small and meek.

"The Monday after Thanksgiving."

"Don't bother coming to see me again." The voice was still small, but no longer meek.

"Mom, don't be unreasonable. I . . ."

"You heard me."

Putting a hand on her shoulder, he leaned down to kiss her lips, which were cold and limp as giblets. "I'll be back."

"I told you, don't bother," she screamed. "Don't bother, you selfish bastard."

Her door slammed behind him. The elevator opened. Greased gears to the ground floor.

As the TR-3 coasted down the driveway, the patients puffed uphill toward the sanitarium, their thin, tired bodies striving for it as if for a distant but hollow goal. The ones on the terrace—those who looked like frankfurters cushioned on buns—had already been wheeled inside, for dusk was settling with a rush of cold air that sent dead leaves skittering like spiders over the asphalt. Suddenly a chill forked down Walker's spine, and thinking ahead to the promise of San Francisco, he prayed that if he failed to make it there, he could at least be spared another visit to Oak Knoll.

Chapter 2

At first, reaching open road on Washington-Baltimore Parkway, Walker felt better. He was, of course, still worried about Mom, still wondering about the future, still remembering what Grandmother Hawley had told him, and still reluctant to face Dede Clinton. But he was moving. That was the point. At seventy miles an hour nothing, except progress, seemed inevitable, and despite past history, he believed he could make it this time—get away and stay away.

But then he glanced out the window, and even speed couldn't shield him from ugliness. There were blighted acres of Baltimore, Anne Arundel and Prince George's counties, where the trees had been slaughtered, the top soil stripped away, and mounds of sucking red clay turned to the sky. Something going up? Something being torn down? Progress or defeat? Who could say? Even where the forest remained, the leaves had fallen, and in their bare upper branches the trees were threaded with ragged nests of mistletoe. Cobwebs holding old skeletons intact. The essence of summer burned to its bones. On the median strip, colorful cabbages of trash and broken beer bottles sprouted from the dead grass, while overhead a bright evening sky mocked the dull earth which was whistling and whirling like a comet toward the cold extinction of winter, carrying Walker and the TR-3 along with it. His mind might fondle its memories of palm trees and ocean beaches, ice-capped mountains and open plains, but this was where he always wound up. Maryland with its mimosa and crape myrtle bled of life, the black branches waving like evil wands in the wind. Matted straw and stumps of corn, stubble and rubbish in the fields. Yellow porch lights to kill bugs in neighborhoods where nothing else stirred.

That was the bad thing about flight—the return. And yet

Walker remained addicted to motion, to sudden trips. Short sprints down Bladensburg Road to Jerry's Hot Dog Stand. Summer drives across the Chesapeake Bay Bridge, through the brackish tangle of Kent Island, to Rehoboth Beach. Month-long hauls to Canada, Alaska, the West Coast. He liked to load the luggage rack of the Triumph, strap himself into the cockpit, and set out, alive to each crack in the concrete, to the pleasant pressure of hairpin curves, to the feel of his shoulders pressed against the bucket seat. Open to the sights, sounds, and smells of the land, it often seemed there was no asphalt beneath the tires and he and the TR-3 were racing barefoot and breathless over cool grass.

So despite the return, the reaction to motion, he persisted, moving simply to move, his heart a helium-filled balloon that often slipped its string and dragged him along for a ride.

But today, since speed and motion carried him from one sad encounter to another, he let the TR-3 idle, and thought, I'm a bastard. That was what Mom had said. And yesterday, in a drier tone, her malice aimed both at him and a dark hour in the Hawley history, Grandmother had implied the same. A bastard made legitimate by late vows. But when those vows were broken, where did that leave him?

Two days ago the call had caught him as he was leaving for work.

"May I speak to Matt?" asked a voice worn smooth as silver by age and constant use. He knew at once it was Jordan Oliver, Grandmother Hawley's lawyer, confidant, and companion, for the two of them alone insisted on calling him Matt. "Your grandmother would like to see you tomorrow."

Walker couldn't suppress a puzzled "Oh?" He hadn't heard from her since last year at the Christmas party. "What time?"

"Let me check." He cupped his hollow palm over the receiver, leaving in Walker's ear the sound of surf, then said, "Any time that would be convenient."

"I have to be at work by noon."

The paw formed a seashell again before Mr. Oliver said, "Mrs. Hawley suggests you skip work."

"I don't know whether I can."

"Certainly you can, Matt." He pitched his voice lower, as if to keep Grandmother Hawley from hearing, but, as Walker knew, she was standing beside him. "It's important. She's leaving for Boca Raton in a few days and wants to get this matter settled before she goes."

"Would three-thirty be okay?" asked Walker, anxious to work at least the evening shift.

"Fine, Matt. We'll be waiting."

Walker was one of few Hawleys—at least of that line that mattered to his grandmother—and the absolute last likely to produce a male heir to carry on the name. She never failed to remind him of the precious genes he carried, and over the years had grudgingly—as if fearful too much friendliness would drain his masculinity—maintained an interest in her grandson. Every year at the family Christmas party, with a frankness that embarrassed him and annoyed the others—although they tried not to show it—she reminded him, "Matt, you're a Hawley. It's a good name and we're a proud family. My money is Hawley money, you know, and I intend to leave it to a Hawley."

She was enormously rich by Cottage City standards. Or by any other standards, for that matter. And with her brownstone on Massachusetts Avenue, her palace of pink stucco in Boca Raton, and her Lincoln, driven by a Negro named Earl Warren Boggs, she was held in reverential awe by Mom, Nancy, and Ben—when, that is, the three of them weren't bitter with envy of her or resentment for Walker.

Grandmother Hawley was also generous. In her fashion. Walker couldn't remember a time he'd gone to see her when she hadn't given, or tried to give, him something. But in the end her generosity always seemed to cost more than it was worth, and therefore on Tuesday, as he drove into town, he felt reluctant, almost afraid, and tried to think of a way he might refuse her, for his grandmother's presents were usually little more than demands—personal, difficult, and confusing.

He had only to remember the annual Christmas party to know this. Each year Jordan Oliver would phone in early

December to make sure he was coming, and if Walker showed the slightest hesitation, would lower his soft, hired voice and say, "You know, Matt, your grandmother's flying in from Boca Raton just to see you. Don't disappoint her. It'd be a pretty sad party without you."

And each year it was the same. Boring and depressing. When he was a kid, Mom would instruct him how to act and what to say. "Whatever you do, don't tell them any of our business." He'd nod. He didn't even know what it was, their business. Then in the pickup truck Daddy Dick would drive him to town, drop him at the front door, and go to a bar to wait. While Walker kissed half a dozen old, nameless ladies who said, "Doesn't he look like his father?" While he shook hands with dark solemn uncles who said, "Hello, Matt," then turned back to the television. And while his unfriendly cousins ignored him completely. When gifts were exchanged, Walker invariably received two. A hundred-dollar savings bond from his grandmother, and from someone who'd drawn his name out of a hat, a professionally wrapped package containing something impersonal and sexless —a book, stationery, a gift certificate from Lord & Taylor's— for from one Christmas to the next no one, except his grandmother, could remember how old he was or what size he wore.

Toward evening of those interminable days, he'd stand at the front window and wait for Daddy Dick, but often someone else would notice the pickup and ask, "Claire, are you expecting a delivery boy? There's a truck in the driveway."

And there he'd be. Slumped behind the wheel. Somehow malevolent and three times larger than life in his green and black car coat. Eyes shaded by a Washington Senators baseball cap. Face red as a brick from weather and whiskey.

"Why," Grandmother Hawley would say, as if not quite sure, "I believe it's Mr. Murdock."

"I have to go."

"Oh no, Matt. Not yet. Won't you ask him in for a drink?"

"I think I'd better go," he'd insist, obedient to Mom's instructions. ("Don't you dare let him go into that house. I'll be damned if I'll have those Hawleys giving him liquor, then laughing at him when he leaves.")

So he'd dash out to the truck, which smelled of stale tobacco, wood shavings, and cheap bourbon.

23

was. From his grandmother there was no word at all. The silence of rage and rebuke. But the following December, Jordan Oliver made his annual call. "Your grandmother isn't getting any younger, you know." His voice became reedy and thin, as if in empathy. "You have to come, Matt. Don't you want to make an old woman happy?"

Two weeks later he was led into the library, and his grandmother—solid and impregnable in a low-cut gown of red and green brocade, her shoulders a healthy brown from a month in Boca Raton, her nails long and lacquered as claws, and her hair frosted and piled atop her head like a miter—asked him the same question.

"Of course I'd like to make you happy. If I can."

"Matt, I assure you, you can make me the happiest woman in the world if you'll enroll at the University of Virginia next fall."

"I'd like to, but I'll still be in the Army."

"No, you won't."

"Grandmother, you already tried to get me out, and it didn't work."

"You can get out by yourself. It's very simple. If you've been accepted by a university, you'll receive an early discharge. Jordan checked on this for me . . . I mean, for you."

"Hmm." In the last year he'd come to regret he hadn't gone to Berkeley or accepted the commission she'd arranged, for although he hadn't been sent to Vietnam, he'd been sentenced to a desk in Biloxi, Mississippi, which often seemed hotter, more savage, and less secure than Danang. "But I don't know if I could get in. My marks weren't . . ."

"Don't worry. There's been a Hawley at the university for nearly a century. They wouldn't dare refuse you." She reached out and took his hand. "And if you'll do this for me, Matt, I won't refuse you either. I'll pay your way, and see that you have money to spend. I know we've had our disagreements in the past, but . . ."

"Grandmother, I . . ."

"Don't apologize. There's no need to dredge up the past. Despite your childish stubbornness, I care for you, Matt, and I want you to have the best. You're a Hawley, and you deserve it. There's a whole world you've never seen. But I'm going to help you to see it and know it. Yes, you're going to discover there's a way of life different from the one you've been leading."

If nothing else, he learned this at Virginia: that there wasn't just another life, but hundreds he hadn't led and, in fact, hadn't known existed. Suddenly it seemed to him he'd spent his first twenty years in a vacuum, sealed within the ugly, high boundaries of Cottage City, and that now he'd burst out of it into a new world. He watched, listened, studied, and gradually learned. At night he stayed in his room, the radio tuned to WNEW, New York City, and submerged in a private canister of sound, read compulsively anything he could lay hands on. Through the mystery of other men's words he slowly began to work his way into his own past, to discover there not only an insecurity, but an emptiness that had to be understood as well as filled. Perhaps that was the most important, and most painful, thing he learned his first year—the need for a counterweight to life in Cottage City.

But by spring he'd also learned he didn't belong at Virginia either, and that summer, after buying the TR-3 with Grandmother Hawley's money, he started his search for a place that was like neither home nor the university. He never found this middle ground. Not that summer. Never in the ones that followed. And so the return to Charlottesville each fall became a painful rebuke, and every trip home a conscious renunciation.

Walker remained an outsider all four years at Virginia, and to his grandmother's disappointment, never pledged a fraternity or was asked into a society. Although he graduated with honors, she seemed to regret she'd wasted her money on him, while Mom was blunter and told him he'd wasted his time and turned into "a wise-mouth punk." Daddy Dick, as usual, was silent.

There were only two things that he looked back on with pleasure. Those first few months when the pace of his learning had yet to force upon him the inevitable crisis of choosing. And the short story, "Drowning Voices," which he'd written in senior year, telling of his choice. He thought then it read like a graph of his life, but in the last paragraph the young hero had gathered his belongings and, like so many of his kind, headed for the lights of a distant city, whereas after graduation Walker himself had borrowed Daddy Dick's truck, loaded it with his books and baggage, and driven back to Cottage City.

. . .

27

Now, two years later, as he drove into Washington, struggling to think how he could refuse whatever his grandmother might offer, Walker suspected his efforts would be futile, not simply because she could be so persuasive, but because she always seemed to offer what he wanted, or what he thought he would need, to find his way out of Cottage City for good.

Walker went around to the alley, but found the rear gate locked and a sign painted in foot-high letters on the fence: "The Hawleys are racist, honky pigs." When he sounded the horn, Earl Warren Boggs, wearing his winter uniform of navy blue, opened the gate leading to a driveway where his grandmother's Lincoln stood like a polished block of onyx.

"Sorry, Mista Hawley, but we been having trouble and don't dare leave the gate open no more."

"Trouble?"

Earl Warren nodded. "Bad trouble. Colored problems."

"The sign?"

"Yessir. Effie, the cook, got her boyfriend to do that sign after Miz Hawley told Effie she wasn't taking her to Florida this year."

"It's a civil war, then?"

"Something like that. When you go in, walk light. Effie's still touchy and might wallop you 'longside the head with a skillet. Miz Hawley and Mista Jordan are waiting on you in the library."

Over the crunching white gravel and up the back stairs. No sign of Effie, or anyone else, in the kitchen or dining room. The chandelier, its prisms of crystal-like angular, frozen tears, tinkled softly as he stirred the air in passing. Long polished table with basket of wax fruit, set for no one. A house without dirt, smells, shadows, and despite its age and his grandmother's claims, curiously without history. The living room, too, was empty, and Walker wondered whether it was ever used except for the Christmas party. A portrait of his grandfather, Herbert Hawley, hung over the fireplace. A slender man with blue eyes and tapered fingers that propped up a law book. When they'd buried him, he'd weighed eighty pounds, half of that in cancer cells, and those tapered fingers were stained a coffee color from tobacco.

Walker paused at the library door, heard voices he couldn't understand, and finally knocked.

"Come in."

Jordan Oliver wore a dark suit that hung limply from his shoulders as if from sharp hooks. In the last year he'd lost weight, and seemed to have shrunk an inch in height. Age was whittling him down and pounding him into the ground. But on his face he'd grown a white floss of whiskers, a beard to hide his stringy jowls.

"Hello, Matt." He offered a dry stick of a hand, then held Walker at arm's length. "My goodness, Mrs. Hawley, I think he's gotten taller."

"No, I don't believe I . . ."

"Yes, he's nearly as tall as his father. Come and give me a kiss."

Going to where she sat next to the shelves of leatherbound books, he kissed the powdered cheek she offered. Whereas Mr. Oliver had bent, shriveled, and turned grey with the years, Grandmother Hawley had grown more robust. The flowered bodice of her silk dress couldn't contain the tanned exuberance of her bosom. Wrinkled and dark cleavage, deep as the mystery of how she flourished in old age. Her nails and lips a polished pink, and her hair a new color. A beautician's mistake—although Walker couldn't have guessed what had been intended—gave it a purple tint.

"It's good to see you," she said. "Walk over to the desk and back, and let me have another look. The image of his father, don't you think, Jordan?"

"Without a doubt."

"You're both looking fine, too," he forced himself to say.

"What do you think of Jordan's beard? I say it makes him look like a billy goat." She ended with a seismic burst of laughter that shook her dewlaps.

"Very distinguished."

"Thank you, Matt." Mr. Oliver stood beside his grandmother, a hand on the back of her chair, as if posing with her for a photograph. "I'm glad someone likes it. I grew it out of dire necessity. Something had to be done before I slit my throat and bled to death." He held out his hands, which couldn't be made to stop trembling. "Shaving had gotten to be a very risky business."

"It looks good on you. But at first I thought you'd become a a hippie and painted that sign on the fence."

"That's Effie's doing," said his grandmother. "She had the

nerve to demand that I take her to Florida, or else let her live here while I'm gone. I'm having new locks put on all the doors, and the minute I leave, she's through. Out of a job and out of my house."

"Calm down, Mrs. Hawley. It's just a phase."

"I'll be damned. This time I've had it." Then, turning to Walker, "Bring a chair over from the desk, Matt, and let's have a drink."

As he sat down he noticed the smile on her face had skipped over her pale eyes, as though the lids were dead, or as if she were, just under the surface, savagely serious and waiting patiently to make her point.

"That's better," she said. "Pull a little closer and tell us how you've been."

"Fine."

"I hope you're telling the truth." There was doubt in her voice.

"Oh, you can be . . ." But then Mr. Oliver, with a decanter of whiskey, a bucket of ice, and three glasses balanced precariously on a tray, passed between them, and Walker said, "Let me help."

"No thanks, Matt. I've been pouring bourbon for Mrs. Hawley for thirty-five years, and I'm not too old for that yet."

"Careful of the carpet," she said, extending her glass. Her arm solid and brown as mahogany.

Hands shaking, he tilted the decanter and splashed out a shot. "Ice, Mrs. Hawley?"

"No. Straight."

As he served Walker, his hands made a sudden leap like startled little animals, and a few drops of liquor dribbled to the rug.

"Didn't I tell you to be careful? Now see what you've done."

To help, Walker put a hand on the old man's wrist, which felt like the fretted neck of a guitar, bones and veins thin and pliable as catgut.

"I think that does it," said Mr. Oliver. "Thanks for the assist." Then, taking up his post behind Mrs. Hawley's chair, he raised his glass. "Here's to you, Matt."

Walker barely touched the glass to his lips, knowing he had to stay sober if he hoped to stand up to his grandmother.

"How's your dear mother?" she asked.

"Fine," he said, not caring to mention Oak Knoll.

Slowly the rest of her face went as dead as the wrinkles around her eyes. "I was told the poor woman had been committed to a mental institution."

"Not committed." Walker stiffened in the chair and fought not to ask who'd told her. "The doctor said she needed a rest. She hasn't been well, and she'd developed a . . . a nervous disorder."

"Is she at Oak Knoll?"

He nodded.

"The state sanitarium?"

"Yes, but . . ."

"I've heard it's a marvelous place," said Mr. Oliver.

"She seems to like it." A soothing swallow of bourbon to calm his suddenly jangled nerves.

"What's her favorite flower, Matt?" Her head was cocked to one side as she tried to pull the appropriate expression of sympathy.

"Azaleas, I think. "

"Oh my, they'll be hard to find this time of year." Turning to Jordan Oliver, "But try to have half a dozen plants sent to Mrs. Murdock."

"Of course."

"How's the family doing without the poor dear?"

"We're all right."

"Her husband must be frantic."

"Yes, Daddy Dick's a little worried, but . . ."

"Daddy who?"

"Uh . . . Daddy . . ." Walker fumbled, wondering what he'd said wrong.

"Are you speaking of Mr. Murdock?"

"Yes, I mean Mr. Murdock." Another sip and the bourbon started to burn, bubbling like steam in his blood. But something checked his anger. Perhaps it was the sight of Mr. Oliver standing by the chair like a delicate doll that a mischosen word would shatter. Or even the urbane civility of his grandmother's voice. Those modulated tones that seemed to prevent anyone but her from speaking his mind.

"It's such a shame. The poor woman has had so much trouble in her life."

"Not much more than anyone else."

"Yes, we all have our . . ."

"But the tragic thing about her," she cut in on Mr. Oliver, "is that she always gets caught in her own traps."

"Traps?"

She smiled, gazed down at her lap or into the mystery of her cleavage, and smoothing an imaginary wrinkle from her dress, said, "Like most women—we're all so single-minded—your mother probably knows what she wants, but unfortunately she hasn't had the means to go about getting it. So she does what comes naturally to a female." Still smiling, she glanced up.

"And what's that?" Walker asked, surprised how civil his own voice sounded, for deep down his lungs ached to shout, What in hell are you trying to say?

"Oh, feminine wiles as old as the earth. You know, your mother wanted your father very badly. So badly he had to drop out of dental school and marry her. I tried to warn him. But by that time he had no choice."

The bubbles in his blood turned to ice. "No choice?"

Her mouth fell open as if she was shocked. "Your poor mother was two months pregnant when she married. Didn't you know? I haven't . . . Oh my God, Jordan." She reached for the withered hand on the back of the chair.

"Of course I knew," he lied, and finished his drink.

"I'm relieved to hear that. It was such an unfortunate mess, but a person of your intelligence can draw the obvious conclusion. People often get caught in their own traps."

"Yes."

She smiled. "Dear, dear Matt. Sometimes I think you're the only good that came of all that trouble." Then, drawing a deep breath, "But I guess there were other small favors we should be thankful for. The shock of the marriage and the quick divorce jolted your father out of his prolonged adolescence. And as for your mother we should be thankful Matthew refused to marry her in the church. He had nothing against Catholics, you understand, but thought a church wedding would make things more difficult if the marriage didn't work out. I know how important religion is to your poor mother, and it would have been such a shame if she'd been excommunicated. It must be a great comfort to her now, don't you think? Well, don't you?"

"Yes, it must be," he mumbled, telling himself it didn't matter why his parents had gotten married or divorced. But his mind seethed. He was their mistake. A trap that had sprung on the wrong person. On him.

"Where were we? Oh yes. I'm leaving for Boca Raton next week, and there's something I'd like to get settled before I go. Sit up and listen, Matt. This is important. It's about money."

"You're leaving early this year." He got up to pour himself another drink, hoping to sidetrack her.

"Yes, I can't stand winters in Washington. They seem to come earlier and earlier every year."

"It must be all that atomic testing," said Mr. Oliver.

"Jordan, don't talk like a silly old fool. We leave next Tuesday from Friendship, and Earl Warren will drive the car down to meet us. I can't put up with that long, exhausting ride any longer."

"Mr. Oliver's going along, too?"

"Yes." He gave a hollow-faced smile. "I'm almost retired now, and I thought it was time I took a little vacation."

"I'm sure Grandmother's grateful for your company."

"Hold your tongue, Matt. Don't go playing cupid with us."

"I . . ."

"Never mind. We're adults. We've talked it over. I've already buried one husband, and I don't intend to marry another sick old man."

"Matt understands," said Mr. Oliver, patting her on the shoulder.

"Yes, I suppose he does." She drew back her head to get a better look at her grandson. "He's got a good mind, just like his father. You know I have a great deal of money, don't you, Matt?"

"Yes, I . . . I assumed you . . ."

"You don't have to stutter and stammer and blush like that. Let's be honest. I *am* rich, and I'm not going to live forever. someday you stand to inherit a lot of money."

Walker looked down the tube of his glass to the bourbon which lay at the bottom like a tarnished coin.

"Look at me, Matt," she commanded, face solemn with thoughts of money and mortality. "You're my only grandson. I want to make sure you have a good life. But"— she leaned forward in the chair— "you worry us, Matt. You worry all of us."

33

"Don't worry about me. I'm happy. I couldn't . . ."

"Are you really?" she asked. "Are you really happy? Really satisfied? You can be honest with me."

"To tell the truth, I don't think much about happiness."

"Oh, Matt, don't try to fool me. How old are you?"

"Twenty-six."

"At your age your father was already married."

"Yes, and divorced."

"Don't act defensive. I'm only trying to help. What do you want to be?"

"You mean when I grow up?"

"This is no time for jokes. What do you want to do with your life?"

Twisting his hands around the glass, he said, "I'd like to do something different. Something special. I'd . . ." His voice trailed off.

"But what?"

He shrugged.

"Do you have a job?"

"Yes, I'm still with Safeway."

"Oh, Matt." She shook her head. "Why? Why Safeway? You're a brilliant boy. You're handsome. You could do anything you wanted."

"It's not a bad job."

"But why?" Her voice soared, and finally cracked. "Why spend your life putting cans and boxes on shelves?"

"That's not what I do. I'm a cashier."

"That's just as bad. Please, Matt, why?" She was straining so far forward, the wattles on her neck had stretched tight. Mr. Oliver tried to calm her, but she brushed aside his hand like a dry leaf. "Why?"

"I took the job at Safeway because I thought it'd leave me a lot of free time."

"Time to do what? To write? We were all so proud of that little story . . ."

"Short story."

"Your father said it showed promise. Why didn't you keep writing?"

Walker finished his drink and said, "I did. I tried. I worked like hell, but . . . It's not easy, you know."

34

"Nothing's easy, Matt."

When he held out his empty glass, Mr. Oliver shook another shot of bourbon from the decanter. "I know, and I still haven't given up. But sometimes I wonder if . . ."

"Don't tell me you don't have talent, because I know you do. But do you know what you don't have?"

Wearily he shook his head.

"Despite the job with Safeway, you don't have the time or the freedom, and you certainly don't have the right atmosphere. You could do anything you wanted if you had the chance. But first"— at last she sat back in the chair— "first you've got to get out of Cottage City."

"That has nothing to do with it." The anger he'd held for an hour burst out as she struck the mark.

"Just calm down and listen. I didn't say there was anything wrong with your home or with Cottage City. God knows I've never even seen the place. But if you want to be a writer, you should seek interesting places and intelligent people. Give yourself the chance to grow. What you need is experience. Doesn't that seem reasonable?"

"Yes, it does," he admitted.

"I knew you'd agree. So here's what I plan to do. I want you to have part of my money now so you can . . . can enjoy yourself, and start writing again. In the top drawer of the desk is a check for five thousand dollars. Take it. Quit your job. And go someplace better than Cottage City."

The skin at the back of his neck tightened. "And where would that place be?"

She puckered her lips, and after a pause, said, "Where do other intelligent and talented people go? Where would you go?" she asked Mr. Oliver.

His grey skin turned a transparent red as Walker glanced up at him. "Well, I tell you, Matt, if I was young and had my health . . ."

"Get to the point," she said.

"And I wasn't worried about climbing up and down all those hills, I'd . . ."

"You'd got to San Francisco," said Walker.

"That's exactly where I'd go."

"That's where all the young people are going. Think of the

atmosphere and inspiration," said his grandmother, who'd never thought of either.

"I don't suppose this has anything to do with the fact that Dad lives there?"

She looked at him with wide, wondering eyes. "After all, Matt, he is your father."

"That's what I'm told."

Her eyes flared like struck matches. One could almost smell sulphur. "I can assure you he is, and the greatest sadness in my life is that you have never gotten to know each other. My God, you haven't seen him more than six times in your life. Don't you think you owe it to yourself to get to know your own father?"

"I guess I do." But Walker had little feeling about the matter. Even after he'd visited his father that summer six years ago, he could never believe the strange man with the mustache and the hard blue eyes was anything but an acquaintance. At most, a distant relative. Certainly never as paternal as Daddy Dick. Walker had more feeling for Tanya. Sometimes so much it frightened him.

"Of course you should. So take the money and go out to see your father. Buy yourself some clothes. A car. Anything you want."

"I've got a car."

"Oh, yes. That little blue thing. Looks dangerous to me. But you will go, won't you, Matt?"

Stirring uneasily, he wanted to sit up straight and, kindly as he could, tell her no. He couldn't go. But her offer had gotten to him, and it took great effort to murmur, "What about Mom? I couldn't run out on her."

"What can you do for her if you stay? It may be years before she can be let out."

"Wait a minute. She's not a psycho. She . . ."

"Matt, please. Of course she's not. But it takes time to care for these little nervous disorders. And at your age time is precious. Don't let it slip away. Besides, she has her other children."

"Not really. Nancy's married and has a baby, and Ben's in the Army."

"Well, then, she has Daddy-what's-his-name."

"It'd be hard on her," he mumbled.

"Matt, would you like me to tell you what I've learned after a long and full life? After seventy-five years I've finally learned you have to accept things as they are. You've got to take advantage of what you have, and forget what you could have or what you think you should have. You've got to be yourself, and, Matt, you're a Hawley. Don't waste this chance."

"Your grandmother's right, Matt," Mr. Oliver's seamless voice reassured him.

"Yes, but this time I want to make sure I don't disappoint you. Exactly what do you expect of me, Grandmother?"

"Nothing. I just want you to be yourself, go out to San Francisco, and stay with your father."

"How long?"

"What?"

"How long do I have to stay with him?"

"You talk as if it were a punishment."

"I don't mean to, but he's married, and busy with his shop. I don't want to intrude. I'd like to have a life of my own," he said, thinking of Dede.

"Certainly. What could be more natural? Let me see." She put a finger to her upper lip. "Let's say until the first of the year. Less than two months. That shouldn't be a strain."

"Your grandmother's right, Matt," Mr. Oliver repeated wearily.

Walker sighed. "Yes, I think she is."

"Then you accept?"

"Yes," he nodded. "Yes, I do."

Tonight, after visiting Mom, as he headed for Dede Clinton's apartment, he still accepted, and although he knew it would be difficult to get away, he was desperate to do just that. Flee. Escape. Run from Maryland and Mom and this last meeting with Dede.

Chapter 3

Away from the parkway the Beltsville exit led to the world of contradictions where Dede Clinton flourished. First it passed through Greenbelt, where little was green except the mold on the barracks-like buildings of this community spawned by the Depression, later overrun by war babies, and finally abandoned by all but the aged and destitute. Beyond it stood a new development of garden apartments, where nothing grew, and high-rise apartments, which rose no higher than two stories. Dede herself lived in a project called Ashtree Townhouses, where there were no ashes, no houses, no towns, and certainly no trees. Instead, walling an immense moraine of parking space, a narrow fence of red-brick apartments conformed to the nameless architect's low-budget notion of what Georgetown might look like if it were transported eight miles out of Washington to the center of a pasture. During the day, when the tenants were at work, a deadly silence hung like a corpse over this homing spot for childless couples on the make, but now, even through closed windows, televisions, radios, hi-fi sets, electric can openers, and toothbrushes made a whirring noise in the night air. The sound of a great machine, the steady buzz of transistors unscrewing the tense lid of suburban minds.

Walker parked the TR-3 beside Dede's snub-nosed Corvair. The cars were identical in color, Carolina blue, as she called it. He'd met her three years ago late one misty March night in Charlottesville, when he'd seen her standing on West Main Street in front of the Rotunda, huddled for warmth in a poplin raincoat.

"Do you want a ride?" he'd asked, pulling the Triumph to the curb.

"Are you headed for Chapel Hill?"

"What?"

"Back to the university." Then, bending down to look through the side curtain, she'd said, "I'm sorry. When I saw the color of your car I thought you were from North Carolina."

"I see," he muttered, although he really didn't.

"I missed the team bus." She chuckled through chattering teeth. "I *am* with the team, you know. Cheerleader." Opening the raincoat, she showed him her uniform. Short pleated skirt the color of his car. White knit sweater with UNC across the front. "We played UVA in basketball tonight. Afterward I got lost in the crowd, and the bus left without me. I thought if I waited here, some kids heading back to Chapel Hill might pass by."

"I see," Walker muttered again, and this time he did. The shapely legs with chubby cheerleader knees. Seckel-pear breasts under the sweater. A face with black eyes, upturned nose, and lips that smiled even as they shivered with cold. The mist had soaked her dark hair, pressing it in curls along her forehead and cheeks. "I don't think you'll get a ride now. It's after midnight."

"I don't guess I will." She laughed.

"Why don't you get in the car while you decide what to do."

"Okay. Thanks."

"I could take you to the Trailways station, but they won't have a bus out of here until morning," he said when she'd settled into the bucket seat beside him.

"I don't have any money anyway. My purse is on the bus. Geez, am I soaked." She slipped out of her raincoat, and on her thighs were beaded drops of water. "Hope I don't ruin your car."

"Wish I had some money to loan you, but I'm broke. Do you know anybody in Charlottesville?"

"Just you. I'm Dede Clinton." Smiling, she put out a hand which was small and moist as a baby's.

"Walker Hawley." Then, as the TR-3 sputtered out wreaths of exhaust, he said, "You could stay at my place tonight, and tomorrow I think I can scrape together enough money to buy you a bus ticket."

"Actually, in the morning I could call my roommate, and she'd send me the money. But if I had a place to . . . I mean, if I wouldn't be putting you to any . . ."

"No trouble at all." Jamming the TR-3 into gear, he sped down West Main before she had a chance to change her mind.

"Do you have roommates?"

"No, I live alone. Out in Keswick."

A minute passed in silence, and Walker kept his foot poised over the brake pedal, certain she'd say she wanted to get out. But then she gave a nervous laugh. "Well, I hope you're a gentleman."

That first night he was. He stayed in his room rereading Wallace Stevens while Dede took a bath, then, wearing one of his old shirts, curled up on the living-room couch, saying she preferred to stay there near the fireplace.

"You're welcome to my bed."

"No, this is fine."

"Do you like Wallace Stevens?"

" 'Esthetique du Mal' is my favorite."

"It is?"

He read it three times, but decided she must be joking.

In the morning she cooked him breakfast and called her roommate for money, but postponing the trip into town to the Western Union office, said she'd like to go for a walk in the woods, where hard shiny leaves had burst out overnight on all the trees. Willow branches beat in the breeze like buggy whips, the marshy fields, coming out of their winter coma, sprouted violets and pokeberries, and overhead the sky slowly cleared. Having left her uniform in front of the fire to dry, Dede wore a pair of his Levis with the cuffs rolled up to her calves and a crew-neck sweater with the sleeves pushed up and bunched at her elbows. Her face was tan from a week she said she'd spent in Nassau over semester break, her eyes were bright, and a smile remained perpetually on her lips.

Walker immediately suspected her of insipidness. No one could smile that much. Then she told him she, too, was an English major and had been a Phi Beta Kappa since junior year. Next fall she planned to go to Columbia for her master's degree. This seemed so far out of keeping with how she looked and acted, he didn't believe her at first, but by the end of the day he'd decided her smile was actually a mask which allowed this girl of rare determination, and even rarer intellect, to do and say exactly what she wanted.

40

When they got back to the cottage, Walker asked her to stay again that night.

"I'd like to, but what'll I do for clothes?"

"Don't you like the ones I gave you? If not, you can put your uniform back on. The idea of talking about D. H. Lawrence with a cheerleader fascinates me."

Later that night he settled the question of her clothing by slowly taking it off her, and they slept in each other's arms before the fire.

But now memory of this night three years ago, and of all the nights and talks that had passed since then, and of the changed plans—particularly her decision to enroll in the University of Maryland's graduate school to be near Walker—came to weigh upon him like the demands of his mother, the gifts of his grandmother, and the strange, conflicting influence of his father and his stepfather. He didn't want to tell Dede he was leaving, but couldn't bring himself to go until he had. Maybe she'd follow him again, he thought. Transfer to Berkeley or Stanford. He wouldn't ask her, but if she offered . . . Slightly disgusted with himself, Walker climbed out of the car and went up to her door.

A solid rap on wood. The rush of her bare feet across the floor. "Who is it?"

"It's me."

"Why didn't you use your key?" she asked, breathless but smiling, as she opened the door.

"I didn't want to scare you."

"You wouldn't have." Standing on tiptoes, she kissed him. "Have you eaten? There's some leftover tuna casserole I could heat for you."

"I'm not hungry." Taking off his coat, he tossed it over the back of a chair.

Dede was wearing black slacks, tight as leotards, and a soft wool sweater, Carolina blue. He was tempted to take her in his arms and return her kiss, but thought better of it. If he did that, he'd never get around to telling her. Never get around to leaving.

"What's wrong?" she asked. "You look upset."

"I've just been to see Mom."

"How is she?"

"Healthy enough to call me a selfish bastard."

Slipping her arm through his, she said, "Let's go into my room," as though the living room belonged to someone else, which, in a sense, it did.

Dede tried to keep it the way it was two years ago when her parents agreed to pay for the apartment, for it reassured them to see this clean room full of early American furniture each time they drove up from Chattanooga. Having a daughter in graduate school was strange enough by Tennessee standards—especially if, like Mr. Clinton, one owned a chain of used-car lots—but at least they could be certain she lived in a safe neighborhood. Not a rancid garret where some wily Nigra was likely to rape her in the hallway. Here the beige carpet and egg-white walls were spotless, the fringed lampshades unruffled. Across the back of the couch a monotonous parade of stagecoaches was frozen forever with the front hoof of the lead horse lifted, and a spotted hound pointing the way west.

"How are you coming with the thesis?" he asked as she led him into the bedroom.

"Not too bad. I should be able to start a first draft by January. But Dr. Portis told me the next volume of Leon Edel's critical biography may come out this spring, and I'd hate to do much before looking at it."

Dede sat on the double bed, leaning against the headboard. There was room for him beside her, but he resisted temptation again and went to the ladderback chair at the desk.

"I'm rereading *The Tragic Muse*," she said, "and finding it more helpful than I'd expected. Have you read it?"

He shook his head. "Never got to it."

"Philistine! Imagine not liking Henry James."

"It's not that I don't like him. It's just that he doesn't agree with me. Like cucumbers. Or buttermilk."

"The simile sours."

They both laughed.

When she'd first told him she planned to write on Henry James, he'd decided to read the books along with her, but after finishing *The Ambassadors,* he fell upon *The Wings of the Dove* as if upon an iron spike. It knocked the wind, almost the life, out of him. Each page brought a shortness of breath, a steady constriction of his lungs as the plot moved with a dreamlike, mannered slowness reminding him of underwater ballet, of sea fans waving in deep currents, of rosebuds blooming for time-lapse cameras. His mind ripped loose of its mooring and sailed into strange waters, so that when he'd finished the last page he wasn't sure where he was, and this dislocation started a nervous tic at the corner of his mouth.

Thirty pages into *The Golden Bowl* the tic took possession of his body, and he developed an itch he couldn't scratch. It wasn't that he disliked the book. Had that been the case, he'd simply have set it aside. But it terrified him, like paintings of endless, exact fields done by meticulous madmen who labor at each blade of grass, each drop of dew. The flawless technique made Walker despair of ever writing a masterpiece himself, and finally of ever writing anything. Once aware of the difficulties, how could one choose the first word, the proper tone, the correct nuance?

At last, when Maggie Verver asked for the sixteenth time, "For what do you take me?" he'd let the book crash to the floor, and for two hours found it impossible to move, knowing that if great literature was difficult and complex, life was even more so. Shifting like sand, disappearing like mist, its shape and direction could only be sensed in shadows.

But tiny Dede dived to the depths of James and came up with dark eyes smiling. She not only understood, she liked what she read, and never seemed to suffer the intellectual bends in shuttling between the surface of her life at Ashtree Townhouses and that other world contained in books. Somehow she'd made allowances for both.

"You have the most peculiar expression on your face, Walker. Are you sure nothing's wrong?"

"I told you I'd been to see Mom, and she called me a bastard."

"Did that surprise you?"

"It shouldn't have, but yesterday my grandmother said the same thing."

"What did you do to her? Or should I say what wouldn't you do *for* her?"

"She wasn't mad. She was serious. She told me Mom was pregnant with me when she got married."

"What a terrible thing to say." Dede straightened, eyes flashing. "I feel sorry for your mother, and can understand why she says the things she does, but your grandmother just sounds mean and disagreeable."

"Well, she's that, all right, but I'm glad she told me."

"It doesn't bother you, does it? After all, they did get married before you were born."

"And divorced three months later." He smiled ruefully. "I'm barely legitimate."

"It does bother you then?"

"Yes, but in some crazy way it also makes me feel free. Maybe like an orphan would."

"Now, Walker, don't start feeling sorry for yourself."

"I'm not. But knowing this does give me a sense of freedom."

"To do what?"

He shrugged. "To try something new without feeling guilty about Mom."

"She's still your mother." Dede's voice had grown cooler, for perhaps she suspected what he'd come to tell her.

"Don't I know it. I read a sign on a men's-room wall that said something like that. 'Remember, no matter how dark the night is, she's still your mother.'"

"You're leaving again, aren't you?" she suddenly asked.

"What do you mean?"

"I mean just what I say. You're getting ready to go." She swung around to sit on the side of the bed facing him.

Walker looked at his hands. Flexed them once, then folded them together. "Grandmother offered me a lot of money so I could be free to . . ."

"What?"

"Do what I want." He didn't look up, for he knew the menace her small eyes could hold.

"And what do you want?"

"To be free."

"Walker, you're talking in circles. Do you want to write? Is that what you're saying?"

At last he looked up. "You're the third person in the last two days who's asked me that. But it has nothing to do with writing. Or it has to do with more than just writing. I simply want to get away from home and my family. They're dragging me down. How in the hell could I write there?"

"You can write anywhere if you want to badly enough. If nothing else, you could write about your home and family. Maybe that would . . ."

"That book has already been written and is an all-time best seller. It's called the Montgomery Ward Catalog."

"That's not fair, Walker. Nobody can make you do any . . ."

"Okay, it's not fair. I've got nobody to blame but myself. But I do know I'm unhappy there."

"Then why do you keep going back? Why do you stay?"

"I . . . You know I have feeling for them. It's just that . . ."

Dede reached out and took his hands in hers. "Honey, why don't you move in here?"

"Dede, we've been through this before. I don't want to get married until I get my feet on the ground and decide what I want to do."

"I didn't say anything about marriage." Her voice had an edge to it.

"I don't see any difference between that and living with you. It would lead to the same . . ."

"Look, Walker"—she jumped off the bed, and folding her arms, went to a far corner of the room—"the only place it would lead is to a different arrangement than the one we have now, where you pick up and leave whenever the mood strikes you. If you don't want to get married, that's fine. We'll live together. But we've got to do something because"—her voice cracked—"I can't go on this way. After three years I think I have a right to know where I stand."

"You know where you stand. I love you. But if we get married or live together, nothing will change. We'll be stuck here or in Cottage City, or someplace like it, with you wasting your time pounding iambic pentameter into college sophomores, and me . . . me, I'd be . . . It just wouldn't work."

"We could go somewhere else," she said eagerly, coming back to the bed. "I've got some money, and if your grandmother's given you some, we could go any place you like. Maybe Europe."

Walker stood up and began to pace. "I have to find out first if there is any place other than Cottage City."

"I don't understand."

"That's because you don't live there. But I do, and I want to

45

get away from it and every place like it before it's too late." For a moment he paced in silence, then said, "The Monday after Thanksgiving I'm leaving for San Francisco. Maybe I'll find something there that I like. I mean, there must be someplace ..." He trailed off weakly.

Dede slumped against the headboard. "Where does this leave me?"

"I'll write. And this June after you finish your M.A., you could..."

"Follow you to California? By that time you'll have gone someplace else."

He sat beside her. "No, I won't. I'll be with my father for a while. Maybe I'll catch onto something interesting or worthwhile through him."

"Yes, like a willing coed from Berkeley."

"That's not true," he said, smoothing the sheet with a hand he brought to rest on her bare ankle. "You know that."

"Don't start making promises, Walker. If you're going, then go and we'll just wait to see what happens."

Her voice sounded careless, almost cynical, and it bothered him to think she could so easily part with him for good. Slowly he moved up the bed until he, too, was leaning against the headboard. "Maybe you can fly out to see me over Christmas vacation."

"No, my parents will want me to come home, and I think if we're going to break, we ought to do it cleanly and completely. I don't like people who hang on forever."

Taking her face between his hands, Walker looked into the brown eyes that were brimming with tears. "Do you mean that?"

Reluctantly she shook her head no. "But I wish I did. Maybe I do and I just don't know it. After you leave I'll . . ."

He brought her lips to his and wrapped his arms around her. So small, so fragile. The sleek ribs thin as spring branches. A coolness on the cheeks of her behind. He warmed them with his hands, then reached up to her breasts and found she wasn't wearing a bra under the blue sweater. Perfect miniatures. The pink nipples hardening between his fingers. But when he moved along the flatness of her belly to unzip the slacks, Dede grabbed his wrist.

46

"No, Walker." Tears had begun to flow down her cheeks. "This won't help. You're still going to leave, and . . ."

"Baby, please." He blotted a salty tear with his lips. "I . . ." But there was nothing to say, so he kissed her again, and this time she didn't stop him when he slid the zipper, then her slacks, and finally her panties down.

When both of them were free of their clothing, she stopped crying, and he rolled her onto her back and, more slowly now, rubbed her thighs, and belly, and breasts. "This fascinates me," he said, touching the tight slit of her navel. "It's the only perfect belly button in captivity." Leaning down, he wet it with his tongue.

She laughed and brought him back up to her breasts. "How many have you seen? I didn't know you were a man of such great experience."

"You see them everywhere. At the beach. In magazines and movies. Even on TV. Most of them terribly botched jobs that look like aerial views of tiny bald-headed men. But yours is perfect."

"Quite an honor."

"Really, it is." He spoke lightly, as if to cover what his hand was doing. Combing through the soft tangle of her bush.

Then Dede climbed on top of him, brushed her breasts against his chest, and finally sat astride Walker, her lips half-parted, eyes wide open and looking into his, which were a bright Carolina blue.

"Come here." He reached out for her.

She shook her head. "I like it where I am." And as his hands held her breasts she moved against him and around him, rolling her hips, wishing Walker goodbye. She seemed so faraway herself. Floating there above him. Eyes slowly closing. Mouth opening wider. Goodbye to Walker, who'd shut his own eyes and was almost gone, driving in a warm wind toward the sunset.

Afterward, as they dressed, Dede asked, "Are you still a Catholic, Walker?"

Losing his grip on his trousers, he took this like a poke to the stomach, and leaned over both to cushion the blow and retrieve his Dacron worsteds. "What kind of question is that?"

47

"A serious one."

"Of course I am. Once a Catholic, always a . . ."

"Don't give me that. I want to know if you still believe. Do you go to Mass?"

"I go when I can. And I believe in God. I even love Him, if that makes any sense. But I don't have much feeling left for the church."

"Maybe you should read this book. It's written by a monk." She handed him Thomas Merton's *The Sign of Jonas*. "I bought it at the Book Exchange. Thought it'd help me understand the church . . . and you."

"In that case, Dede, you ought to keep it."

"No. You take it. I won't have time for it."

As always, he left her apartment with more than he'd brought. The book. A pleasant warmth in his crotch. The low-tide scent on his fingers. A cool print of her lips on his cheek. And additional sadness. She'd kissed him goodbye and cut him loose. Click, the door had shut quietly behind him. Now there was only one place to go, home to Cottage City to tell Daddy Dick.

Chapter 4

Although he'd lived there all his life, Walker didn't know the true boundaries of Cottage City. Where it ended and where Bladensburg, or Colmar Manor, or Mount Ranier began, he had no idea. Sometimes it loomed as large as his imagination. At others, as small as the backyard of the Murdock house. As Mom often said, until her own brain short-fused and became filigreed with anxiety, "It's all in your mind."

Walker thought of the town in terms of its landmarks, the limits of his life as a child. Cohen's Junk Yard, where he sold tons of old newspapers and magazines the neighbors saved for him in their basements, where as a teenager he'd stolen hubcaps, and radiators, and strips of chrome for the hot-rod he never built. The Bladensburg Roller Rink, with its weekend crew of randy girls from Rogers Heights, Hyattsville, Landover Hills, and Lanham. The Peace Cross Memorial, a monument of grey stone that erupted volcanically from the macadam of Bladensburg Road. Stained with pigeon shit and with verdigris from a plaque which bore the names of dead soldiers from a forgotten war, the concrete cross stood as a hazard to motorists, and a target for vandals, artists, and the irreverent. High above the pavement someone had painted in indelible orange letters, "King Kong died for our sins." The West Branch of the Anacostia River, where Walker had caught turtles and frogs each spring and gone wading in shallow pools each summer. Now it was the color of teak, thick with sludge and crude oil, beer cans and Coke bottles, condoms and cow turds, all oozing downriver on a skin of dead fish. The apocalyptic moment had come three years ago when someone tossed a lighted cigarette from the bridge and the river caught fire. Next morning in newspapers across the country was a picture of volunteer firemen hosing the West Branch with chemicals, struggling to keep the blazing river under control.

Ten P.M. of a November night, as Walker drove into Cottage City under the cover of darkness, he noticed these landmarks and others. Jerry's Hot Dog Stand. The Firehouse, Pincus' Tavern. The Rayco Seatcover Shop. Fort McHenry Cemetery, with the clock made out of flowers. The Frito-Lay Potato Chip factory, its chimneys belching straight grease. He knew every building on that strip of Bladensburg Road, and mentally ticked off each in passing. Duval's Lock Shop, with its huge bronze key instead of a doorknob. Shapiro's Pawn Shop, where behind plate glass, reinforced by chicken wire, a dozen switch-blade knives stood in a block of wood like a gleaming bouquet of artificial flowers. Wagner's Bicycle Repair, which gave off through its closed door the smell of lubricating oil and the pungent dry rot of old inner tubes.

Then he turned right on Whittier Street, coasted down the block of small, identical houses until he found his own, and pulled into the driveway next to Daddy Dick's pickup truck. On the porch he paused to look at what he'd be leaving. The air was warm, almost balmy, but neither this nor the darkness could hide from Walker the desolation of Cottage City. The asbestos shingle houses, less than twenty years old, already looked ancient, the walls cracked and stained, window blinds badly bent or torn down, screen doors rusting, fences crooked and falling. The yards had gone to weeds, or else were pounded smooth by children's feet, for the neighbors, assuming they ever had, now no longer cared. Dead branches and fallen leaves cluttered the street. Fistfuls of grass grew up through cracks in the sidewalk. Garbage cans remained all week next to the curb—when, that is, they weren't sent thundering down Whittier Street by stray dogs hungry for bologna skins and ham bones. In the O'Reillys' front yard, beyond a gap in the shattered picket fence, a wheel-less '49 Ford sat on blocks, its engine hoisted on a winch built over the chassis. On the corner, at 5308, where no one had lived in six years, the grass was waist-high, and rose bushes had run wild, reaching their mad tendrils for the second-floor windows, while below, a For Sale sign, riddled by B-B guns, fought to keep its pockmarked face free of shrubbery.

At this hour there was little noise. Trucks grinding and pounding from one stop light to the next on Bladensburg Road. Kids talking as they smoked beneath a streetlight. The patter of canned applause and laughter from televisions along the block. Cottage City at peace.

Could there be any doubt he had to escape, Walker asked himself, and went into the front hall, which smelled curiously like a spice shop. Garlic, oregano, and thyme bristled in his nostrils, the scent rising, along with the predictable sound of the TV, from the recreation room.

When he was halfway down the stairs, Daddy Dick called out, "'At you, Walker?"

"Yessir."

"Give a holler next time. I don't like people creeping up on me. You're liable to get coldcocked doing that one night."

In an armchair, three feet from the TV, circled by empty beer bottles, Daddy Dick watched wrestling from Capitol Arena. On the table beside him lay a half-eaten pizza, which in the purple light of television, looked like vomit thrown from a second-story window. "Where you been? I thought we'd have dinner together tonight. But when you weren't here by nine, I got so hungry I went up to the bowling alley and ordered a couple of pizzas. There's some left, if you want it. Pull up a chair, and have a beer."

"Sorry I'm late. I stopped to see Dede and couldn't get away."

Daddy Dick gave his deep rumbling laugh. "I see. What kept you there all this time, boy?"

"We talked awhile," said Walker, opening a beer.

"You're always doing a lot of that with her, aren't you? And what else?" he needled.

"She gave me a book."

"I'm telling you, Walker, you keep reading them books and your eyes are going to fall out and your dick's going to shrivel up like a leech." Another rumbling laugh. Then, as the next match started—Killer Kowalski versus Haystacks Calhoun—he turned to the screen, bathing in the purple light, a miniature reflection of the picture set like a jewel in each of his eyes.

Daddy Dick was a big man, even taller than Walker, and at two hundred and thirty he outweighed his stepson by at least fifty pounds. In his chest, arms, and hands he possessed a frightening strength which Walker knew quite well, for every night after dinner he and Ben used to wrestle with him on the recreation-room floor, and after toying with them for an hour— squeezing their arms and legs until they cried out for mercy, tickling their ribs in a way that left bruises, and rubbing their peach-fuzz faces raw with the emery board of his own jaw— Daddy Dick would invariably pin them the moment Mom yelled down the stairs, "For Christ's sake, will you stop that racket? Nancy and I are trying to knit."

But he wasn't a violent man, not even when drunk, and Walker had rarely seen him angry—especially not at Mom, which was amazing when he remembered how often she'd provoked him. There was that time two years ago when during the second quarter of the Notre Dame–Michigan State game she'd raced down the stairs and switched off the television, screaming, "I can't stand it. If I hear one more minute of football, I'll go insane."

"Mina," Daddy Dick had said quietly, "Notre Dame is losing by ten points. Will you please turn the game back on?"

"No, goddammit. I hope they lose. Do you hear me? I hope to hell they lose."

Even now Walker winced at the memory. But Daddy Dick had simply got up, lifted Mom bodily from in front of the set, stood her in a corner, and gone back to the game. Then, as she stayed there open-mouthed, he turned and said, "Don't ever do that again, Mina. I might just break every bone in your body."

Or there was the weekend he'd spent thirty-six hours in the recreation room, having passed out after the Late Movie Saturday night and awakened just in time for the Redskin game Sunday afternoon. At half-time Mom had crept down the stairs and thrown a pitcher of ice water in his face, but Daddy Dick scarcely moved. Glancing up into her wild dark eyes, he'd said with infinite restraint, "I didn't mind that, Mina. It cleared my head. But don't ever do it again. I don't like to be pushed."

As a matter of fact, Walker had seen Daddy Dick hit Mom

only once, ten years ago at the St. James parish picnic. A sudden thunderstorm had driven everyone into the central pavilion, and as rain and wind churned Chesapeake Bay against its shores, most adults began feeding the slot machines, while children stood under rainspouts or raced forks of lightning across the badminton court. Teenagers, no older than Walker, danced in their bathing suits on the cool concrete floor, pumping goose-pimply thighs back and forth to the tune of "Secret Love," "Rags to Riches," and "Kokomo."

But Walker stayed with Mom and Daddy Dick, who were talking to the pastor, Father Relihan, and every few minutes Daddy Dick handed him his Dixie cup and told him to bring another draft. Hoping the kids thought the beer was for him, Walker strolled to the keg, drew the lever, and watched the foam carry chips of wax up from the bottom of the cup.

When he came back, Mom said, "Daddy Dick, don't you think you've had enough?"

But listening to Father Relihan, Daddy Dick didn't answer.

The next time he handed Walker the cup, Mom shouted, "That's enough, I tell you. Fourteen's enough."

Nodding at something Father Relihan had just said, Daddy Dick turned, raised his fist, and poked her solidly to the point of her jaw. Back she staggered, but shifting to a widespread stance, kept her balance and wailed, "Did you see that? Father Relihan, you saw him. Do something!"

He didn't say whether he'd seen or not, for linking arms with Daddy Dick he led him over to the keg, where they both had another beer.

"Walker, he hit your mother. Do something!" Then, holding her jaw, she'd turned in an errant circle, appealing to the dancers, slot-machine players, and children, all of whom had seen the deed but were afraid to come to her defense. "Isn't anybody going to do something?" she whined.

"I didn't see anything," said Walker, and ran out of the pavilion, across the badminton court, with thunder crackling overhead, and didn't stop until he'd reached the pickup truck. Switching on the radio and turning the volume high as it would go, he'd cried for an hour amid the smell of hot dusty silk from the frayed speaker and the sound of the Senators playing the

Red Sox in faraway Fenway Park. The crowd had jeered and hooted all afternoon, as Walker sobbed and Ted Williams gestured obscenely at the stands.

That was one of many bad moments, but Walker held no ill feeling toward his stepfather, for usually, after a day of digging foundations or laying patios, Daddy Dick was content to pop a bottle of Budweiser, descend to the recreation room, and remain in front of the television until the Tonight Show came on. He never shouted, never quarreled, never complained. He was slow, shy, and kind. A rare man, one who kept quiet when he had nothing to say. Perhaps if he'd talked, Walker would have disliked or resented him as his own wife and children seemed to, but since he never offered advice or encouraged him to find himself, Walker loved him. The lone exhortation he gave both Ben and Walker before he kissed them good night, was to "Get a lot of sleep and grow up to be six feet tall." At times Walker was prouder of this than anything else; that he'd obeyed, and even exceeded, Daddy Dick's wishes.

"Daddy Dick, I've got something to tell you," Walker said at last.

"What?" As his eyes turned from the TV, his great, loose-limbed body gave a lurch like a puppet that had been cut down from its strings. "What did you say?"

"I'm leaving home after Thanksgiving."

Daddy Dick showed nothing on his stolid face. Nothing in the small green eyes. But Walker knew his words had struck bottom and were reverberating somewhere in the man's massive chest. "Does your mother know?"

"I told her today."

"This is going to be hard on her."

"It will at first. But I think it'll be better if I'm not around. I only seem to upset her. Maybe she'll learn to depend on herself again . . . and on you."

"She always could depend on me. She knows that."

"I wouldn't go if I didn't think it was for the best," Walker tried to convince himself as well as Daddy Dick.

"No, I guess you wouldn't. Where you going, anyway?"

"Out to San Francisco."

"To be with your father?" For once there might have been emotion in his voice.

"Not really. I'll probably see him, but I'm not going out there just for that."

"I wouldn't blame you if you was." Daddy Dick glanced down at his lap and rubbed away a speck of mortar. "I never met him, but I reckon he's a nice enough fellow."

"I don't really know him myself," Walker struggled. "And at my age I don't need another father."

"No, I don't guess you do. You always been like my own boy, Walker. Sometimes I even forget you're not mine. I was just telling Jimmy Durslag the other day how much I'd love to have you come to work with us so I could put another Murdock on our sign. Murdock, Murdock, and Durslag. But then I remembered that Murdock ain't your name. I guess I'll just have to wait for Ben to get out of the Army. But don't get me wrong. I wouldn't mind putting a Hawley on that sign. I'd do it in a minute. You just say the word . . ."

"Thanks, but . . ."

"Construction business isn't what it used to be those summers you worked with me. A lot of the riffraff's been cleared out. We got a good bunch of guys, and they all make money. Now if we had a man with your brains, we'd . . ."

"I really don't think . . ."

"It's a good life, Walker. Healthy, outdoors work."

"Sounds great, but you'd better save that place for Ben. I want to try my luck in San Francisco."

"If that's what you want . . ."

"It is, Daddy Dick. It really is."

"Well, I won't try to talk you out of it. I'm glad you've found something you like. But it's going to be lonely around here without you and Mina."

"I'm . . ."

"No, don't be sorry. I'm happy for you."

"Thanks, Daddy Dick."

"Don't mention it. Have another beer. The news'll be on in a minute."

As always, the news was awful. Trouble in Vietnam, bombing in the north, guerrilla raids in the south. Half a dozen new "gaps" had chopped the nation into hostile chunks. In Indiana at the Paraplegic Olympics a team of American World War II veterans had won the wheelchair basketball championship.

There was a note of sadness here, too, however, for a competitor in the field meet had put the sixteen-pound shot into the stands, breaking a spectator's leg. Then on the Sports Round-Up, talk was all of The Game—this year's battle of the century. Notre Dame versus unbeaten Southern California in O. J. Simpson's last regular season game. The Trojans were favored by twelve points.

"Bullshit," snorted Daddy Dick. "Notre Dame's going to eat that guy alive. Wait and see. Put your money on the Irish."

With this, he pried himself out of the chair, gathered his empties, five in each hand, and staggered over to Walker. Eyes swimming with emotion and the effect of ten Budweisers, he said, "I'm proud of you, boy. You're going to do real good out there. Just don't forget the rest of us when you're famous."

"I won't. I promise."

At the foot of the stairs, he paused again. "Jesus, they get steeper and longer every night."

"Take it easy, Daddy Dick," cautioned Walker, who'd seen him take many a thumping backward tumble. "Do you want a hand?"

"No, I'll make it." But after a limber little bounce on the balls of his feet, he settled back on his heels. "Tell you what, Walker. I think I'll leave a couple of bottles for you to carry." Setting the five in his right hand on the floor, he grabbed for the banister, and using it like a lifeline, slowly dragged himself up the steps. "Night son," he called from the landing.

"Good night, Daddy Dick."

At once the recreation room seemed to grow cooler, even though Walker's heart was making noisy slaps at his ribs and pumping hot blood to his temples. Despite all he'd told Mom and Dede, and all that Grandmother Hawley and Daddy Dick had told him, he didn't feel right in leaving. He wanted to. He knew he had to. But . . .

Concentrating on Johnny Carson's monologue, he managed to pass a few relatively painless hours until the Tonight Show ended, then, turning off the television, he stood for a moment in darkness, watched the white dot fade, and listened to the tubes snap and fizz as the old Zenith settled for the night.

He left the beer bottles on the kitchen table and started for his room, knowing he'd never make it all the way to the attic.

At Ben's room he pushed open the door, crumpled onto the bed, and lying there in the semi-darkness, looked up at the walls that were weighted with pennants, pictures, and other youthful memorabilia. They seemed to be closing over him like the lid of a box. Groaning, he turned onto his side and shut his eyes.

"'At you, Walker?" Daddy Dick called from his room.

"Yessir."

"Sometimes it gets so lonesome you don't even feel like leaving the recreation room, do you?"

"No sir."

"I may put my bed down there after you leave. Night now."

The sound of bodies straining uneasily in an empty house. The creaking of dry timbers. A maple tree rapping its branches on the roof. Trucks on Bladensburg Road. Dogs in the garbage, gobbling and growling. Then silence. In search of sleep.

Chapter 5

In the morning Walker felt better, and on a sudden, unquestioned impulse, phoned the *Washington Post* and, only half expecting a reply, placed a classified ad. "Wanted: Rider to San Francisco. Male or female to share expenses. Call Mr. Hawley." Then he went out to the TR-3. Another warm, clear day. Weather unusually fine for late November. An apple-sweet scent of Indian summer still in the air. Folding back the convertible top, he slid behind the wheel and went to Suburban Trust to deposit his grandmother's money and purchase two thousand dollars' worth of traveler's checks. A glance of respectful envy from the pimply teller stirred a sense of rare well-being in his heart.

He couldn't have admitted to himself, much less have explained to anyone, why he'd placed the ad, but the next day, after passing an unbearable morning trying to ignore the telephone's black, silent rebuke, he'd sadly resigned himself to traveling alone when it rang and a girl said, "This is Lila Caine. About the ad in this morning's *Post*, I hope you haven't found a rider."

"As a matter of fact, I haven't."

"Oh, beautiful," she sighed. "And you're going to San Francisco. Wonderful."

"Well, it is . . . it does . . ." Walker fumbled.

"I mean, that's exactly where I'm going."

"I'm glad too . . ."

"When do you leave, Mr. Hawley? How long will the trip take? Can I bring my hair dryer?"

"Well, I have a TR-3, you understand, and that'll limit . . . plus, I want to make it clear . . . I'm a man, and . . ."

"I presumed as much, Mr. Hawley." Dry wit, and a touch of malice at his bungling.

"What I'm trying to say, Miss Caine . . . It is Miss, isn't it?"

"Yes."

"Good. I wanted to say the car is small, but I have a luggage rack. If I can ever find it. I plan to leave the Monday after Thanksgiving, and take a week or more to get there."

"Hmm . . ."

"But we can discuss that," he said, anxious not to lose her.

"No, you make the plans. I'm not in a hurry. Not any more. I don't live my life by a schedule. Is it a convertible?"

"Sure is."

"Great. I can't wait to get a suntan, can you?"

"I hope we have good weather."

"So do I. When can we get together and talk? I'm sure you'll want to meet me before you get stuck with me for a week."

Certain it was she who didn't want to get stuck, Walker faltered again. "You name the time and place."

"I'm out in Maryland. Near the university."

"A student?"

"Not any more." A shameless surge of triumph and jubilation in her voice. "Why don't we meet tomorrow in front of the College Park Hot Shoppe at . . . Do you work, Mr. Hawley?"

"Not any longer."

She laughed. "A couple of drop-outs. I like that. I'll see you at the Hot Shoppe at noon. Okay?"

"Fine."

"Oh yes! One other thing. Will we be camping out? Should I bring a sleeping bag? Or will we stay in motels?"

"Uh . . . umm. Motels. Separate rooms, of course," he felt compelled to add.

"Yes, I guess it'll be too cold to camp. Too bad. Well, I'll see you tomorrow."

Walker was dripping perspiration when he hung up. Sleeping bags? Camping out? And on top of that her breathless enthusiasm? He was glad he'd have a chance to meet Lila Caine. If she turned out to be a dud, he could always . . . He'd think of something.

Late the next morning Walker came downstairs to find Nancy in the kitchen feeding her three-year-old son, Skip. Pausing in the hall, he knew why she was here, and was tempted to run. Yet it seemed foolish and demeaning to sneak away. She didn't look threatening in checkered slacks, a man's shirt, and a pair of battered tennis shoes run over at the heel. Mean and stringy, yes, but not threatening. Unlike her husband, Chip, she'd lost weight since that day—exactly nine months before Skip's birth—when she'd become a teenage bride. Now she was washed out, her girlhood gone, and her startlingly red hair looked three shades brighter.

"Morning, Nancy." He plunged into the kitchen. "How's the little bugger?" He pinched the baby's cheek.

"My God, you scared me!" She clasped a hand to her chest like a young girl hiding meager cleavage, then gaining a grip on herself, said, "And quit calling him a little bugger."

"Hi, Unca Walky." Skip, in his high chair, sputtered shreds of apricot into her face. A chubby, towheaded baby, he looked like his father. Same slack mouth. Same piggish little eyes.

"Hi, Skip." Going over to the sink, he chased a cockroach off the drainboard. "Any coffee left?"

"Yes. And there's plenty of date-nut bread, so eat it before it gets stale."

Walker poured himself a cup and sat in Daddy Dick's chair, where the morning *Post* lay open to the Sport Page, just as he'd left it. When there was a story, score, or picture he wanted Walker to see, he circled it with a red magic marker. His way of communicating. One of the pathetic few.

"Get your hands out of your pants," said Nancy.

"Who, me?"

"No, Skip. And keep them out."

"Okay, Mommy."

A fat fly trapped in a milk bottle under the sink whammed itself to death against the glass, while the cockroach emerged, antennae waving from behind the stove.

"Mommy, why can't I touch my peanuts?"

"Shut up and eat."

"Do girls have a peanuts?"

"Skip, I told you to shut up. Besides, it's a penis, not a peanuts."

"Do girls have one?"

"Open your mouth. Here's another bite." The spoon made a clinking noise as she dug for the last scraps.

"Do they?"

"Do they what?"

"Have a peanuts?"

"We've been through this before. Be quiet and eat."

"Careful," said Walker, "you'll stunt his sexual development."

"You keep out of this."

"Yes indeed, Mommy."

"He called you Mommy." Skip giggled.

"He's silly," she said, sneaking in the last mouthful of apricots.

When he'd swallowed them, Skip asked, "Mommy, do you have a peanuts?"

"Oh, Christ, not again. It's a penis. Not a peanuts. And I've told you little girls have something else. Something inside where they make babies."

"It's not a penis inside them, is it?" asked Walker.

"Keep out of this with your filthy remarks."

"Just checking."

With a washrag from the sink she wiped Skip's face, then lifted him out of the chair. "Go into the living room while I have a little talk with Uncle Walker."

On fat bowlegs he waddled out the door.

"Now," she said, turning to Walker, "there are a couple of
. . ."

"Look, Nancy, I'd like to have one of our little talks but I have to be in College Park in half an hour."

"Maybe when you hear what I've got to say, you won't go." The words came out slowly, each hard and cold as a link of chain. A spoon was still in her hand, pointed at Walker like a weapon.

Setting aside the coffee cup, carefully folding the newspaper, he cleared his throat. "Nancy, you've obviously got something on your mind, and I think I know what it is. Now, there are two ways we can go about this. Holler and scream, like we usually do. Or like mature adults. I'd prefer the latter, but I'd also appreciate it if you'd be quick about it, because I'm in a hurry."

"Okay, if you know why I'm here, quit making speeches."

"I will, when you start minding your own business."

Scrawny face twisted in anger, Nancy rushed forward. "This is my business. I—but not just me. I'm talking about everybody else, too"—which meant Chip—"we're all damn sick and tired of your irresponsibility, and think it's time you took other people into consideration."

Walker shook his head. "You're wasting your breath. No matter what you say, I'm going to California."

Nancy bit her lip, and started again. "Jesus Christ, for two years you been living in this house like a goddamn zombie, and suddenly you get this wild hair up your ass to go to California. Leaving Mom at the worst time of her life. Don't you know what menopause does to a woman? Hasn't she told you about her hot flashes?"

"Only about ten times a day for the last twelve years."

"Then show a little consideration."

"Same to you. Remember, I have a life to lead too. And, for your information, I've had a job for the last two years."

"Oh, bullshit. You did nothing but . . ."

"Look, Nancy, I don't care what you or Chip or anyone else thinks I was doing. The whole lot of you don't have the brains to pack sand up a rat's ass anyway. So why don't you . . ."

"Watch your tongue in front of my child."

One of Skip's pig eyes darted around the kitchen door.

"Who are you kidding? It'll be another fifteen years before he learns to hold his water much less speak English."

"Why you son-of-a-bitch, I'll . . ." Her fist flailed out, but Walker caught it by the wrist.

"I knew it." He jumped out of the chair. "Didn't I tell you? Now why don't you knock it off?"

Wrenching free, she went to the table, sat down, and crossed her arms and legs. "I want to make it clear I don't give a damn what you do. It's Mom I'm thinking about."

"She has Daddy Dick."

"Cut the crap. He needs more looking after than Skip. You've been here all these years—rent-free, I might add—and now that Mom needs help, I think you ought to pitch in."

Walker sat down and tried to be calm. "Nancy, you're right. I shouldn't have been living here rent-free. I should've gotten out on my own. That's what I'm trying to do now. Be truthful. Don't you think I should go? Don't you think everyone would be happier if I left?"

"Yes," she said, and Walker had the answer he wanted, though it hurt to hear it. "But what I think doesn't matter. Mom's the one who wants you to stay. She doesn't want to be stuck here alone with Daddy Dick when she gets out."

"I think we can trust them. After all, they are married."

"Very funny! I'm talking about his drinking."

"Jesus Christ, when will you stop trying to make him out to be an alcoholic? Drinking's the only thing he's got, and if you and Mom had any sense, you'd know it's what lets him give in to you on everything else."

"Say what you like, he's disgusting and he's dangerous. Mom's afraid he'll pass out with a cigarette in his mouth and burn the house down."

"Is my presence supposed to prevent that? I guess I could call the fire department, but ..."

"Oh, hell, I give up." She slapped her bony thighs. "Do what you want. You always have and you always will."

"Look, I ..." But Nancy was stuffing Skip's food into a leatherette handbag, then she fetched him from the other room and wrestled him into his snowsuit. Walker got up and leaned against the sink, feeling let down and edgy.

When she'd finished, she turned for a parting shot. "You want to know something, Walker? I feel sorry for you. Sure, you've got a rich grandmother and a college degree, and that little car and a lot of opportunities Ben and Chip and I never had. But you're miserable." She shook her head, whipping the stiff wires of her red hair. "You're really miserable, aren't you? I mean, despite everything, you aren't even happy. So what's the good of that diddly-ass story you wrote, and all your running around? What the hell kind of life is that for a man?"

"But I say good riddance. Let your father put up with you like we've had to all these years."

"I ... You don't understand."

"I understand enough to know you're not happy."

"In my own way I'm ..."

"Look, you don't have to convince me. Convince yourself—if you can." With this, she scooped Skip up in her arms and stalked out of the house.

Walker was tempted to run after her, but knew it was no use. She'd never understand. She was caught herself. She'd married and moved away, but only to another Cottage City. Here or there, it was the same. One either became a clenched fist of raw, angry nerves, like Mom and Nancy, or a likable but listless man, lobotomized by beer and TV, like Daddy Dick and Chip.

Another day of Indian summer. But the season long and dangerously overdue for change. Time wasn't far off when ferns of frost would blossom on the windowpanes. Everyone at work except Walker, troubled and truant, heading for the TR-3. He no longer knew anyone in the neighborhood. Old people had died. Young ones wed and gone away.

"How's it hanging, Walker?" asked Nelson, the mailman. "Couple of bills here for your old man. And a card for you from San Francisco."

"Thanks." He took them over the closed gate.

"Out of work?"

"No, I'm leaving for California."

"Don't say? Running off again. 'At's the way. Do it while you're young. When I was your age I was banging like an old screen door. Now I'm bone-tired, and scared a mad dog'll bite my dick off before I retire."

"I'm sure you'll make it intact." Walker edged toward his car.

"Don't know. Not with Christmas coming. 'At's always a ball-breaker for us full-timers."

"Good luck."

"Same to you. Don't let your meat loaf."

At last into the car. Once on the road, there was no time to think. Cares steamed off in a haze of exhaust fumes, or were ground fine as sugar by passing trucks. Motion released the mind's burden. Past the firehouse. Pictures of orange turkeys pasted in the windows for the fall dance. Past the Rustic Cabin and Jerry's Hot Dog stand. Over the West Branch bridge. The river smooth and thick as chocolate.

A red light stopped him at the Peace Cross, where a starling, misled by scent, pecked at an empty lunch bag, gave it a peevish shake, and clattered off on lacquered wings. Green light, and traffic rotated around the monument, onto U.S. 1 toward Hyattsville. Easing out of second gear, Walker squeezed between two tractor trailers, past the white brick house where George Washington supposedly slept but no one had since. Its windows were opaque with grime, shingles and beams shattered by the rumble of trucks. In the distance Cohen's Junk Yard smoldered. The guts of old upholstery burning. Abandoned Chevrolets hollow as locust shells. Bald tires baked grey like elephant hide.

Into Hyattsville. Gathering speed past Pep Boys, the Armory, Lustine-Nicholson Chevrolet, the Coffee Cup, and Spiller's Tavern. Plastic pennants waving and pinwheels spinning. Everything for sale. And in Riverdale more of the same, a nightmarish collision of old and new, of suburban towns growing and dying at the same time, like fruit left too long on the vine.

In College Park at the Hot Shoppe, he stopped and slouched against the front fender to read his father's card.

Matt,

At last you're acting like you have good sense. Tanya and I are delighted, and look forward to seeing you in December. The weather has been cool and clear, good for sleeping. The shop was raided twice this summer. The cops looked in all our pots, but found no pot. Ha ha! We don't need dope. We've got each other, and that's a constant source of inspiration and mind-expansion. I don't see how the atmosphere can do anything but help you, too. If this place doesn't inspire you, nothing will. Let us hear from you.

M & T

That's what he needed. Atmosphere and inspiration. Not College Park, crowded with students on this warm autumn day. The last chance for coeds to wear Bermudas and march along Baltimore Boulevard, showing off their tans. Smug, dumb chicks marking time until they became airline stewardesses. He needed someone like Tanya. Mind-expanding. And tall. Her pelvis looked chest-high. But that night in Carmel when his father told him to dance with her she'd felt weightless in his arms, and he realized he was wrong. Her pelvis rode snug as a small saddle

65

against his thigh. Expansion and incest by proxy. The way creative people live, she'd said, tossing back her head and letting her hair unfurl over his arm, must be free. Then she'd told him of the time Ferlinghetti asked for her phone number.

For Walker, the way he lived had always been painful. Not from creativity, but from the desire and its frustration. The jewel that burned annoyingly inside him. That night in Carmel, eighteen years old and eager for art and life, he'd stumbled after three drinks into the lavatory to stare at himself in the mirror, and he thought he saw, behind his blue eyes, a second self longing to be let free.

The chimes of University Chapel struck twelve, played a few bars of "Maryland, My Maryland," then died. Maybe Lila Caine would be his Tanya. An inspiration. But she still hadn't arrived. He'd seen no one who looked as he imagined her. No one at all in front of the Hot Shoppe. He checked his watch, and a fear that she might never show passed like a knife blade over his throat. Suddenly so much depended on this girl he didn't know, as if without her he couldn't make it to the West Coast.

Then, glancing again toward the Hot Shoppe, he saw her. It had to be she, and if it weren't, he'd take this girl instead, for she was the Lila Caine of his mind's eye. Tall, blond, high-breasted, she stood next to the Pappy Parker Fried Chicken sign, combing a hand through her long hair. Strangely dressed, but beautiful, aloof, and younger-looking than he'd expected, she wore a suede jerkin with fringes that moved like fingers over her bare thighs, and she carried a colorful woven-wool bag over her left shoulder. She turned, and their eyes met for an instant before they both looked away. God, it had to be she! But she made no sign, just kept her hand moving through the bright hair, feeling its warmth, pressing its softness to her cheek. He'd have to make the first move, which couldn't be done of a sudden or without thought. Too much depended . . .

She bared her wrist to stare at a gold watch that lay on a wide red-leather band. Though she'd seen him—that was sure—she wouldn't wait much longer, Walker feared, and so he slid off the fender, glad that he hadn't had time to shave or put on a coat and tie. A baggy brown sweater, knitted by Nancy, and a pair of old corduroys, that was better. He ran a hand through his hair, leaving it tousled, shaggy.

Still she refused to make things easy. Turned for no reason and glanced across the street. Slender brown legs, tight and smooth in the calf, then a wider softness halfway up the thigh. A suggestion of lighter skin at the inner leg where summer sun never shone. Standing a foot from her, he smelled perfume, and a breeze, stirred by a barreling Fruehauf on the boulevard, caught her hair and brushed it across his face. Somehow it gave him the strength to deliver his tired line.

"You must be Lila Caine."

A stiffening of the shoulders. With a precise manner, as if practiced, she turned and smiled. "Mr. Hawley? Yes, I remember the voice." She shook his hand. "I thought I'd missed you, and couldn't imagine what I'd do if I had. Hitchhike to California, I guess."

She had dark eyes, and brown roots barely visible in her hair. Not a true blond, and yet an effective one, for the bright hair and brown eyes struck a delicate balance, lending her face a volatile appearance, and with lips half-parted, as if about to speak, she gave the impression something amusing and unusual had just happened or was about to.

"Would you like to go inside and have lunch while we talk?"

She grimaced. "It's always so crowded. And the food's greasy."

"Well, we could . . ."

"I know a little vegetarian place on New Hampshire Avenue where we could get soup and salad."

"Sounds great. Let's go." Taking her elbow, he guided her toward the car.

"Don't you just love pure food? Oranges and nuts. Things like that. What a beautiful shade of blue," she said of the car. "Almost della Robbia."

"I think it's Carolina."

"What?"

"The color."

"Oh."

Even with Walker's help Lila did a poor job of getting into the TR-3. She folded her long limbs, the leather fringes fluttering higher up her thighs, and when he came around behind the wheel, she was still struggling to pull the suede over her bare legs.

"Having trouble?" Seeing her difficulty, he felt surer of himself.

"I just love your car, but these seats make it hard to be a lady."

"Don't try. It'll get you nowhere."

Lila laughed a little too loudly. "I guess we're in for a snug three thousand miles."

"It'll keep us warm." What the hell was he trying to do? Sound like an operator? Liable to scare her away. "I hope it's not too uncomfortable." He pulled out onto U.S. 1, turned up through the campus, and onto East-West Highway. "Where are you from, Lila?"

She glanced out at the community of Adelphi. "Oh." A pause. "That's not an easy question."

"It's not?"

"No. I've roamed around a lot in the last few years."

"That right?" Looking at her profile, he knew she couldn't be more than twenty-one. "Where?"

"Oh, just, you know, around. Georgetown. I lived in Ocean City awhile. All over the place."

"But where are you from?" he repeated, puzzled.

"You mean where was I born?"

"That'll do."

"Is it important?"

"Not as important as you're making it sound."

In a lisping singsong, like a five-year-old, she said, "I was born in Catonsville, Maryland, in a red-brick house with a white picket fence around it."

Catonsville was Cottage City north. Newer, nicer, more money, but essentially the same. Now he understood her reluctance.

"And you?"

"Cottage City. A few miles south of College Park."

"You don't have to tell me. I know the place. A couple of girls and I rented a house there one semester. Pretty grim, if you don't mind my saying so."

"I don't."

"I see why you're going to California. This is the dullest place in the world. You'd think with the university there'd be something happening, but there never is."

"Never that I can remember," he said, warming to her now that they were in agreement on this point. "But why are *you* going to San Francisco?"

"It's a long story. There's Crank's"—she pointed to the restaurant—"over by Woolworth's. You can park in back."

When Walker came around and opened the door, Lila didn't move.

"Anything wrong?" he asked.

"Just trying to decide how I can get out of this seat without losing my dignity." She laughed, then after some preliminary wriggling about, took his hand, and vainly attempting to restrain her hem, extended a foot toward the pavement. The legs flexed, the leather fringe rode up to her hips, and Walker got a glimpse of floral panties before her red sandals touched ground. Perhaps it was an awkward movement, but Walker had lost objectivity, and it seemed beautiful to him. The flawless, tanned, and flexed leg, the lighter flesh of her inner thigh, and that fleeting, triangular print of panties destroyed any delusion that he held the upper hand, for he knew when one felt a desire so keenly, he couldn't have things entirely his own way. Her body gave her a big advantage, and he suspected she knew it.

Crank's was a small cafeteria, gleaming with stainless steel and plate glass, crowded with students and old women in sensible shoes who'd come to eat muesli, yoghurt, artichoke hearts, and nut cutlets. At the cashier's desk a sign read, "We are your escape from the white bread world." And it was true. Not a slice was to be seen. Whole wheat and Russian brown instead.

"Do you eat here often?"

"When I can."

"Are you a vegetarian?"

"Not really, but I go through stages where I can't stand the sight of meat and I just crave natural food. It cleans out your system." Then she asked, "Why are you going to San Francisco, Mr. Hawley?"

"I asked you first. And please call me Walker."

"I will, if you'll answer first."

"I've . . ." In her brown eyes he noticed darker flecks that sparkled beneath Crank's fluorescent bulbs. "I've been offered a grant to go to the West Coast and work."

"Oh?" She speared an artichoke heart. "What kind of grant? What do you do?"

"I'm a writer," he said, seeing no advantage in telling her he worked for Safeway. "It's a grant given by a very rich old lady interested in the arts."

"How interesting."

"Yes," he mumbled, and scraped a walnut shell out of his rissole.

"What do you write?"

"Short stories. But let's not talk about me," he said hastily, not wanting to see her false recognition when he told her of "Drowning Voices." "I'm more interested in you."

"I'm afraid I don't make a very interesting story," she said, but obviously didn't believe it. "You see, I don't have an ending, a dramatic climax."

"The climax is very important, isn't it?"

"Have you published, Walker?" Lila pushed her artichokes aside and took a pack of Benson & Hedges from the woven-wool bag.

"Yes. One of my stories just came out in an anthology," he said. "But now it's your turn. Why are you going to the West Coast?"

She stared at the filter tip of the cigarette she'd lit, and after a drag, said, "I don't know. I guess I just want to get away. I feel so"—her shoulders rose, fell—"so restricted. I want to breathe, to grow. I've changed a lot in the last few years, and I don't want to stop now. Once you stop changing, you're dead. You know what I mean? You must, you're a writer."

"I think I do."

She shook the loose blond hair back from her face, and spreading her fingers like a fan, said, "I want the option of California living. Not a life lost in appearance. That's such a drag. And of course"—she knocked an ash from her cigarette— "if you're interested in my field, San Francisco's a good place to be."

"What's your field?"

"Drama. The theatre."

"I'd have thought you'd rather go to New York."

"No. Never." She sat up straight. "I've had New York up to here. I've got too many bad memories."

70

"I'm sorry to . . ."

Smiling, she shook her head. "Don't be. Who was it who said, 'Be anything, but don't ever be sorry'? That's my motto. One of them, anyway. I learned a lot in New York."

"I guess if you're interested in the theatre . . ."

"I don't just mean the theatre. I'm talking about, you know, everything. Life. I met this fantastic man there. Actually, I went there with him. He's a professor in the Drama Department at Maryland. I won't mention his name, because I'm sure you'd know him."

"I don't know anybody at Maryland. But don't tell me about him, if you don't want to." Ill at ease, Walker pushed aside the uneaten walnut rissole. Lila unnerved him. He didn't know how to react, perhaps because she seemed to expect something different from him each time she spoke.

"That's all right. It doesn't hurt me to talk about him. He wrote a play last year that was put on by the Falls Church Players."

"I missed it." Or had he? But no. He'd never seen the Falls Church Players. Whoever they were.

"Well, all that's over, anyway." She made a fist and rapped the table. "It was an enriching experience, but it doesn't do any good to look back. We were as close as two people can get—always serious and analytical about ourselves. We were like abrasives on each other, buffing and polishing our love. But when Herb told me he wanted to divorce his wife and marry me, I knew it'd gone too far. We were using each other as oxygen tents, avoiding the responsibility of growing. Suddenly I was suffocating. I'd grown beyond him. Has that ever happened to you?"

"I'm not sure." He wondered about Dede. Who had outgrown whom? Abrasives somehow sounded relevant. No buffing or polishing. They'd rubbed each other raw.

"Last summer I decided to spend some time alone. You know, I'd almost forgotten who I was. I was so out of touch with the real me." She put a hand to her leatherbound bosom. "I went to Ocean City to my family's place. I read, sketched, photographed, and hiked through the dunes. One day I did nothing but sit on the beach and make a pile of sand and stones. It was a rich summer."

"It sounds like it."

"Then in September I felt this . . . this thing growing inside of me."

"You weren't . . .?"

"No." She chuckled. "Nothing like that. It was my new self blossoming, and I realized I had to build my own truth. Everyone does. Everyone who doesn't want to regret his life."

"I guess no one does."

"Some people act like they do. But not me. Never again. I came back to school, and got the lead role in *Antigone*. After that I knew I was ready for something bigger. A new challenge."

"I understand," Walker said hopefully.

She gave him a quick smile, reached across the table, and laid on his hand a light touch that made the hair on back of it stand on end. "Of course you do. I shouldn't be rambling on like this."

"No. I enjoy listening to you, and I think you're doing the right thing going to San Francisco. That's where all the young and talented people are heading," he quoted Grandmother Hawley.

"Have you been there?"

"Yes. My father lives in Sausalito. He and his wife are . . . well, I guess you'd say they were sculptors."

"How interesting. I'd like to meet them."

"You will as soon as we get there."

Between slender fingers she slowly rubbed a lock of blond hair, and as she rubbed, a taunting smile narrowed her eyes. "I hope they won't think it's funny that we're traveling together."

"I hadn't thought of that. I wouldn't want to . . . to compromise you."

Lila burst out laughing, showing a mouth full of healthy white teeth specked with sparkling saliva. "That went out with the nineteenth-century novels. But you're the famous writer. Won't it hurt *your* reputation to be seen with a mysterious lady?" Pulling the lock across her upper lip, she made a villain's mustache and laughed again.

Walker felt gooseflesh at the back of his neck. "Being seen with you could only enhance my reputation."

"In that case, I'll do my best to play the part."

"Don't play it. Live it!"

Taking out a compact to touch up her lipstick, Lila looked up from the tiny mirror with suddenly serious eyes. "We'll see how things go."

Walker thought it best to say nothing.

He drove her back to College Park and dropped her in front of her apartment on Knox Road. She asked him in for coffee, but he declined, fearing the longer he stayed, the more likely he was to ruin the bantering familiarity which, for no reason he could understand, linked them with something like static electricity. "I'll see you the Monday after Thanksgiving."

"I can hardly wait."

"Neither can I." And as he coasted down Knox Road, he whispered again, "Neither can I," watching her walk up the steps, the fringes of her suede jerkin and the ends of her long hair waving in the autumn air.

Chapter 6

Thanksgiving Day the weather broke. Snapped like a branch and fell with a crash to the ground. All night a high wind whined in the maple trees, skinning the sky of its autumn haze and blasting cold air through the cracks in the house. Walker and Daddy Dick woke with the feel of winter in their bones. There was frost on the front lawn, and low black clouds were folding like a dome over Cottage City.

"Snow by nightfall," said Daddy Dick, slurping his corn-flakes.

"Too early. It'll rain."

"Wait and see. I remember a Thanksgiving it snowed so deep, people had to climb up trees to take a shit. No indoor toilets in those days."

"Not around here?"

"No. West Virginia. Half a dozen football games on TV today. So let it snow."

"You going up to see Mom?"

"Yeah, right after the Packers–Lions game."

"Good, I'll go now, so she'll have two visits."

The TR-3 battled a headwind all the way to Baltimore, but the loss of speed didn't bother Walker, who was mentally preparing himself for a farewell to Mom. Of course, she'd told him not to come again, but he had to try. Not for more explanations, or an apology, but to wish her a heartfelt, low-key, goodbye. Locked in a snug carapace of indifference, safe from subterfuge, he pulled through the main gate of Oak Knoll.

The last leaf that was going to fall had fallen now, while the others, brown as old cigars, clung to the upper branches, prisoners for winter. The mad nun, alone, stalked the frozen ground, wimple waving, black skirts billowing. Everyone else was inside, many of them in the lobby reading, or painting pictures by the number—more ducks and geese, brindle cows and spotted dogs to hang on the wall—or talking to visitors, or to themselves, heads shaking, lips fluttering, hands thrashing the air.

As he started for the elevator, a strong hand grabbed Walker by the elbow. It was the fat switchboard operator. "I've got orders not to let you go up."

"What?"

"Your mother doesn't want to see you."

"She doesn't mean it. She'll be happy to . . ."

"I have my orders. Signed by Dr. Wolter."

Inside the carapace Walker felt himself going to mush. "I'm her son. She . . ."

"She left a note for you." Between fingers splotchy and red as sausages she held an envelope.

"There must be some mistake." But he read:

Walker,

I thought I told you not to come. Don't you ever obey? I don't want to see you. Never! No matter what you say, you'll just run off and leave me. If you have any feeling for me at all, pray for my special intention that you'll live to regret and repent what you're doing. If I wasn't stuck away here, I'd go to Mass today and beg God to forgive you. Maybe you'll have sense enough to do it on your own.

Mom

"She doesn't mean this," he pleaded. "She's sick. She doesn't . . ."

"That's why she's here."

"Yes, but . . ." It was no use.

Back in Cottage City, he stopped at St. James, where a special Thanksgiving Mass was being said. Surprisingly the church was full, and on the altar beside the priest stood four teenage boys with guitars. After a sermon titled "The Teen Ten Commandments; or Help Me Lord Not to Go All the Way," they strummed and sang "Sometimes I Feel Like a Motherless Child," "Summertime," and, during the consecration, "The Theme from Mondo Cane."

Walker's mind wandered, and his eyes roved from pew to

75

pew. He was sure he loved God, but he couldn't stand religion, the church, or the other parishioners. What did they have to do with his soul? The bald, beefy-faced men, straining as they knelt on one knee like defensive tackles. Members of the Holy Name Society. Bingo players. Women in their mangy winter coats. Half a dozen kids sandwiched between each husband and wife. Nothing but distractions. Was he to repent leaving them?

He knew these people. Men and women whose lives thudded always in the same groove like blunt needles. Every Sunday as an altar boy he had seen their pointed, dovelike tongues quivering for the Host, their morning breath fogging the gleam of Father Relihan's Chalice. And he'd seen them Friday and Saturday nights, too, drinking at the Rustic Cabin, Pincus' Tavern, and the Dixie Pig. Falling off chairs. Fighting on the parking lot. Thank God, they'd soon have nothing to do with his life.

Strange the thoughts that religion roused in him. Always anger, guilt, and resentment. Never joy or love. Memories of confession, or of Dede, a Methodist, who after intercourse often asked, "Do you still believe?"

"Of course I believe. I've seen it."

"Not that, Walker. I mean in God."

"Yes."

"Oh, Walker." She'd hug him in relief. She believed, and knew this was a serious sin, not to be taken lightly by either of them. Commitment made concrete by guilt.

Walker raised his head. Almost over now. "Please, God," he murmured, "I don't know what You expect of me, but I can't believe it's what I see here. I want to do good and avoid evil. Help me learn the difference." This allowed him to endure until the priest intoned, "Go in peace. The Mass is ended," and joining the others for the first time, he responded, "Thanks be to God."

On Whittier Street, Nancy and Chip's Rambler blocked the driveway, so Walker parked at the curb and went inside. With Daddy Dick out, he had no chance to escape them. They'd come early to prepare Thanksgiving dinner, and, no doubt, to try to persuade him to stay in Cottage City.

Finding the house steeped to its rafters in the aroma of roast turkey, Walker took off his coat and made for the kitchen, where Nancy, wearing a blue cotton dress and high heels, stood at the sink slicing apples and oranges for fruit salad. Her red hair, skinned back into a bun, drew her thin features into a petrified smile. "Has it started to snow?"

"Not cold enough. It'll rain."

"That's not what the weatherman says." She began to hum "White Christmas."

"How's it going?" asked Chip, who sat in Daddy Dick's chair, smoking a cigar and reading the newspaper.

"Not bad."

"How's Mom?"

"About the same."

Chip clucked his tongue. "That's a shame. I guess Nancy and I'll drive up Saturday. I think it does her a world of good to have visitors, don't you? A trip to Oak Knoll makes a man realize how lucky he is."

"Doesn't it though?" Prying open the refrigerator, Walker got a bottle of beer. "Want one, Chip?"

"No, he doesn't," said Nancy.

Blam! the door slammed, and Chip stared at the crease in his grey gabardine trousers. He was a round man, thick in the waist, with thinning straw-colored hair and a face that looked as if it'd been pinched out of a lump of dough. Beneath a high forehead he had quick dark eyes the size of pennies, indeterminate in age. Although younger than Walker, he could have passed for older than Daddy Dick.

From his belt dangled a two-way radio which he carried at all times, for he was on twenty-four-hour call at Goddard Space Agency, where he worked as a systems analyst. "Nancy owns my heart. The Lord owns my soul. But Goddard has twenty-four-hour call on my brain." Such as it was. He could always be counted on to start long anecdotes about his job, then stop before he'd made a point, and whisper, as if reminding himself, "Geez, I shouldn't mention this. It's classified."

"I'm going downstairs to watch the game," said Walker.

"Wouldn't you like to . . . ?" Nancy started.

But he was gone.

In the recreation room, always damp, cool, and dark as a root cellar, winter had most certainly come. Maybe it had never left, but instead lurked all year in the corner next to the dehumidifier, waiting to spring like a cat with frozen claws on the rest of the room, and insinuate itself up the stairs and throughout the house. Walker turned on TV for the warmth and diversion that might be in it, fell deeply into an overstuffed chair, and grabbing a ragged square of carpet from the floor, wrapped it round his knees. Ready now! Let Nancy and Chip stay upstairs, plotting in hushed, conspiratorial tones. He'd remain here, feeling safe, even if his toes fell off from frostbite.

"Today's game should be a thriller," promised Lindsay Nelson, "pitting unbeaten, bowl-bound . . ."

Footsteps thudded on the stairway. Chip had summoned the courage to risk the frigid humidity of the recreation room. "What's the score?"

"Just started."

Waddling over to fetch a chair, Chip couldn't hide the weight he'd gained, for it had all settled in his rump, and no matter how far Nancy let out his trousers, they always looked as though someone had stuffed two loaves of bread into them.

"Guess I'm putting myself right on the firing line," he said, dragging a hassock next to Walker. "Probably you'll lord it over me for months."

"I don't know what you're talking about."

"No, no." He chuckled. "Don't act like a gracious winner. We'll get you next year."

"Don't know what you're talking about."

"Come on. Don't play dumb." He gave Walker's shoulder a solid punch. "The Game! Virginia clobbered Maryland last Saturday. Don't know what's wrong with the old alma mater. The Terps haven't had a winning team in years."

"Didn't hear about it."

"Oh." Studying the palms of his hands, Chip waited a minute before making a new start. "You know, I been wanting to talk to you about something."

"Save it until half time."

"Nothing really important. I just want some advice. You see, I been thinking of writing a book. This story's been knocking around in my brain for a couple of years, but I haven't had time to put it on paper. Fact is, I don't know how to start. How would you go about it?"

"How would I know? I haven't written anything in two years."

"Well, if you were writing, how would you do it? I mean, would you do it longhand or type it?"

Walker looked at Chip, but as close as they were to each other, he couldn't trap and hold the small, darting eyes. "Longhand."

"Hmm. And would you take care of the spelling and punctuation, or let them?"

"Them?"

"You know, the publishers."

"You'd better do it yourself."

"What I ought to do, since I'm pretty busy and you're not doing too much, is let you have the story. It's about . . ."

"Look, Chip, I don't . . ."

"Just listen and see what you think. It's about this guy who goes off to war and gets wounded and loses his memory. Afterward he doesn't even remember his name, because the Japs stole his dog tags. So he goes back to the States to start a new life, and meets this girl and marries her, but it turns out that she's . . ."

"His mother."

"No, now listen, Walker. This is the important part. She's his sister, and when he finds out, he doesn't know whether to kill the baby or not."

"The baby?"

"They've had a kid. But when they find out they're brother and sister, they can't figure out whether to shoot it or not."

"Can I ask something, Chip? Why didn't this woman, this sister, recognize her brother?"

"Well"—he pulled at the putty of his face—"that's where you'd have to do a little research. Maybe they'd been separated since childhood. The important thing . . ."

A light tapping on the stairway as Nancy, unsteady in high heels, descended, and at the bottom step paused, smiled, and acted surprised to see Chip and Walker. Hands on hips, she shook her head. "Wouldn't you know it? When there's work to be done, they hide," she said in a loud, directionless voice, as if speaking to an audience.

79

"Guess she caught us." Giving Walker's knee a squeeze, Chip got up. "Here, honey, take my seat. There's a real good game on."

"What's the score?" She smoothed her skirt as she settled onto the hassock.

"Four to one in the bottom of the fifth," said Walker, seeking refuge in the TV screen.

Nancy sighed. "It's good to sit down. I've been on my feet all day. Finally I got Skip to take a nap."

To Walker it'd begun to sound like a dress rehearsal for the high school play. He knew the two of them had worked out this little scene up in the kitchen, but couldn't decide how they planned to suck him in with their moronic patter.

When Chip had found a chair, the three of them pretended to watch the game, until Nancy asked, "How's work coming, Walker?"

"I quit last week."

"I mean your writing."

"I quit that two years ago."

"What a shame! Especially after you fixed the attic into a study."

"Maybe you'll bear down and work on that plot I just gave you," said Chip.

"You know what I'd like to see you do?" asked Nancy.

"I can imagine."

"Write a story about President Kennedy and Jackie. Maybe a long book about the whole family. Wouldn't that be wonderful, Chip?"

"Hey, I think she has a point, Walker. It couldn't help being great. And you could save the story I gave you until later."

"He was such a great man. So handsome and articulate."

"It'd be a subject equal to your talent. Personally, I'd buy anything written about the man. That's how much he meant to me."

"Plus you'd be here, near Washington, to do research and go to..."

"Nancy, I..."

"And you'd have a place to live, and the attic where you could work. There'd be no one to bother..."

"Nancy, I'm going..."

"Think it over," said Chip. "This is a big opportunity to . . ."

"You wouldn't be paying rent, and if you . . ."

"Goddammit, shut up! I'm going to San Francisco."

Jumping from the hassock, Nancy flicked off the television. "Why? Why are you leaving, you selfish shit?"

"Because I want to write."

"Oh, bullshit. You haven't done a . . ."

"Please, honey, calm down," said Chip. "You'll give Skip nightmares."

Nancy folded her arms and prowled about in front of them, while Walker stared at the blank picture tube as if expecting to find in it a secret source of strength. The recreation room was growing colder. Nancy and Chip would weaken, he knew. Exposed to the damp drafts, with no rug to wrap around them, they wouldn't last much longer. But he'd stay all night, would move his bed down here until Monday morning, if necessary.

"Walker"—in a weary voice Nancy said his name softly, dragging it out to about eight syllables—"don't you think you owe Mom something?"

"No."

"Eearri . . ." She growled through clenched teeth. "You are a miserable prick."

"Nancy! Please . . ."

"He is. Show me one other . . ."

"Please," said Chip, squirming in the chair as if trying to get a grip on it with his prehensile buttocks. "I shouldn't stick my nose into a family squabble, but I think you're both being unreasonable. Nancy, there's no reason to lose your temper, and . . ."

"No reason! What the . . .?"

"And, Walker, if you're honest, I think you'll admit you owe a lot to your mother."

"You're goddamn right," said Nancy. "She carried you for nine months, nurturing you with her own flesh and blood, gave birth to you, raised you, trained you, taught you, fed you, cleaned you, clothed you, protected you . . ."

As Nancy proceeded with her enumeration, crushing Walker beneath the weight of his indebtedness, he struggled to find a loophole. An escape clause. An asterisk. There had to be something. Otherwise each man's life would be twisted and finally extinguished by continued gratitude for his existence. Generation after generation scribbling thank-you notes in blood to their mothers. "Wait a minute. I don't want to hear another word. You shut up and listen to me for once. I didn't ask to be born. As a matter of fact, I represent little more than an errant sperm."

Both of them gasped.

"Hey, Walker, show a little decency," said Chip.

"You gutter-mouthed, ungrateful turd. How can you say . . . ?"

"Will you let me finish? Okay. I've depended on Mom, and Daddy Dick, too. In your words, I owe them a debt. But I couldn't pay it off in a million years. The only thing I could do . . ."

"Would be to show a little concern for your mother in her hour of need."

"Christ Almighty, how do you turn her off? Is there a button or a switch?"

"Honey, let him finish."

"The only way I could repay Mom is to have kids of my own, raise them, provide for them, and do everything for them that . . ."

"You'd never do as much for them as she did for you."

"You're right! In fact, I'd refuse to do all the things to my children that Mom did to me."

"What are you . . . ?"

"Nancy, he's got a point." Chip's face was pulled tight by a look of fierce concentration. "It sounds logical."

"I don't give a damn about logic. This leaves us right where we started. Somebody has to look after Mom."

"She's got a whole sanitarium. Nurses, doctors, psychiatrists. She has you and Chip and Daddy Dick and Ben."

"She wants you, and you know it."

"Did you ever wonder why she wants me?"

"I don't care. She wants you, and that's all that matters."

Walker sprang out of the chair, letting the rug fall to the floor, and at once goosebumps spilled like cold urine down his legs. "What about me? Am I some kind of yoyo for her to play with? Something she can always drag back?" Turning to Chip, he asked, "Suppose Mom was in a sanitarium on the West Coast. Would you quit your job and move three thousand miles to be near her?"

Slowly his dough-ball features reddened, for, trapped between his honest systems-analyst's mind and what he knew Nancy expected of him, Chip couldn't answer.

"Shut up, and quit trying to confuse things," she shouted.

"Face it, you wouldn't move, and you know it. And I don't intend to . . ."

Beep-bleep. Beep-bleep. Beep-bleep.

"What the hell's that?" asked Nancy.

"My radio," said Chip. "Quiet, they're trying to contact me." Taking the radio from his belt, he pressed a rubber plug to his ear. "Seven one six. Blue Jay Bill. I read you loud and clear."

"Tell them you're busy. You're not going. I don't care what's busted this time."

Chip shook his head, pleading with her for silence. "Mad Dog Don, I don't read you. Repeat that last part. Have you called Am Pac Control? Did you try Cedar Rush Red? It'll be hard for me to come in."

"You're not going. Let them call someone else."

"No, Mad Dog Don, I cannot advise over the phone. No, not even on Thanksgiving Day. That information is classified. There are people in the room."

"Oh Christ, we won't listen. Tell him anything, so long as you don't go."

"Ring Linear Six on Wallop's Island and ask for Hard Hat Henry. I can't! We have . . . my mother-in-law's just been sent to a mental institution. I told you I can't."

"You won't!"

"I won't. There's too much static, Mad Dog Don. Over and out. Blue Jay Bill signing off."

"If they call you one more time, I'll personally . . ."

"It's okay, honey," he said, looping the radio over his belt. "I'm not going." Then, to Walker, "Sorry about this."

"Quite all right. There's nothing more to say."

"That's what you think, brother dear. I'm not finished. Not by a long shot. If you . . ." The back door slammed. "Oh, shit." She looked to Chip.

"Could it be Skip? Maybe he fell out of bed."

"No, dammit. It's Daddy Dick. You lucky bastard," she said to Walker.

Broad and flat as shovels his footsteps fell on the kitchen

floor, shaking the storm windows and rattling a rotten beam. The refrigerator was opened, then shut, with a popping sound from the door's gummy rubber stripping. He was coming down the stairs when Chip and Nancy drew their shoulders in close and froze.

"What's going on?" He eyed them from beneath the bill of his Washington Senator's baseball cap, a bottle of Budweiser all but hidden in the palm of his hand, and leaning back, took a swig, then wiped foam from the bristles of a two-day beard. "Well?"

"Just watching the football game," said Nancy.

"Here, Mr. Murdock," Chip leaped out of the chair. "Have a seat."

Daddy Dick studied the empty television screen a moment, grunted, and leaning down to flick it on, fell into Chip's seat.

"Guess I'll go check the bird," said Nancy with a brittle laugh that shattered in midair. "Don't ruin your appetite, Daddy Dick."

"Need any help, honey?" Afraid to be left without her, Chip floundered up the basement steps.

"What did they want?"

"They wanted me to stay."

"Hmpf!" Removing the cap, he set it on his knee and twisted the little felt button on top. "That's what Mina wants, too."

"Did she know I tried to see her this morning?"

"Yeah, and she was plenty pissed off. Said if you'd really wanted to see her, you wouldn't of let them stop you."

"What! That bull-dyke at the desk could toss a piano out a window."

"Mina's not herself these days."

Daddy Dick's face hadn't changed expression. Not in the last few minutes. Never in the last two decades. But Walker knew he was troubled and so asked, "Do you want me to stay?"

The florid jaw moved slowly back and forth. "No. I want you to go and have a good time. You worry too much. That's why you're so skinny. Take it easy and put some meat on your bones. Maybe after you're settled and Mina gets better, we'll drive out and visit. I hear they got dual-lane roads now all the way to the Coast." Then, after watching a few plays in silence, Daddy Dick asked, "When you were off to the university, did you take any medicine?"

"Do you mean pills or shots?"

"No, I mean did you learn about it? I was wondering about Mina. You suppose what she's got is serious?"

"The doctor told me she needs rest. That's all. But . . ."

Sighing, he clapped the cap onto his head backward like a catcher would. "Seems like she could rest just as good right here. I'd take care of her."

"I think it's easier on her up there. You couldn't keep her still. She'd want to clean, and cook, and help Father Relihan in the rectory."

"I guess you're right. But, you know, the way I see it, it won't take her no time to throw off this bug, or whatever she's caught, and get home by Christmas."

"I wouldn't count on it, Daddy Dick. She's . . . she's more worn down than any of us imagined."

"You think so?"

"I'm afraid I do."

"I see. Sure is lonesome around here without her."

"We'll just have to be patient," Walker muttered inanely, and wondered whether the sorrow he felt for Daddy Dick had ever touched Mom. Couldn't she see how he loved her, and how utterly he depended on her? Why wasn't this enough for her?

Daddy Dick drained the last of his beer, forced a loud belch, and asked, "You want a cold one?"

"Yeah. Sounds good."

Together they watched the second half, and for a while Walker felt better, as if through a few muddled sentences they'd come to an understanding. But as afternoon grew old and evening came to the recreation room on a breath of dampness and decomposition, Walker felt trapped, shut off even from his stepfather. He turned the dehumidifier a notch higher, but this was no help. Nothing could keep pace with the doom that worked at him from the inside out, sprouting like mildew and ravaging the fabric of his will. Soon the ceiling of plasterboard, sagging like a wet blanket, and the walls of green Sta-Dri which gave the room the look of an empty swimming pool, and the cold grey floor, seemed the limits of his life. All he'd ever known. Or the things he knew so well they outweighed everything else.

There was only this room, and television, where the football game continued—a nip-and-tuck battle, said Lindsay Nelson.

And he was right. It went down to the everloving wire, which somehow seemed to tighten around Walker's throat, choking him on the residue of all the cliff-hanging pressure-packed games he'd seen this season. And yet, although the noose pulled tighter, Walker couldn't stop watching. Better those flickering images than nothing. The illusion of progress in the high leg motion of a breakaway runner. Faster and farther over a field of green toward the goal line. Desperate for victory, but if victory were impossible, then for violence, any absolute to shatter the stalemate of an empty life.

Finally Nancy called them to the table, but this was no reprieve. Bloated with beer, Walker watched Chip carry platters of food from the kitchen, and felt his throat clench like an angry fist. It was impossible to beg off, to refuse the challenge. Before the night ended they had to devour this fat brown bird. Crack off its crust. Dip out its roasting innards. Gnaw its flesh. Suck its bones.

After Chip strapped Skip into the high chair, they lowered their heads, and joining hands, said grace. "Bless us, oh, Lord, and these . . ." Holding Daddy Dick's calloused paw in his right hand and Skip's wet fingers in his left, Walker stared at a plate of stuffed olives whose pimentos glared like bloodshot eyes. ". . . Amen." Slightly embarrassed, since they rarely said grace aloud, they raised their heads and went to work.

"Chip will do the carving this year," said Nancy. "He just got a new electric knife with green stamps."

Disappointed, Daddy Dick set aside the brass fork and butcher knife with which he'd attacked so many turkeys and roasts in years past.

"Too bad Mom and Ben can't be with us," said Chip, sawing slices of breast meat and arranging them fanlike on a platter. "But I guess we should be thankful for . . ."

"Small favors," said Walker.

"Yes, this year we'll just have to be thankful for what we've got," said Nancy, passing a dish of celery stalks daubed with peanut butter. "Even if a lot has gone wrong, a lot of other things have . . ." Celery suspended over gravy boat, she paused, sensing that if a lot had gone wrong and a lot had gone right, there was no point in talking. Like most, this year had been a draw. But disapproving of ambivalence, she plowed on, bent on filing

1968 in her mental debit-credit sheet. "In many ways we were lucky. If you think about people who . . ."

"Want a beer, Walker?"

"Oh no, Daddy Dick, you'll spoil your dinner." A grim, panicked look came to her face as she tried to figure how many he'd already had. "Why not have some cider?"

"Naw." He rose unsteadily. "That stuff gives me the runs."

He brought a bottle for Walker, as well as for himself, and although Walker didn't want it, he accepted and drank deeply, cauterizing his tongue with the taste of copper tubing, as Nancy and Chip continued their solemn antiphony. It'd been a joyous year, yet a sad one. A depressing one, yet hopeful. Full of sudden shocks and disappointments, yet also full of lessons. One that they'd like to forget, yet would always remember. Long, yet short. Cold, yet somehow warm. Troubled, yet . . .

Like characters in a soap opera they trampled each other's lines until the phone rang.

"I'll get it," said Walker.

"No, let me . . ."

"I said I'd get it, and I will." Throwing his napkin to the table, he dashed.

The phone was in the hallway on a wrought-iron table, and next to it, serving as a paperweight, hunched a green porcelain frog Ben had made in high school shop class. Because it reminded Walker of him, he wasn't surprised to hear Ben's voice long-distance from Fort Campbell, Kentucky.

"Say, how's it going? Man, Airborne School's a bitch. I made my first jump last week. Nearly tore my ass off in an apple tree. But . . ."

"You know Mom's at Oak Knoll," said Walker pointlessly—or perhaps just to calm him—for Ben, of course, already knew.

"Yeah, that's one reason I called. I hope it isn't a schizo type of thing. I read this book once called *I Married a Maniac* and . . ."

"She needs a little rest. A couple of months. That's all."

"Maybe she'll be out by Christmas. Do you think she'll recognize me? Her letters have been awful strange. I got one last week that started, 'Dear Jacob.' "

"Probably a joke. Let me call the others, and have them say hello."

But he didn't need to call. Weakening in their assault on the turkey, they were on the way.

"How've you been?" he felt free to ask, since he wouldn't have to listen to the answer.

"Great! I'm up to one-ninety."

"Pardon?"

"I put on fifteen pounds last month. All muscle. I been on a new isometric program. I've never been in such good shape."

"Here's Daddy Dick."

"Put him on the extension, so we can all talk."

Chip, with Skip in his arms, stayed with Walker in the hall, while Daddy Dick and Nancy went upstairs to the bedroom phone.

"Hello, boy. How you doing?"

"Hi, Daddy Dick. You saving me a drumstick?"

Handing Chip the receiver, Walker slipped away to the living room. Dingiest room in the house. Across the carpet a threadbare path led from hallway to kitchen. An oval mirror reflected a painting of the Sacred Heart of Mary—skewered with seven dolors—which hung on the opposite wall. Tops of end tables showed circles left by glasses and bottles, and the black smudges of cigarette butts that had burned away the varnish. In the corners, curled rollers of dust, for now that Mom had gone, the room was seldom used. And yet Walker could feel her presence, sense it in the ugly egg-white walls. It'd been a bad day, but it would have been worse if she and Ben had been home. For while Ben always reminded him of what, without a few chromosomes and chances, he might have become, she forced him to admit just how murky and unsure his future still was.

Chip held the receiver to Skip's mouth. "Say hello to Ben."

"Hello, Uncy Bing."

"Did you hear that, Ben? Sure, we miss you. We're having a great time."

When Ben's three minutes were up, they returned to the table and fell upon the bird with renewed appetites. Soon bones began to show. Chip loosened his belt. Skip gnawed a wing. Nancy had another slab of white meat. Daddy Dick snapped off a drumstick.

"Dressing, anyone?" asked Nancy. "Didn't Ben sound in fine spirits?"

"Good to hear from him," said Chip, "but I wish he hadn't decided to go Airborne. He should of tried to learn a trade. Electronics. Typing. Management."

"Don't worry about him." Daddy Dick wielded the drumstick for emphasis. "That boy won't have no trouble. He always could handle himself. Jesus Christ, can you imagine? He's up to one-ninety. Wait till Mina finds out."

Walker ate silently, tasting little. This does it, he thought after each bite. No more peas or pickles, potatoes or dressing. Enough is enough. Then he shoved in another mouthful.

Chapter *7*
_____

It had begun to snow, falling in scraps like bread dressing, or flakes of white meat, or globs of whipped cream. Sight of it made him sick. Eddying, whirling, and changing shape, it swept down Whittier Street and blew against the window of Walker's room. Daddy Dick was in the recreation room, waiting for the final football game. Nancy, Chip, and Skip had left early for Takoma Park, afraid of being snowed in. "So long, Mr. Know-it-all," she'd called over her shoulder. "Hope you freeze your butt off tonight."

But he wouldn't. Not here under the eaves where heat gathered like the wooly wings of bats. Although it looked cold and austere—an artist's garret with narrow cot, small desk, and straight-backed chair—the room was sultry as the tropics, and the lampshade, which cast green light on the sloping roof, created the impression of a bamboo hut or a lean-to of palm fronds.

Yet if he was certain he wouldn't freeze, there was little else he could be sure of in the solitude of his attic study, for despite all he'd eaten and drunk, he still felt an aching, unknown appetite. Was it Dede? he wondered. Did he miss her already? Or was it the thought of Lila Caine? He knew he needed something to deaden his awareness of this empty day.

The snow was no help. From the window, he could see it had fallen four inches deep on the grass and laid a slick glaze on the street. Clinging to telephone wires, it traced white lines like the thick filament of a spider's web over the night, holding Cottage City a prisoner of its wet embrace. A car careened around the corner and fishtailed toward Bladensburg Road, splashing slush

90

into the gutters and trailing ribbons of black. At once a flurry of new flakes covered the tracks.

As a boy, Walker had loved snow and hoped one winter a blizzard would bury the ugliness of Cottage City in blocks of polished blue ice that would never melt. But the sun always reappeared and stripped the town to its withered bones, leaving in puddles of grey slush a skeleton like that of the turkey which lay on a plate in the icebox on a film of congealed grease. Now he had no faith in snow, especially not in this storm, which had come too early in the year and would last no longer than a day.

Like so many things, snow had let him down. Was all surface and no substance, little more than dreary rain decked out in a winter coat. Lifted his hopes, then crushed them, filling his ears with metallic laughter as it melted on rooftops and chuckled through drainpipes. Every time he'd seen his dream dissolve and swirl down the sewer, he'd come to hate snow more. Hate it, yet hold his breath and try to hammer down hope as if it were an erection he'd gotten in church.

It wouldn't free him. Just the reverse, he thought, remembering a morning of snow when he was nine and had sat in Sister Catherina's class daydreaming of sleigh rides after school. Outside, black clouds coiled and twisted, squeezing loose the heaviest fall he'd ever seen, flakes the size of large daisies tumbling to the ground in solid lines, like ropes to moor the clouds to earth. His memory was of a whirling white motion without sound, a silence which grew more profound by the hour, until at noon recess, when he floundered over the playground, knee-deep in drifts, yelling so that his throat burned, his voice didn't carry much beyond the mushroom of his breath. He thought this at last was the blizzard he'd hoped for. Tomorrow there'd certainly be no school. As for the day after, and the weeks to come, who knew what might happen?

When the bell rang and lines regrouped to march back to class, Walker hurriedly packed a snowball and tossed it at the sliding board. In a perfect arc it glided across the yard—barely perceptible, like the scribble of a sky writer on a hazy day—and with a soft thump burst against the board.

"Matthew Hawley! Step out of line." Sister Catherina had caught him. Taking his ear in the pincers of her fingers, she led him into the building and down the hall toward Mother Superior's office. Since he hadn't thought the offense was that serious—especially not for someone like him who seemed always to be in trouble—he was frightened, for boys were often taken to Mother Superior before they were suspended or expelled. But just outside the office, Sister brought him to an abrupt and painful stop with a twist that left his ear ringing. "One moment, Mr. Smart Aleck. Come with me." They moved beneath a statue of the Infant of Prague, a pink porcelain baby Jesus robed in royal garments, who held in one hand the globe—such as one might a snowball—while the other was raised as if to say, "Peace." "Look up at Him, Matthew. Do you think He'd ever fight on the playground, or talk in class, or chew gum, or throw snowballs in the schoolyard?"

"No," he whispered, lowering his eyes.

"No what?" Roughly she lifted his chin. "Don't stand there with your nose to the ground like a puppy dog."

"No, Sister."

"Matthew, you're such a disappointment to me. To all of us. We expected so much of you."

"Who did?"

"Who did what?" She squeezed his jaw till his eyes watered.

"Who expected so much of me, Sister?"

"We all did. And still do. God does. You know the parable of the talents. To whom much is given, much is . . ."

Pressure to his jaw popped the answer out, "Expected."

"Correct. You know, Matthew, I've been offering up my prayers for you all this year, hoping the Lord would help you become an obedient and attentive student, and during this time I've come to a surprising discovery. What do you think I found out?"

"My jaw hurts, Sister."

She released her grip. "Now then, what do you think I discovered?"

"I don't know, Sister."

"Matthew, I think God has chosen you. I think you have 'the call.' Haven't you ever considered devoting your life to Christ and becoming a priest?"

"No, Sister," he lied, as though with one sin he could shed the destiny which, on this snowy day when he wanted only to be a boy at play, weighed too heavily on him.

"You'd better start thinking about it."

"Yes, Sister."

"Have you chosen a confirmation name?"

"Jerome."

"Why don't you change it to Christopher? Do you know what that name means?"

"Yes, Sister. Christ bearer." And a picture from his *Catechism* came to mind. The brawny saint carrying the Christ child on his shoulder. But the nun's solemn eyes bearing down on him caused a strange inversion, and he imagined himself the size of the baby Jesus, staggering beneath the weight of a grown man.

"Keep that in mind when you're tempted to sin, and St. Christopher will help you. And pray for guidance. It would be a shame if you threw away a vocation because of your poor conduct."

Walker returned with Sister to the classroom, feeling guilty because he had "the call"—there was nothing he could do about it—but didn't want it. Particularly not today when snow was piling deeper and packing harder. Soon the police would barricade Longfellow Street for sleigh-riding, and tonight at the bottom of the hill someone would build a fire and roast marshmallows. The smell of burned sugar and wood smoke would mingle in the frozen air while kids stood beneath the streetlamp to lick the sweetness from their fingers and watch golden flakes slant through the cone of light.

Yet to Walker, who had "the call," all this seemed already forsaken, and he wondered what priests did in their free time. Father Relihan played softball with the eighth-graders, but at night when snow fell heavy and luminous as sparks from a Fourth of July rocket, and Cottage City grew quiet and close, what did he do? Stay in the sanctuary, where Walker had seen him after Mass, kneeling in the darkness, head buried in his hands which smelled of wine, unleavened bread, and beeswax?

When school let out, everyone raced home for his sled, and Walker ran too, but felt himself not really a part of what he saw. Even when he came to the crest of Longfellow Street for his first ride of the winter, his mind was elsewhere, his thoughts turning back upon themselves like the curved spine of Father Relihan, who on Saturday afternoon, after hearing confessions, paced with stooped shoulders next to the rectory reading his breviary. Then one kid after another belly-flopped to the sound of steel runners, until finally it was Walker's turn and he, too, flung himself downhill, snow needling his face, stinging his eyes, and bowling him over like high surf as he piled into a drift.

Without brushing off, he charged back up the hill, determined to have a better, faster ride this time, but after a second and a third and a fourth try, his breath rattled like ice cubes in his rib cage, his legs quivered, his feet thudded against ruts, his hands were numb, and he knew not even his Flexible Flyer was fast enough to outdistance "the call." Flopping down onto the sled, he scooped up a handful of snow, pressed it to his feverish cheek, and whispered an Act of Contrition.

Now, as ever, falling snow left him heartily sorry for some sin or evasion, but just as anxious to outrun "the call." No longer the priesthood, of course, but any "call" that would limit his future. He had to be free. To do what he wanted. At least to find out what that was. But on Thanksgiving, a day of forced gratitude and comradery, made more difficult by memories of disappointing snows, it was impossible. Better to be alone at such a time, for at home, faced with a fifteen-pound turkey and a year's supply of platitudes, he didn't have a chance.

The phone rang, a loud rasping noise like a rusty zipper ripping the house in two. It rang again. With the TV tuned to a football game, Daddy Dick would never leave the recreation room, so Walker raced down the narrow steps, past the bedroom extension, and descended the stairs to the hall phone, to be closer to the door, ready to leave. He had a premonition it was Dede calling to say . . . to say . . . what? Or maybe Lila Caine, calling to ask him . . .

"Is that you, Walker?" A woman's voice.

Eager and out of breath, "Yes."

"Oh, Walker." The woman broke into tears. It was Mom.

Groaning, he squatted on his haunches, leaned against the wall, and although not cold, began to shiver. "What's wrong, Mom?"

"Nothing, baby. Nothing at all. But I had to talk to you. I couldn't let you leave like this. You shouldn't have listened to that nurse. I didn't mean what I wrote." She flung the words like fishhooks, a facile flycaster of emotions, and Walker could feel her trying to reel him in. Why couldn't she make up her mind? One moment she was a harridan, the next the nicest woman you'd want to know—if you didn't already know her as he did.

"How did you get to a telephone?"

"I bribed the nurse's aide. I knew how bad you must of felt about that note. Please don't hold it against me."

"I won't hold it against you."

"You promise?"

"Yes."

"You forgive me?"

"There's nothing to forgive, Mom. Everything's all right."

"Walker, you're not mad because I called, are you?"

"No." But he spoke wearily, as if pushed to the limits of his patience. Then immediately he felt ashamed of himself. After all, what was so trying about a desperate call from a sick, lonely woman? His mother. "You scared me," he added in a gentler voice.

"I didn't mean to. I keep forgetting how I affect you. If I'd thought this was going to bother you, I wouldn't of called, but I had to say goodbye. Have a wonderful time out there. Enjoy yourself. But don't forget who you are, Walker. You've got Walker blood in you, so be . . ."

"Thanks, Mom, but I . . ."

"Sure, you've had troubles in the last two years, but you haven't found yourself. That's all."

"That's enough."

"What?"

"Good to hear from you, Mom, but I think you'd better go back to your room. I wouldn't want you to get in trouble."

"Please, don't hang up." She started to sob again. "I don't have anybody to talk to. Nobody in the whole world."

"That's not true. You've got Daddy Dick and Nancy, Chip and Skip. And there must be patients you can talk to."

"Yes, but you and I always seem to have such good conversations. Remember the time right after Ben . . ."

"Mom, it doesn't help to think of those things," he said, unable to recall one of their conversations that hadn't ended in an argument.

"I guess you're right, Walker. I'll just have to learn to accept this cross. A long time ago I read a book about . . ."

"Yes, that's a good idea." Legs throbbing, he stood up.

"Actually, I've already accepted it. That's the only thing I can be proud of. The way I accept. But you probably don't believe that, do you?"

"I believe it, but I think . . ."

"What were you doing when I called?"

"I was about to go to bed."

"At ten o'clock?"

"I'm tired."

"Okay, I'll let you go. Pull the covers up over your shoulders so you don't catch cold."

"Good night, Mom."

"Do you ever put JMJ on your pillow?"

"What?"

"You don't, do you? I knew you didn't."

"What are you talking about?"

"The sign of Jesus, Mary, and Joseph. I used to put it on your pillow every night before you went to bed. Now you'll have to do it for yourself."

"Mom, take care of yourself. I'll write."

"Please do, Walker. I'll miss you."

"Goodbye."

In the darkened hall, with the dead phone in his hand, Walker paused, not wanting to return to the attic. Before his mind could tell his frantic fingers what fools they were, he'd dialed Dede's number. It rang three times. Eight. Twelve. Ten o'clock and she was still out. Where? Maybe home in Chattanooga.

Breaking the connection, he listened to the dial tone drill at his ear. In the distance there was static on the line, a whispering mockery, an open invitation to call anyone anywhere on earth. But who? Slowly he picked out the number of the weather bureau. Cloudy and cold tonight. Snow accumulating four to six inches, with more in the western suburbs. Hazardous Driving Plan Number Three in effect. Tomorrow clearing and warmer. Barometer . . . He hung up and dialed Time. At the sound of the tone, 10:16. Bong! Then the Sport Report, to hear a recorded announcement of the football scores he already knew.

" 'At you, Walker?" Daddy Dick shouted from the recreation room. "How about bringing me a beer and the other drumstick?"

He lopped the last limb off the carcass, opened a beer, and started down, feeling at each step as if he were descending to the core of an iceberg. Cold air from the concrete floor had forced Daddy Dick closer to the TV, to seek in it the warmth of tubes and transistors. Slumped in the chair, he wore his car coat and baseball cap, and had pulled the carpet up over his knees.

"Daddy Dick, you'll freeze to death down here."

"Colder than a well-digger's butt, ain't it?"

"Why don't you go to bed?"

"I got one more game to see."

"You'll feel like hell in the morning."

"If this weather keeps up, I might stay home tomorrow. Take a long weekend. Pull up a chair and open a beer. This here's a pretty good ball game."

"Who's playing?"

"Don't know. Couple of West Coast teams."

"I think I'll go to bed. Careful with your cigarettes. Don't stay up too late," he said.

"Going to bed already?"

"Yeah, I'm beat."

"Want me to call you if the game gets better?"

"No, thanks. See you in the morning."

"Wait a minute, Walker. Before you go . . ." Setting the beer and drumstick on the end table, he dug into his pocket. "I got something for you. Here." He reached out and pressed a ten-dollar bill into Walker's palm.

"Daddy Dick, I can't . . ."

"No, keep it, and when you get to California, buy yourself a steak dinner."

Walker put a hand on the man's shoulder, a gathering of muscle as lumpy and thick as an oak limb. "Thanks, Daddy Dick."

"It's nothing. But"—dragging his eyes away from the game again—"I want you to promise to write your mother. She's going to miss you."

"I promise."

"Good boy. Get a good night's sleep."

From the stairway, he glanced back and saw Daddy Dick's

97

breath condense in the dank air, forming a wreath around his head.

As usual on nights when he felt lonely, and when being with Daddy Dick only made it worse, Walker didn't return to the attic. To that crooked coffin where he'd spent so many nights confronting blank pages which seemed a perfect reflection of his mind. That narrow space beneath the sloping roof where Mom had come to him two months ago, having crawled on hands and knees up the steps and clawed at the door, moaning like an animal. "Walker, please, help me." He'd carried her to the cot, and turning on a lamp, seen dark eyes that shone like squashed beetles. "Help me."

"My God, what's wrong?"

"I'm dying." Her sparrow-claw hands scrabbled the air, then fell to her throat. "I can't breathe, Walker. Help me."

"I'll call a doctor."

"No." She grabbed his arm. "Don't leave. I don't need a doctor. I need you."

"Mom, I . . ."

"Not a doctor, Walker. He'll put me in a hospital." The cords of her neck stood out thick as pencils. "I can't stand it any more. I've got to get away from this house."

"Let me get help."

"Don't go!" The claw tightened.

So taking her in his arms again, he carried her down to Daddy Dick, who sat up in bed, blinked, and said, "What the hell?"

"Mom's sick. She needs help."

"I'm not sick," she screamed, writhing and thrashing till she fell from his arms and thudded to the floor. "It's you two. It's all of this. I can't stand it any more. Get away from me. Don't touch me."

They'd wrapped her in a blanket, carried her out to the pickup truck, and with Daddy Dick struggling to restrain her, Walker had driven to Prince George's Hospital. In the morning she'd been sent to Oak Knoll.

No, tonight he didn't dare climb up there where mad thoughts would flicker batlike through his brain long after he'd fallen asleep. Better to stay in Ben's room. Solid, safe, and familiar. Barbells in the corner, half a dozen copies of *Playboy* hidden under the mattress, and a picture of Ben's girl, Cherry, taped to the mirror. Tumble into bed, thinking of Ben, concentrating on Ben. Bore yourself to sleep. The way he cracked his knuckles. Or came to the door of Walker's room, pressed his hands against the jamb, and after an isometric contraction, asked if he could borrow the TR-3. Yes, Ben with that scar beneath his nose, which sometimes made you think he needed a Kleenex, or should, at least, sniff it back. It'd given him a camel's smile ever since that day when he was five and had nearly harelipped himself running into a wall. Out to the truck for a trip to Prince George's Hospital. Mom had held Ben in her lap, his head pressed against the front of her dress, leaving bloodstains like lipstick prints. Daddy Dick desperately driving to Cheverly, while Nancy and he stayed at home, half convinced Ben would bleed to death. To be helpful they'd mopped the trail of blood from the kitchen floor, then decided to have dinner waiting when the family returned. Three watery bowls of lime jello. The only thing they knew how to make. Ben, forbidden to eat solid food, sucked it up through a plastic straw the next day. Yes, Ben. Ah . . .

He slept in peace until, dragged down to a deeper darkness by the turkey he'd eaten, the beer he'd drunk, and the spartan firmness of Ben's bed, he dreamed he was on a beach where at low tide the sea had drawn back for miles, leaving mud flats and sandbars to bake in a bright sun. Pants legs rolled to the knee, he padded out where the water had receded, a long way off. A blue line below the horizon. All around him on the sand lay stranded fish desperately pumping their gills, and clams and crabs blowing bubbles of foam. They would die there, unless . . .

Daddy Dick, in a bathing suit, his legs surprisingly pale and thin as pipestems, appeared with a shovel. "Let's help them, son," he said, and scooping up the fish, tossed them back into the sea. But as they tried to pry a starfish loose from a rock, they heard a dull rumble and, turning, saw a tidal wave rushing toward shore. Daddy Dick grabbed his hand and the two of them raced for high ground, their feet slipping on the mud and falling into pools of quicksand, while overhead the massive wave curled higher until its crest left them in a deep green shadow.

At the last moment Walker saw it wasn't a wave after all, but a wall of tangled bodies about to crush them. Mom, Nancy, Ben, Skip and Chip, Dede, Grandmother Hawley and Jordan Oliver, even Dad and Tanya were tumbling in a mass that finally broke over them with a roar that dashed Walker to the foamy fringes of sleep, then rocked him more gently, pulled him away from consciousness and back into a dream.

This time Daddy Dick and he were running breathless and barefoot over cool wet grass. A football field before thousands of fans who cheered as the two of them outraced everyone toward the goal line. So fast it seemed they were in the TR-3, driving with the top down, feeling like test pilots who while breaking the sound barrier watched sonar waves slip over the wings of the plane and disappear. It was a dizzying experience, faster than sound or light, so that their hands reached out vainly for what was passing. And for an instant all their troubles were gone as he and Daddy Dick began to soar, sailing toward a . . .

Walker's body gave a lurch, spilling him out of the dream and back to Ben's room. Silence. He lay listening, but heard nothing. The house, the town, the world were all asleep. He glanced at his watch. Ten after twelve. He'd dozed less than two hours. Good, that meant more time to . . . But he remained on his back, eyes and ears poised. Curiously, no sound of Daddy Dick. Shivering, Walker sat up. By this time he should have been in bed, dead drunk, snoring through the stiff whiskers of his nose.

"Daddy Dick, are you all right?" he shouted, ashamed of the quaver in his voice.

No answer.

This time he called louder. "Daddy Dick, where are you?"

Stupid to cry out that way. It would only scare him. He'd go to bed when he was ready. Walker lay back, shut his eyes, but wondered, What about his cigarettes? Suppose he'd passed out in the recreation room. He was likely to freeze to death down there. No. That was silly. He was pickled in alcohol, bone, muscle, and marrow. But Walker sat up again, threw back the covers, and started down the hall to the bathroom. No reason to worry. Check his bedroom on the way.

The floor was frigid, forcing Walker to step gingerly, prance like an elf. But it made his heart pound harder, so he stopped.

What if Daddy Dick saw him walking like that? Be sending him to Oak Knoll next. He rapped on the door. "Daddy Dick, you okay? I didn't hear you come up, so I . . ."

As the door swung open, Walker switched on the light to reveal an empty bed. He was downstairs, of course. Why worry? Bug him and bother him as Mom had always done? He was a grown man.

He stepped into the bathroom, onto the tile which felt like an ice-skating rink. Teeth chattering, he told himself he was cold. That was all. A well-digger's butt. A witch's tit. A brass brassiere.

He glanced behind the door, but there was no one there. Of course. No one in the linen closet. He hadn't tripped and fallen into the bathtub. Best to give the teeth one last brushing, though, before bed, and chase away the foul taste which grew like mushrooms on his gums.

But reaching for the toothpaste he noticed how badly his hands were trembling. Oh Christ. Feeling faint, he clutched the cold porcelain sink, then pushed away from it and thundered downstairs with a sound like breaking surf. The crash of a high wave. God, please, no. He rushed toward the recreation room, opened the door, and called out, "It's me, Daddy Dick. I didn't mean to scare you, but . . ." Finally he looked down.

What he saw struck him like a dizzying blow to the forehead. He grabbed at the banister for balance, but it ripped free from the wall, clattered down the steps, and fell beside Daddy Dick, who was sprawled at the bottom of the stairwell, his back and head flat against the cold concrete floor, his legs slanting against the steps. The cuffs of his workpants had wrinkled back from his shoes to expose swaths of hairy calf. In his right hand he held four empty beer bottles, which amazingly hadn't broken, and in his left the remainder of the drumstick. A warrior who'd gone down wielding his weapons. The baseball cap had been pushed far to the back of his head and was fast filling with blood.

"Daddy Dick," Walker shouted, then must have fainted, for he came to lying on the landing, and thought to himself as his eyes rolled open, "He's dead." He knew this even before he got up and almost tripped down the stairs.

Coming closer, there was no doubt. Blood formed a thick pool about his crushed skull, dribbled from his flared nostrils, and dried in crooked lines across his face, describing with rusty brown each net of wrinkles. It'd also curled from the shells of his ears and was still falling with a soft plop to the floor. From where else it flowed—no doubt from a massive hemorrhage somewhere at the back of his head . . . Walker couldn't bring himself to remove the soaking cap and find out. Instead, he put his fingers to the thick wrist, which was lifeless and cold.

Strangely, the feel of it had the effect of calming him, of allowing him to move with the meaty unimaginative self-assurance of a doctor at the scene of an accident. Next he pressed a hand to the motionless chest, and leaning down, held his cheek above the open mouth to detect the faintest exhalation. Nothing. One of Daddy Dick's eyes was shut, the other half open, gleaming like a chip of green glass. A silverfish, flecked with blood, flashed from the tangle of sandy hair, and after two wild feints, leaped to the floor and escaped into darkness.

"Ooh," Walker moaned, and fell back on his haunches, but was still curiously calm. At least he wouldn't faint again.

Balling up his fist, he thumped Daddy Dick's chest in a melodramatic effort to jar the heart to life. The sound was of a crowbar striking an inflated tire. Whoomp! Whoomp! Whoomp! The body made a little bounce with each blow, so that finally Walker had to stop. His aching hand had started to shake and the blows had done nothing but hasten the beat of his own heart.

Only one thing left to try. Leaning down, he caught a whiff of stale beer and turkey dressing, and lowering his face closer still, felt the weather-chapped and blood-encrusted lips against his chin as he summoned a breath of life-giving air and blew it into the mouth. A moist, flatulent noise escaped the lips and from inside Daddy Dick rose a rank coppery stench of death. Walker pulled back, jumped to his feet, and ran upstairs. There was nothing more to do.

Switching on the light, he went to the kitchen and collapsed onto Daddy Dick's chair. Yesterday's sport page lay on the table. "Packers Take on Lions in Turkey Day Delight." At once he realized, even through the fog of his trauma, that he was wrong. There was a lot more he had to do. Close Daddy Dick's mouth and eyes with a damp towel, then start making phone calls. An undertaker first. Nancy and Ben . . . Oh God! Maybe he would faint again.

Instead, he raised himself from the chair, went to the sink, and doused a dishtowel under the spigot. But when grainy dots spun in front of his eyes, he hunched forward and stared down the drain. Dark and scum-colored, it made a gurgling, sucking sound like the flutter of dead lips. What the hell was going on? Daddy Dick lay cold as a side of beef in the basement, yet here he stood like someone watching himself through the wrong end of a telescope. Distant, studied, and precise, his motions had the grave confidence of Dr. Kildare in his greatest role, while deep in his heart a scream stood on tiptoe straining to be let out.

At last his larynx burst open, but vomit rather than a cry of anguish gushed out, as his stomach heaved up chunks of half-chewed turkey, undigested potatoes, peas and bread. All the pap and slop he'd stuffed down that day simply to be rid of it and get away from the table. It came out now in strings and strands and blobs on a stream of beer and bile, a poisonous taste of rotting liver. He stuck a finger down his throat to bring up what was left. The last bits of this horrible day. Angrily he spat everything out. The decayed matter of so many years. The soggy, death-dealing substance of his life.

When his guts could yield no more, he turned off the spigot and fell back into the chair, pressing the damp dishtowel to his brow. Had to calm down and get a grip on himself. Sick, empty, frightened. Things were bad, but they could only get worse. Shocked and stricken with grief, he'd soon have to do better, and be sorry both in his own and everyone else's way.

Yes, tomorrow they'd come. The O'Reillys and the Durslags. The Luxfords and the Lyonses. Father Relihan and a clutch of nuns from St. James. They'd tell him to be strong, or ask him to have a stiff drink with them and for a moment forget. Nancy, of course, would be here. Ben, wearing his Airborne patch and weighing one-ninety, would come home from Fort Campbell to stand at attention and ask, like everyone else, why Walker hadn't prevented it. Chip would wait, jangle the two-way radio on his belt, and wonder whether Walker was up to being man of the family. Well, he wasn't! And he'd never wanted to be. Especially now that Mom . . . Good Christ! She'd have to be told. They'd let her out for the funeral. Furious rather than sorry, she'd see this death as another tragedy he'd caused by wanting to leave home.

And as for leaving home, there wasn't a chance now. He'd have to stay. Later he'd wake fully to this realization, wake with a sense of bewilderment not so much at what had happened to Daddy Dick as to himself. At least Daddy Dick was dead, while Walker, with all hope lost, would have to go on living, alone here in Cottage City, trapped between attic and recreation room, afraid to spend the night in either. Spend those dark, silent hours when strange thoughts and fears drove like tenpenny nails through the soft underbelly of his brain. Good God, he couldn't stand it!

His shoulders sagged. Things were closing in. Soon the kitchen would be the only safe room. The only one not haunted by bad memories, not tainted by failure, madness, and death. His life would be reduced to the beam of light let down by the circular fluorescent bulb. A luminous ring like iron. Nancy and Ben, Skip and Chip, even Mom, would have lives of their own, but he'd have nothing. The dream of California would wither, Grandmother Hawley's money would go to waste, and as for ever finding himself, coming into his own, he could forget it.

Wrapping the cold wet rag around his neck, he hunched forward in the chair, a sharp cramp, a labor pain of sorts, gnawing with jagged rat teeth at his belly. Like a woman nine months gone, he felt another life kicking and thrashing about inside him, desperate to be born. Another self which if it didn't get out now, never would. He wanted a chance to live before he wound up at the bottom of a dark stairwell, shattered like Daddy Dick.

At last a scream broke from his lips, not a high keening wail of despair or sorrow, but an angry cry, a roar. "I won't do it," he shouted, and threw the wet wad of towel through the kitchen window and out into the yard. Gone. The explosion of glass brought him to his feet and he was running. Out of the kitchen and up the stairs. Moving. He had to get away, and do now what he'd never been able to do before. Escape.

In the attic a suitcase lay half-packed on the desk. Grabbing what he could easily find—a few more shirts, another pair of pants, some underwear, *The Sign of Jonas,* and a copy of *Best Short Stories on Campus*—he filled it and strapped it shut. No time or need to take more. Travel light and travel alone. Tore his raincoat off a hanger. Pair of gloves. Scarf. Traveler's checks, they were what mattered. Stopped for a brief look to see what he'd left, but it was dangerous to pause too long. The hot, heavy blood his heart was pumping threatened to drag him down. Move and burn it off. Down the stairs he galloped, leather suitcase banging his knee. What now? Car keys, yes. Three-A card. Registration and driver's permit. Then, drawing a deep breath, he went to the recreation-room door for a last look and felt that dizziness again, as if he expected to discover it'd been a nightmare. A dyspeptic delusion. But there he was. Spraddle-legged, bloated, and turning blue. So long, Daddy Dick. You'd have understood. Not completely, of course, because everything you ever wanted seemed within your grasp. Beer and food, he clung to them even in death. But you'd have forgiven. At any rate, goodbye.

Leaving the door unlocked, he slammed it on the dark house, a hollow boom resounding in his ears. Then, racing to the TR-3, he tossed the suitcase onto the jump seat, started the engine, and while waiting for it to warm up, cleared the windshield. Snow was falling fast in small icy pellets that stung his face and made a ticking sound through the bare trees. What he needed was a drink. Slogging his way up the drive to the pickup truck, he found in the glove compartment a full pint of J.T.S. Brown. The first swallow sliced like a blade through his chest, and piercing the lining of the stomach, put to death all his doubts. He'd make it now, thanks to Daddy Dick. Holding tight to the bottle, he hurried to the TR-3, ground the cold gears, and was gone.

Chapter 8

Walker gained Bladensburg Road, a heavy fall of sleet pinging at the fenders, rutted snow on the street raking the underside of the car. Delicate lines of frost spun like gauze over the windshield, yet when he switched on the wipers, arunk! arunk! arunk! the rubber blades rattled uselessly. He had to stop and scrape clear a patch of glass. But the touch of his toe to the brake sent the rear tires skidding out from under him, swung the TR-3 in a broad arc, and left it pointed toward Whittier Street. A jarring about-face blatant with meaning he wouldn't accept. Wrenching the wheel, he gunned the engine till he was heading once more toward the West Branch Bridge. Then, at its crest, as he glimpsed the sluggish brown river, the tires lost their grip again and sent him sliding backward down the other side, to come to rest at the Peace Cross Memorial.

Another tug at the wheel took him around the monument once, twice, three times, and whirling like a broken record, he repeated, What about Daddy Dick? What about Daddy Dick? What would happen to him? It might be days, even weeks, before he was found, putrid and moldering. Walker gagged, but nothing came up except the bitter taste of bile. He had to stop. The windshield was completely fogged. His brain no less. Had to think. About what? He couldn't go back. Perhaps a funeral home . . . That was it. Call Chambers Brothers, friends in your hour of need. A million satisfied—or at least silent—customers.

Breaking his orbit of the monument, he pulled into the Cross Roads Nite Club, where a lighted phone booth stood outside. No way a call could keep him from leaving. Yet he paused and took a shot of J.T.S. Brown. The club, a windowless cinder-block building, looked like a garage. Or, because of the neon cross over the door, a Negro storefront church. A place where . . .

Jesus Christ, why was he stalling?

Capping the bourbon, he abandoned the warmth of the TR-3 and trudged through the snow, past the cars and trucks on the lot. In the back seat of a Plymouth a middle-aged couple lay fondling each other through winter clothing, while from the club came the sound of a juke box, muted, blurred, perhaps played at the wrong speed. When the door opened, a truck driver stepped out onto an orange bar of light, and the music focused for an instant. "Oh, the fool on the hill sees the world going round, and the eyes in his head . . ."

As he leafed through the directory, an icy wind raised from the floor the smell of dust and urine. Who'd peed here where a fluorescent light burned? Its brightness visible from the road. On a night like this piss would harden to cubes, or a curving yellow icicle. Caddy. Caine. Camber. Carr. Chambers. He lifted the receiver. Everything in order. A dial tone, at any rate.

Then, hesitating, he hung up. He had to be absolutely sure. Once he made the call, the cord would be severed. There'd be no going back. Never. Even if years from now . . .

Weakly he leaned his cheek against the cold aluminum panel and began to shiver. He sounded as if he was trying to talk himself into staying. Wasn't this what he'd always wanted? To escape with no hope of return. Jesus Christ, what was wrong?

In answer, the phone rang, jabbing like an ice pick at the fragile membrane of his mind. He lifted the receiver and was about to let it drop on the hook when a gruff voice demanded, "Say, what is this, Julie? First it takes you five minutes to answer, now you won't talk. What's wrong? Julie, say something."

"You've got the wrong number."

"Who's this? Carl? I thought I told . . ."

"No. You have the wrong number."

"Don't hand me that shit. If you know what's good for you, you'll put Julie on the goddamn line."

"Julie doesn't live here. It's a phone booth."

"A comedian! Okay, punk, you want to get your ass whipped, stay where you are. I'll be right over."

"Will you please get off the line? My father just died and I have to call an undertaker."

"What'd he do, croak right there in the booth?"

"He . . . I . . ." Walker hung up.

Back to the directory. Cabio. Caccias. Caddy. Caine. Car . . . What about Lila Caine? What would he tell her? Nothing. Obviously. And that was a shame. He remembered the moment her blond hair had blown across his mouth, nearly taking his breath away. Could he make it through three thousand miles of desolation without her? Alone, how long could he last? This time he couldn't risk returning.

Frantically he dialed her number. Insanity! She'd have to be crazy to consider it. Probably she was at home in Catonsville with . . .

But someone answered.

"Sorry to call so late. May I speak to Lila Caine?"

"Speaking."

"Sorry to call so late, but . . ."

"You said that."

"I did, didn't I? This is Walker Hawley, the guy who . . ."

"Oh yes! Hi!" Her vowels were like thick syrup spilled on snow. Slow and thick. Friendly? Drunk?

"Something's happened. I . . ."

"Yes, it's snowing. I just love it and hope it keeps up for . . ."

"I've got to leave for California tonight."

"California? It'll be warm there."

"Lila, are you listening? Do you understand?"

"I hear you, but everything you say sounds so, you know, so bright and blurred."

"What?"

"Kind of red and orange and . . ."

"Look, I don't have time to talk. Do you want to come?"

"When?"

"Now."

"Okay, but I haven't packed. Gimme a few minutes to . . . You mean tonight?"

"Yes. Right now."

She chuckled. "I didn't think . . . I mean, you want to go tonight? Okay. Why not? Tomorrow we'll be in California. See you in a few minutes." Clunk! The receiver at her end fell to the floor. "Hey, Lenny, I'm leaving for California. You can . . ." Then the connection broke.

What the hell? He shook his head and stamped his feet to get the circulation going. His legs were numb. Knees welded. Finally he dialed Chambers Brothers Funeral Home, to tell a weary voice the address on Whittier Street.

"Be there soon as we can. My man's putting chains on the hearse. It's the earliest and heaviest snow in thirty years."

"I'll leave the door unlocked for you. My mother-in-law's an invalid and I want to get her away from the house. There won't be anyone here when you arrive."

"And may I ask, where's the deceased?"

"At the bottom of the cellar stairs," Walker blurted. "Call me in the morning about the arrangements. The name is Arbuthnot. Chip Arbuthnot at 973-3572."

"But Mr. Arb . . ."

Walker dialed Dede, desperate to explain why he was leaving, but again there was no answer.

His fingers were stiff and blue, lips purple, eyes stinging with tears that froze to crystals on his lashes. Biting a knuckle, he tried to remember what he might have forgotten. Nothing. He remembered everything only too well. Daddy Dick heaped at the bottom of the stairs, blood pooling in a halo around his head. Total silence in the house. Complete darkness. Emptiness. Maple branches, sheathed in ice, rapping the rafters, but with no one to hear, no sound at all. A tree falling in the forest. A noiseless crash searching for an ear. Daddy Dick. Nothing to do but run.

The TR-3 caromed over the treacherous streets like a rudderless boat shooting the rapids of a swollen river, and since of a sudden the steering wheel and tires seemed to bear only the vaguest connection, the car made its own way, plowing through drifts, skating on patches of ice, and tacking from curb to curb. Fortunately Baltimore Boulevard was deserted except for tractor trailers that had been abandoned beside the road. But in Hyattsville an electric line was down, popping sparks as it coiled and uncoiled around a telephone pole. With a bright flare that bled hissing dollops of phosphorous to the snow, a state trooper waved Walker by.

On no account would he have stopped or turned back. Before dawn he had to put distance between himself and Cottage City, if he hoped to escape the horde of cunning devices Mom might use to catch him. The pull of family blood. Her keening cry

109

pitched too high for other ears. A scream like a dog whistle.

Racing an amber light at U.S. 1 and Amherst Road, he'd plunged into College Park, when suddenly the tires let go again, and after lashing the car from side to side, sent it into a slide, then a dizzying spin. With hands locked on the wheel, feet planted uselessly on the floor, too dazed to brace for the crash that seemed inevitable, Walker searched for a landmark, a fixed point, but found none. The world appeared to orbit the car, in motion with no scheme or reason. Rubber screeched, burned, and bumped. His past life didn't flash before him—no time for such boredom—but a telephone pole and a parked car did, and just as quickly were behind him, as the TR-3 righted itself at a red light in front of the Howard Johnson.

When the light was green, Walker eased into first gear, turned left on Knox Road, and felt as if he'd splashed into the tidal wave of fright that had gotten ahead of him. His arms quivered, drops of perspiration fell from the tip of his nose, and deep inside, his heart labored back up a staircase of ribs to its proper place. At Lila Caine's apartment, he was out in the snow before he noticed he'd left the motor running. He switched it off, but got out again, forgetting the headlights. Falling heavily onto the bucket seat, he took a deep breath, a long pull on the bourbon, let his shattered wits coalesce, and checked every button and switch in the TR-3 before going up to her door.

The instant it opened, he said, "Jesus Christ, you wouldn't believe what . . ." before noticing it wasn't Lila. Not at all.

Lenny Cohen, a small, bearded graduate student whom Walker had met through Dede, motioned him in. Stunned, he did a double-take when he saw Cohen was wearing only a pair of jockey shorts. With spindly arms and legs covered by tufts of black hair, he looked like a diapered tarantula.

"Come on, Hawley, if you're coming. You're letting cold air in and smoke out."

"I didn't mean . . . I didn't know Lila had company. Just in the neighborhood and thought I'd drop by."

"She's in the bedroom packing."

Cohen's pupils were large and whorled as fingerprints, and as he shut the door behind him, Walker dredged in the sweet scent of pot. Between ceiling and floor a thin stratum of smoke halved the room. Staggering through it, Lenny returned to a nest of cushions and pillows on the floor. The TV, volume turned down, was tuned to the Late Late Show, *To Have and Have Not*, and Bogart muttered the words which Walker, who'd seen the film many times, knew by heart. "Walk around me, Slim. See any strings?" Seeing none, Lauren Bacall fell against his chest. In the corner a stereo was playing "Sketches of Spain."

"Is that you?" called Lila. "Be right out . . ." She giggled. "I'm packing."

Both of them high. By morning maybe Lenny wouldn't remember, but Walker had to be sure. Put him on guard so he wouldn't mention any of this to Dede.

"I didn't know you were a friend of Lila's." And, after a pause, "Where's your wife?"

"Home drinking beer and watching Johnny Carson."

Lenny rolled a new joint, lit up, and dragged.

"Nice girl, Donna Lu. Always liked her. I'm sorry she's not here."

"Yeah," said Lenny, his eyes narrowing as if in search of a distant object or lost memory. "A great chick. A real princess. Now let's drop it until I get my mind right. I just came down from a bad trip."

"Where would you get LSD?" asked Walker contemptuously.

"Not LSD. Marriage. Donna Lu and I are through. So sit down and blow a joint with me. I'm celebrating the split."

"Sorry to hear that."

"Don't be sorry. I'm free. Whee!" He tossed a cushion into the air. "Jesus Christ, did you see that? One of the most beautiful things I ever saw. Must have taken ten minutes for it to come down. Hey, where you going?" Lenny grabbed the cuff of Walker's trousers.

"To help Lila," he said, unamused, as always, by people who were high. He'd seen Daddy Dick that way too many times to think there was anything entertaining, much less significant and revealing, about a man talking nonsense.

"Don't go. Stay and rap with me. I been out of my skull for two days and need to talk. You like Miles Davis?"

"Yeah." Reluctantly he slumped onto the cushionless couch and tried to relax. What he needed was a nest where he could curl up like Lenny. A place for Dede and him. But only for the night. Tomorrow he'd have to be moving.

"You dig Bogie?"

"Yeah."

"He's beautiful. Doesn't take shit from anyone."

"Not any more."

Lenny exhaled, French inhaled, and shook his head. "Want some advice, Hawley? Don't ever get married. Take it from me, you never know a chick till you marry her. When you see a girl every day, there's no chance things can stay groovy. I mean, you can only walk into the bathroom while your wife's taking a dump so many times before you . . . you just lose it."

"Maybe you should try knocking before opening doors."

His eyes closed to quizzical slits, Lenny paused ten beats as measured by Miles Davis, then wagged his head in quiet laughter. "Great, man. Terrific! The perfect way of facing the problem . . . Pretend your wife doesn't shit."

"You don't have to pretend, but you don't have to watch either," said Walker angrily. "Lila, are you ready?"

Lenny drew at his weed. "You don't understand. You've got to face facts. It's not just shit. It's everything. You take Donna Lu and me. We had it as good as anyone could. You've seen my apartment, haven't you?"

"No."

"A great pad in Cheverly, with a fireplace, a crazy old bathtub with iron legs like lion's claws, a stereo for sounds, a tube for grins, and Donna Lu's pay check from the Suburban Sanitation Commission for bread. We had everything." He shook his head fondly at the memory. "But then it started to fall apart. Just fall into chunks and pieces. First she cut her hair because it kept getting caught in the Verifax machine at work. Next she quit blowing grass on week nights because she had to get up early. Then she started dressing like Little Miss Muffet. I mean, she just threw away her sandals and granny dresses and boots. Said they weren't comfortable. Before I knew it, she was a different person. Finally one day when she came home from work, I looked up from the couch where I was reading Rilke and listening to Otis Redding and I knew it was over. She looked exactly like a cheerleader, or a fucking A Chi O or something—wearing penny loafers, an A-line skirt, blouse with Peter Pan collar, her hair teased into a beehive. So I said to myself, this shit can't keep on, and left."

112

When a few minutes passed in silence, Walker thought Lenny had put himself to sleep, but then Cohen got up and flipped "Sketches of Spain." "I've been listening to this record for seven hours. If you turned it off, I'd still hear it in my mind. What I do is . . ."

"Lila, we have to go," shouted Walker.

"That's another thing I hated about Donna Lu. It started taking her two hours to get ready every time we went out. It drove me nuts. I can't stand to waste time on trivial shit like that."

There was another silence, and feeling uncomfortable and agitated, concerned with his own troubles, Walker mumbled, "At least you don't seem to be taking it too hard."

"Not taking it hard! Jesus Christ, I'm uptighter than a gnat's ass. Even pot doesn't help. I haven't eaten or slept in two days, and this morning I started to piss blood."

"Maybe you should go to Student Health."

"And have a headshrinker tell me to go back to Donna Lu because I still love her? Not on your life."

"You still love her? I thought . . ."

"Sure, but how can I live with her? The next thing you know she'd be begging me to shave, and telling me pot screws up my chromosomes. As if I gave a rat's ass about my chromosomes. All I want is a little freedom. A chance to . . ."

Slouched low and uncomfortably on the couch, Walker was depressed. Depressed, of course, by all that had happened this night and now by Lenny's story. "I think you should go back to her," he said in a weary voice. And this depressed him too.

"Do you really? I mean, do you think I could justify that kind of life?"

Clearly he wanted to do just that. Rationalize and go back to the life he'd had with Donna Lu.

"Why not?"

"Maybe you're right, Hawley. Tell you what, I'm going to blow one more joint, listen to the flip side of Miles again, watch the end of this flick, and make up my mind. So keep talking. Tell me why I should go back."

"Because you want to."

Lenny lay back on the cushions and said in a small voice, "Maybe so. Maybe I should accept it. Stillness. A state of complete stillness. That's what the Bhagavad-gita says men need. I should move in the stream of my desires as if they were the river of life." One bushy leg over the other, his hairy arms folded across his chest, he closed his eyes, and as smoke from the joint nuzzled in the hollows of his body, he looked like an insect, a dead roach swaddled in a winding cloth of dust.

"Lila, for Christ's sake, aren't you ready?" He pushed himself off the couch and paced the room. What was it Grandmother Hawley had said? You have to take advantage of what you have, and forget what you could have or should have. A regular Indian mystic, she was. But she wanted him to leave, not stay. Let Lenny go back. Not him.

Feeling tired, he made himself walk faster. The fire inside was dying and he had to stoke it before it went out. The smell of pot made him drowsy. Thought of Daddy Dick set his blood pounding, but left his legs weak and wanting to fold like Lenny's. He wanted to escape, but had begun to doubt he could. Was he trying again to talk himself into staying? The question started a slow burn in his belly. "We're going to be snowed in if you don't hurry."

He looked around the room. Her pad, Lila in weaker moments might call it. A place like hundreds he'd seen—apartments full of coeds, graduate students, or young instructors, fledgling artists, writers, or even working girls, all trying to keep in touch with a finer life, trying to set up enclaves of beauty, art, and truth in basements, attics, and sublet houses in the wilds of suburbia. And all of them failing. Why? Why did they keep trying? And why did both the effort and the failure anger him?

He could have found his way around in the dark. Two prints tacked to the wall above the sofa. A Van Gogh and a Gauguin. On the opposite wall, behind the TV, a Pan Am travel poster of Machu Picchu. In the corner, along with the stereo, bookshelves of bricks and polished pine boards. A coffee table made from a stop sign stood in the center of the room with a stack of *Time* magazines and a wax-covered Chianti bottle on top of it.

The familiarity of it all, the sickening sense of *déjà vu*, caused his blood to bubble again. Somewhere he had to find the . . . the real thing. Not this confected substitute for a beautiful life.

"Lila, I won't . . ."

"Here I am. Sorry to keep you waiting." Her words were still slow as syrup, and like Lenny's, her pupils struggled vainly to focus. She was wearing faded Levis, knee-high black leather boots, and a white cable-knit sweater drawn so tightly across her breasts the wool was stretched smooth. "My things are in the bedroom." Taking his hand, she kissed him on the cheek. "I'm glad you called."

"I . . . Let's get your luggage."

As Walker carried two heavy valises and a hair dryer to the door, Lila turned to Lenny, who hadn't spoken or moved in ten minutes. "My parents will be down Saturday to get the rest of my stuff. Give them a hand if you're here. The lease runs out Monday. After that you're on your own."

"Thanks, babe." He waved a limp hand. "You saved my life. I think my head's straight now. So long, Hawley. You're going to dig California."

Outside, where a dry, powdery snow was falling, she held his arm and whispered, "Jesus, is he spaced out. Lenny has real head problems. Brilliant, but a brain like plastic."

Walker put one suitcase in the trunk, squeezed another into the jump seat with his own grip, and asked her to keep the hair dryer on the floor between her feet.

"What time is it?" she said when he'd shaken the snow out of his cuffs and gotten in.

"Two-thirty."

"I love this time of night, don't you?"

"Yes."

"Have you ever seen snow that was so . . . so, you know, blue and glowing?"

"Never." As he eased down Knox Road, the dry powder on the pavement acted as a bond. If he drove slowly, he wouldn't slide, and each mile, no matter how slow, was important.

Lila put her hand atop his, which, clad in a leather glove, gripped the quivering gearshift. A tremor moved from it, through his hand to hers. "You're not mad at me for wanting to leave so late, are you, Walker?"

"You've got it wrong. I'm the one who wanted to leave."

"That's right." She giggled, and rubbing a handful of blond hair across her mouth, let a strand remain between her lips. "It took me a long time to pack, didn't it? My mind kept wandering.

115

I've been smoking all day with Lenny. Just social smoking to keep him company. I was glad when you called. I was bored. I like to do things like this, don't you? Do you believe in astrology?"

"What?"

"Astrology. Did your horoscope say you should leave tonight?"

"No. Nothing that rational."

"What sign are you?"

"I don't know."

"When's your birthday?"

"February nineteenth."

"Hmm. That figures. You're unstable, spontaneous, and creative. Born on the cusp between Aquarius and Pisces. Are you sure that's not why you're leaving tonight?"

"Positive."

She seemed to take his answer as a rebuke, and removing her hand from his, let a moment pass in silence. Walker scarcely noticed the absence of her hand or the noise, for he was concentrating on the road, the speedometer, and the fuel gauge to suppress memory and imagination. Above all, he didn't want to think.

Driving slowly north on U.S. 1, he turned onto the Beltway, heading west, and since a snow plow had passed recently, picked up speed until flakes started to accumulate on the highway and the windshield.

"Are you sure you're not mad at me? Was it Lenny that made you mad? You understand there's nothing between us. We're just old friends." Her voice, no longer slow, sounded as if it had sobered.

"I'm not mad at anyone." But when he spoke he sounded angry even to himself. Puzzling. Maybe he was and didn't know it. She was liable to talk him into it. "I'm thinking." A lie. No thoughts at all. Tattered images blew like scraps of trash through his brain. Daddy Dick smashed to the floor. A sense of having been orphaned at the age of twenty-six. Damnable self-pity. The picture of Dede wearing her perpetual decal smile, which when she was unhappy could be the saddest sight he knew.

"Oh," said Lila, putting her hand back on top of his. "You were so quiet. And it's such a sad night. It always is when it snows. Beautiful, but sad. Damn, I think I'm coming down. You're not supposed to feel anything after marijuana wears off, but I always do."

"There's a bottle of bourbon in the glove compartment."

"I don't want to mix. Lenny says alcohol's a bourgeois high."

"True, but it keeps you warm. Hand it to me." Walker took a shot. Maybe a mistake. Driving was already difficult, and liquor might let thoughts leak in and drift like dry flakes to the corners of his mind. Collect there and suffocate him.

"I think I will have a drink."

"That's the girl."

"My mouth's dry." After an audible swallow, she sighed. "It's so sad. People like Lenny, perceptive people with brains, never make out. Sad."

"Yeah. The bottle?" As he swigged, tears squeezed out at the corners of his eyes. It had to be the bourbon. And yet she was right. There was something sad about . . . about nearly everything. About the two of them, strangers locked in the padded silence of Silver Spring. Barely moving. Darkness save for the spears of headlights that impaled flakes of snow like butterflies.

"A boy I once knew—I guess you could say loved—died on a night like this," she said.

"So did my father."

"He flipped over six times in a Corvette. They didn't . . . Your father? I thought he lived in San Francisco."

"I meant my stepfather." He caught himself. So goddamned ridiculous. But when he wiped away the tears, more appeared.

"You're from a broken home?"

"I guess that's what you'd call it." Smashed. Shattered.

"I'm sorry."

"Don't be sorry. It doesn't help."

"Yes, that's what I say. Be anything, but don't be sorry."

They reached Rockville and pulled onto Interstate 70, north toward Frederick. Houses thinned out and were replaced by woods, then the trees thinned out and were replaced by rolling fields. At this time of year corn shucks should have lined the road and placid pink-eyed cows blinked as the TR-3 passed, but now there was nothing. A white waste. Perhaps the most meaningful memory to carry away from Maryland.

"My God, it's quiet," she whispered. "But why would silence

117

make me think of death? I feel a state of complete stillness in the soul. Have you read *Siddhartha?*"

"No," he lied, sick of his own self-indulgence and embarrassed at the conversation.

"It's my favorite book." Another silence. "Who was it who said, 'We die each other's lives, and live each other's deaths'?"

"I don't know."

"I forget too. Yeats? Keats? Joyce?"

"Joyce Kilmer?"

"You're making fun of me." The hand fled to the darkness of her lap.

"No, I'm not." As he reached for it, the car swerved, and he grabbed a fistful of thigh as well as the hand. He kissed the palm of her glove. Why? "No more sad thoughts for tonight. We're at the start of our trip, not the end." Again, why? He didn't mean it. Didn't feel it. Not the way he would if Dede were here. Despite her smile, she lived on sadness and seriousness, and could have helped him through the night.

"You're right. We should be happy. We're lucky, don't you think?"

"Yes."

"Mind if I turn on the radio? Maybe music will cheer us up."

"Fine," he murmured without enthusiasm.

"Hello, Daddyo, this is big old, fat old Dino bringing you stacks of wax from station WPDC, number one with a smile on your radio dial this snowy night. Now for a groovy sound that was a chart climber a few years back, Martha and the Vandellas and 'Heat Wave.'"

"Remember this?" She sang along with Martha, syncopated with the Vandellas, but when he didn't answer, lowered the volume. "You know, I feel uptight around you. Maybe because you're a writer, I'm afraid you'll think I'm stupid." She paused, then asked, "Do you?"

"I haven't known you long enough." Why was he such a prick?

But she broke into laughter. "See what I mean? But I'm not going to let you put me down. We'll be spending a lot of time together and I don't intend to worry every minute what you're thinking, and I won't apologize for my tastes. So there!" She flailed at him with a wisp of her hair.

118

"I'd say I'm sorry, but you'd only tell me not to be."

"I don't want you to be sorry. I want us to have a good time. And what's more, Mr. Walker Hawley, I'm going to buy a copy of one of your books so we can have deep literary discussions."

"Fair enough."

Talk came easier then, at least for Lila, who told him of her aspirations, her acting, and her agony at the University of Maryland. While she spoke, and they drove through Frederick and Hagerstown, the snow continued falling. It piled on the highway and was packed down by passing cars only to be scraped up by monstrous plows and carved into ornate dadoes, scrolls, and glyphs which banked the road. Slender cedar trees held the dry flakes, bent their branches low beneath the burden, then, spilling snow in avalanches, snapped straight to start taking on weight again. Parked cars lost their shape. Small ones bulked their white shoulders higher in the night, while sleek new ones molded to the contours of a drift, and trucks were capped with icy crusts which canted rakishly over their windshields. Fences disappeared. Billboards were obliterated. The web of neon signs and TV aerials along U.S. 40 was invisible, leaving Walker, who'd driven the road many times, with an exhilarating sense of amnesia.

Following a broad yellow snowplow that struck sparks from the pavement, they passed through Hancock and reached the Pennsylvania border at five-thirty A.M. But in Breezewood, a state trooper blocked the entrance to the Turnpike.

"The road's closed between here and Pittsburgh. The plows can't keep up with the snow."

"Is there any other way?" asked Walker.

"Local roads. But they're worse. Better go back to town and get a room."

"Are we going to drive all night?" Lila asked as they turned around.

"It's already morning."

"Then are we going to drive all day? I'm tired. Why don't we stop?"

"Maybe we should." But he didn't think so, for they weren't far enough from Cottage City. When his mother learned about Daddy Dick, she might call the cops. Swear out a warrant accusing him of murder.

Back in Breezewood, they passed several motels, but there were no vacancies. At many places the neon signs had been snuffed and the parking lots were crowded with cars.

"Maybe we should drive on. We're sure to find a room in Pittsburgh."

"You heard the trooper, and I am awfully tired. Why not try there?" She pointed to the Hitching Post Motel, where a life-size ceramic horse with blinking blue eyes stood outside the office.

Irritable and impatient, Walker hurried through the snow. The air felt warmer than it had in the last twenty-four hours, cushioned between deep drifts and a low sky that was brightening in the east. By contrast the office, furnished with plastic and chrome, was frigid.

"Do you have two single rooms?" he asked the clerk, a young man with a long crooked nose.

"No. A lot of people are snowbound."

Relieved, Walker turned to go.

"But I got a double you can have."

"No, thanks."

"There's not another room in town, and the Turnpike's closed."

"I'll try in Pittsburgh."

"You'll never make it."

Walker hesitated. "How much is the double?"

Craning his neck, he glanced beyond Walker's shoulder to the TR-3 and Lila. "Twenty-two dollars."

"Jesus Christ, I don't want to buy the place. Just rent a room."

"That's the going rate." But his face reddened to the tip of his nose. "It's, uh, you know, high season. A lot of people on the road."

"Forget it."

"Eighteen."

"No." Walker started for the door.

"Okay, fifteen. I'm not going to turn a white man away on a morning like this."

"Let me check with my . . . my sister."

"Yeah, check with your sister."

When he came out, Lila slid back the side curtain. "They only have one room," he said. "I say we push . . ."

"I can't keep my eyes open. Let's take it."

"It's twenty-two dollars."

"That's all right."

"Maybe I can talk him down," Walker mumbled.

Back inside, he pulled three fives from his wallet and dropped them on the counter.

"Now," said the clerk, "sixty cents for Governor Shafer's estate, and thirty cents so all the niggers in Philadelphia can drive Cadillacs, and we're set."

"What?"

"Ninety cents tax."

"Is there a phone in the room?"

"Yeah, there's everything."

Indeed, the room did have everything. Everything, that is, but heat. Imitation leather chairs. A metal bureau with polished-on wood grain. Drinking glasses wrapped in cellophane. A complimentary shoeshine rag from Giordano's Shoe Repair. A Bible donated by the Gideons. A feeble sunlamp in the bathroom ceiling. And one double bed. Narrow.

"Brr. It's chilly. We'll have to bundle for warmth." Hugging her arms across her breasts, Lila sat at the edge of the bed, leaned down to tug at her boots, then fell back wearily. "I don't have the strength to take them off. Will you help me, Walker?"

"What?"

"Help me with my boots?" Her voice had become slow and thick again, each word long as an all-day sucker.

Kneeling in front of her, exasperated with Lila and the stupid delay she'd caused, he asked, "What do I do?"

She raised her foot. "Just pull."

Cradling her calf in one hand, he pulled at the heel with the other, and the boot slid off easily, leaving him holding a bare pink foot.

"Umm, that feels good. Your hands are so warm." She raised the other foot, forming a broad V with her legs, a dramatic funnel toward the crotch of her Levis. "This one's always hard."

"Yes, it is." Although he struggled to control it, Walker's voice cracked, and the strain started a tingling in his groin. Christ, an erection. His awkward position had brought the blood rushing. He was no fetishist. But after sitting for hours in the car, what could he expect? Breathe deep of the cold air. "There."

"Thanks." The feet fell limply to the floor. "Ooh, it's like ice."

121

Pulling them back, she curled onto her side. "You act nervous. Is something wrong?"

"No. Nothing." Unsnapping his suitcase he took out *The Sign of Jonas* and *Best Short Stories on Campus.* "But I'm not sleepy. I think I'll just sit here in the chair and do some work."

"Work? At this hour?"

"A little reading," he mumbled.

"Is that your book?"

"Which?"

"Either?"

"They're both mine. Do you think I stole them?"

"I mean, did you write them?"

"I have a short story in here."

"I'd like to read it."

He tossed *Best Short Stories on Campus* to her.

"Oouff! Not tonight." She pushed the anthology aside, and it fell off the bed. "I'm too tired. Do you want to use the bathroom first?"

"No. You." Falling into the yellow Naugahyde chair, he opened *The Sign of Jonas* and pretended to read, while Lila dragged the smaller of her suitcases into the bathroom. When the door closed, she turned on the tap, filling the room with the sound of rapid running water. Obviously she didn't want him to hear what she was doing, which was all right with him. He didn't want to hear.

Setting *The Sign of Jonas* on an end table, he leaned down to retrieve *Best Short Stories on Campus,* and leafing through it, found "Drowning Voices." Twenty-four pages. One page for each year of his life when he wrote it. Now two years had passed without a word to mark them.

The opening paragraph turned his mouth dry with disgust. A lot of pompous nonsense. Bad! Worse than he remembered.

Hoping to find a well-written passage, he quickly skimmed the story, wondering why it'd been published, who'd read it, how he'd ever done it. He was ashamed to let Lila read this drivel. Better to sneak outside and drop it in the nearest drift.

But before he had a chance, she came from the bathroom wearing a white nightgown with a pink drawstring at the neck. Nothing special. A gown for a little girl. But underneath was a big girl with sizable breasts, and nipples nearly visible as they hardened. Tossing her clothes on the bureau, she looked long and limber in the waist, just like his stepmother, Tanya. On top of her sweater and Levis she left her bra and panties, a bright jungle pattern of yellow, green, and red, like exotic birds about to take wing.

Walker reached for *The Sign of Jonas,* opened it, but couldn't read.

Sitting on the bed, Lila brushed her long blond hair, and with each stroke her uncradled bosom made a startled bounce. Through the gown he could see no hint of brown bush. Maybe she'd brewed a batch to make her snatch match.

"A hundred strokes every night?"

"When I get the chance."

"Thought you were sleepy?"

"I am. But I have to relax first. You know what I mean?"

"Yeah."

"Would you hand me my cigarettes?"

They were on her panties, and as he picked up the pack, the briefs fluttered to the floor, so that he had to retrieve them. Were they perfumed? Soft.

As she leaned out to take the cigarettes, her breasts swung back and forth with a motion like the sea. "Now a match." Her cool fingers guided his hand. "Thanks. Are you sure you're comfortable in the chair?"

"Yeah, I . . ."

"There's plenty of room here." She rolled back the covers. "You're welcome as long as you don't snore." But the honey had leaked out of her voice. Just being polite. Yet she wouldn't have asked unless . . . unless nothing.

"I'm fine."

Still brushing, she crawled beneath the covers. Strange how her breasts bounced so high. Was she keeping track of the strokes? He was counting to himself.

"Do you have a quarter for the machine?"

"What machine?" he asked, wondering what might be in the bathroom. Impossible!

"The Magic Fingers. You put in a quarter and it makes the bed vibrate."

"No kidding." He flipped her a quarter.

"Ooh. It's wonderful." Breasts quivering, Lila slid lower in the bed, which emitted a steady purr to accompany the vibrations. "Absolutely sinful." Hugging a pillow, she rolled onto her stomach. "You ought to try it."

Walker's brow was wet, his throat painfully dry, as he teetered there over the bed, then said, "I have to make a few phone calls."

"Now?"

"Important calls. Business." He rushed for the door before he did something he'd regret. His heart held enough grief already. Heavy horns, heavy heart. He'd bear them both. Bang! Out the door. Pitchforks of pain jabbed from his navel to his knees as frigid air swirled up his pants and got at his gonads.

In the office, the clerk was asleep with his head on the counter.

"Is there a phone I can use?"

"Huh?" A blanched face lifted toward him like the bloated belly of a frog.

"A phone?"

"What's wrong with the one in your room?"

"I need privacy."

"Use this one here. I'm going out back to make some coffee."

When the operator answered, there was a moment of embarrassed silence while Walker wondered whom to call. At last he blurted Dede's number, but for the third time that night no one answered. Next he tried his own number in Cottage City, thinking the undertakers might be there, and that they, more than anyone, could put him in touch with stark reality. Stir his adrenalin and thrust a briar patch between Lila and him. He didn't want love, or whatever he might have in that arctic motel room with her. But there was no answer on Whittier Street either. An ominous hollow ringing.

He thought of Dede's home in Chattanooga. She must be there, but he didn't dare call at six A.M. Who then? He had to talk to someone.

Dialing the operator again he asked for information in Sausalito, California.

A clicking, ratcheting noise like a lead door unlocking, then two rings, and a faint voice said, "Information."

"Sausalito, California, for Mr. Matthew Hawley at 921 Laurel Way."

It was late there too, but his father would be glad to hear from him. Or would he? Cool weather, a breeze off the Bay, perfect for sleeping. He and Tanya, a tangle of limbs. Better than dope.

As he started to break the connection, the operator said, "Mr. Matthew Hawley's number is unlisted."

"I'm his son," Walker mumbled inanely.

"Sorry, but I can't . . ."

"I just got back from Vietnam and want him to know I'm all right." Now that it seemed impossible to talk to his father, there was nothing he wanted to do more. "Can't you give a soldier a break?"

"Let me ring the supervisor."

But Walker hung up. What was there to say? He was probably out anyway. Off somewhere in the Lotus, leaving Tanya alone. How he'd like to see her. No, not now.

He started back to the room. The snow had stopped, and in the west a triangle of blue appeared among burly grey clouds. The air felt almost balmy. In a field across the road a herd of cows huddled in the lee of a billboard and dropped steaming flop to the ground. But silence as deep as the highest drift left Walker lonely.

In the room, Lila was asleep. Quiet now. Scarcely breathing. Maybe it was safe to lie down, on top of the covers, and get an hour's rest.

Then she sighed and turned over, baring the soft flesh of her throat. An invitation to disaster. To calm his nerves, he pilfered a Benson & Hedges from her purse, slouched into the chair, and watched smoke sail through the room like vapor trails, convoluting itself into corners and pressing against the ceiling. That was better. He took up Thomas Merton's *The Sign of Jonas* once again, but before reading, looked at Lila, who was facing the opposite wall, leaving him to stare at her tall, curving hip and her bright hair that had fanned out from under the covers. Her body tensed, as if in a dream, then her legs moved against the sheets. The sound of a whisper. A noise like that of her sibilant breathing.

With great effort he lowered his eyes and at last started the autobiography of a Trappist monk, a successful man who'd abandoned the world and the appearance of freedom to seek peace and wisdom through God. Walker couldn't help but admire such strength of devotion, such charity and acceptance, and yet, other than Brother Merton, who could suck sustenance from the Rock of the Church? A cold hard stone like the one Walker had often knelt on in St. James. Finally, when he read, "Meanwhile, for myself, I have only one desire and that is the desire for solitude—to disappear into God, to be submerged into His peace, to be lost in the secret of His face," he let the book fall shut in his lap. He could understand the desire for peace and solitude, and more than anything, the wish to disappear. But what and where was the face of God? The image suggested to him nothing more than another billboard. Poorly illuminated at that.

He stared again at Lila, who was on her back now, one leg bent at the knee, propping up the covers like the center peg of a tent. Her deep chest labored with each breath, as she scissored her legs against the sheets and rolled over to face him. Her breasts coasted up and over the rib cage, the left falling against the mattress, the right against the left. Her mouth was pushed open slightly by the pressure of the pillow. Moist lips. Scant scrap of pink tongue held in the sparkle of her teeth. She groaned. Or was it Walker?

Whoever made it, the sound brought him to his feet, and as *The Sign of Jonas* fell next to *Best Short Stories on Campus*, Walker swallowed and attempted to choose between the door and the bed, between rushing out and sliding beneath the covers. Just to be near her warmth. The brightness of her hair. To find rest in the lean strength of her limbs. A few hours of sleep were all he'd need. A chance to stop thinking. To empty his mind. Bleed himself of seed.

Suddenly—and spontaneity was important—he shucked his loafers and climbed into bed, bundling Lila in his arms. Although her eyes were closed, she was awake and pressed his face to her breasts. He bit them tenderly through the cotton gown, her nipples like raisins between his teeth.

"Walker, take off your pants. The buckle's hurting me."

When he'd shed the corduroys, she unbuttoned his shirt with fumbling hands, while he reached for the hem of her gown and lifted it up her thighs.

"No," she whispered.

He stopped dead, not really surprised.

She sat up, eyes still closed. "The ribbon. Pull the ribbon."

When he tugged the drawstring, white cotton sloughed from her shoulders to settle like foam at her hips. Lying back, her belly pulled taut, the navel little more than a smudge, oval and flat as a fingerprint on the tanned flesh, while her nipples wrinkled into ridged peaks, and the breasts themselves seemed to expand, spreading away from each other like rings of water on a pond. Then gooseflesh showered them, she shivered, and held open her arms.

Again he paused, this time in disbelief. It wasn't happening. Wouldn't go much further. But when she murmured, "Yes, Walker," he realized he was wrong.

He went first to her breasts, burying his face where it was pleasantly cool until he warmed them with his lips. Moving a hand down her stomach, he plumbed the shallow navel and went lower to the junction of her thighs to find . . . He raised his head. She'd opened her eyes and was smiling. Probing again, he thought he'd missed it, but glancing down, saw she was shaven. A glabrous cleft. Smooth as a child's.

"Walker, come here." Guiding him in, she continued smiling, her eyes open, brown, and depthless till the end.

Chapter 9

Walker struggled to wake himself, straining for consciousness as an underwater swimmer would for light. Then just below the surface of sleep he relaxed and coasted, convinced it'd been a dream. For once he'd be happy to wake and find himself at home. With Daddy Dick still alive.

But rising the last few inches, he reached out a hand, discovered Lila's luscious rump, and awoke feeling an acute guilt and, at first, something like revulsion for the warm body beside him. He moved to the far edge of the bed. With the curtains drawn, he couldn't tell the time of day. His wristwatch read two-thirty, but had it stopped last night? No. Damn! They'd overstayed the check-out hour and would have to pay another fifteen dollars. All because of . . . No, it wasn't her fault.

Lifting the covers from Lila, he watched gooseflesh darken the skin that had helped him through the night. He couldn't blame her. She'd only done what she thought he wanted, and maybe she hadn't been altogether wrong.

Outlined by a dark tan, her breasts—white ovals with pink nipples now tensed—carried the perfect pattern of a bikini halter. Her hands, clenched like a child's with the thumbs tucked under the fingers, rested on the flat plain of belly that flowed in a straight, unbroken line to her cunt. No doubt, in better light, it would bear the triangular blueprint of her shaved bush, but now it looked simple, rudimentary, bare of mystery. Yet somehow it created confusion in Walker's mind. Was it the fount of youth and animal ease she seemed to have but he had always lacked? His fingers plucked and probed the hairless crease for an answer, until, before he'd found one, he'd aroused himself, awakened Lila, and claimed her with his arms.

But when he went to kiss her, she turned her cheek. "Not before I've brushed my teeth."

"I don't mind."

"I do." Holding his cock, she whispered, "Let me help you. I know where it is."

"So do I."

"Last night you almost missed."

"I was surprised and unfamiliar with the terrain."

"You'll learn."

"Yes, with practice."

"Do you like it this way?"

"(...)"

"Are you ready?"

"(...)"

She continued to talk with her eyes open, and had a climax long before Walker, leaving him convinced it'd been her own virtuoso performance, not his grim techniques, which had excited her.

After dozing for another hour, they showered together and went out to eat. The sky had cleared, revealing a sun of unseasonable warmth and roads of glistening black. The sound of metallic laughter—the noise of melting snow gushing from drainpipes—assaulted Walker's ears from every direction, but for once didn't bother him. Walking with Lila to the Wagon Wheel Inn, a diner next to the motel, he thought to himself the blizzard had served its purpose. When it melted, they'd go on their way, changed people. He was happy. That, at least, was a change. Not a small one, either.

The restaurant, paneled in knotty pine, was lit by three chandeliers in the shape of wagon wheels, and while waitresses dressed in mini-cowgirl skirts rushed from booth to booth taking orders, the jukebox played country music.

"I feel like we're already in the West," said Lila as they sat down.

"Too bad we couldn't find a vegetarian restaurant. The food here might not suit you."

"I don't always eat natural food. Sometimes I cheat."

"I'll bet you do. Maybe you'll learn to like grease. It's good for you. Keeps you warm in winter."

129

"We'll see." When the waitress came, she ordered country-fried steak and French-fried potatoes.

Thinking she'd done this to please him, Walker reached across the table and held her hand as they waited for the food.

"What are you thinking?" she asked.

"Wha . . . ah, about you."

"You must be psychic. I was thinking about you. About us."

"You were? That's . . ."

"Yes, every time someone stares into my eyes the way you were doing, I remember a proverb I once read. 'Love isn't looking into each other's eyes. It's looking together toward a common goal.'"

Walker laughed uneasily. "Would you like to sit beside me, facing west, staring off toward California?"

Lila didn't smile. "Who knows whether that's where we're headed, or whether the West Coast is our ultimate goal?"

"I see." He glanced around, wishing the waitress would return. What was this girl trying to say? The only place it seemed she could relax was in bed, where she lay open-eyed and garrulous while she rolled her long loins.

"Square and irrelevant as it sounds, I don't know a thing about you." She grinned slyly. "Oh, maybe a few basic facts, but nothing else."

"That's all I know about you," he said, thinking of the smooth rolls of flesh between her legs.

"I don't even know where you went to school or what you majored in. Not that it makes any difference, but . . ."

"I was an English major at the University of Virginia."

"Is that right? I once dated at UVA. An SAE named Holton Wilkins." Walker shook his head that she needn't ask if he knew him, but she insisted. "You must have. He was a fixture on Rugby Road. Everybody knew him. Holton was kind of a folk hero. He came back every fall, stayed for the parties, then dropped out just before the exams."

Walker shook his head again, this time a bit irritably, disappointed to hear that she'd had anything to do with the fraternity men at UVA.

But Lila went on. "What a hunk he was. It's strange, though. I don't actually remember what he looked like. All I recall is that he was big and handsome and wore a size-sixteen

130

Bass Weejun. He had to have his shoes specially made."

"Is that right?"

At last the waitress brought the steaks covered with thick gravy and onions. Turning to the food, Walker tried to tune her out, for he knew any reminder of UVA might bring trouble. Strange that she, with her heightened perceptions, couldn't see he didn't want to talk about it.

"If you didn't know Holton, maybe you knew Paul Crawlik?"

His fork clattered to the table. "Look, I didn't have much to do with that crowd, and I'm surprised you did."

"Oh. Well . . . I . . . I pledged Tri-Delta in my freshman year. Just to see what it was like." Her hands moved nervously through her hair, a delicate shuttle weaving the wisps. "It all seems like ancient history now. So much has changed. It was a stage, I guess. I never liked it or thought I fit in. I was, you know, too different. Off-beat. Too much an individualist. I didn't want anyone running my life. Telling me what to do or what to wear." She'd worked herself into a mild fit of anger. "I didn't like fraternity parties. The boys always got drunk and vomited, or became obnoxiously gross. Don't get me wrong. I'm no prude. I didn't mind the language. But when they began dropping their pants and"—she struggled for a euphemism, but giving a little shiver, abandoned the effort—"and mooned everyone, I hated it."

"Yes, I can imagine," said Walker. Maybe he'd judged her too hastily.

Picking at her steak, she mumbled, "I think you were smart not to pledge. It's not worth it."

"I should've done it for the experience. Like you did." He met her halfway. "But I'd just gotten out of the Army, and after two years of living in barracks full of men, I wanted to be alone."

She looked at him solemnly, and said again, "I think that was a very wise decision."

Walker was pleased, although he knew there'd been no decision. No plan.

"I mean, you seem too . . . too instinctive and sensitive to be a fraternity man. I think that's what I noticed first about you and"—pausing, she lowered her eyes and her voice—"and that's why I went ahead last night. I knew you were the type who

131

could appreciate a mature, meaningful relationship." She bit at her lip. "It's not good to talk these things to death, but that's how I felt, and I wanted you to know. How do you feel?"

"I'll have to admit I've never felt anything like last night," he said quite honestly, then realizing this didn't amount to a declaration of his ability to appreciate the seriousness of what they'd done, started to add something when Lila interrupted.

"I'm so glad. Usually I don't care what people think. I have my own values. But"—she took his hand—"I was worried what you might think. I don't want you to lose respect."

"Never! I respect you even more now," he said, and tried to think how he could make this sound plausible. "I know you're not bound by a narrow, selfish, unbending, bourgeois code of ethics."

In his fumbling, he'd found the right word. "That's exactly what I mean," she said. "In my own way I'm a very moral person, but I believe in situational ethics. What we did had a justification of its own."

"Certainly." Glancing at his plate, he saw the gravy was congealing.

"This can be an enriching and productive experience. If we're strong and honest with each other."

"Only one thing bothers me," he said, wondering exactly how productive their experience had already been. "I wouldn't want to jeopardize you."

"What?"

"I wouldn't want to . . ."

"To get me pregnant?" she asked with a smile.

"Yes."

"Don't worry."

"I can't help worrying about you."

"Well, don't. I'm on the Pill. I used to have trouble during my periods, and a gynecologist told me the Pill might help. It did."

"I'm glad. Glad, that is, you don't have trouble any more."

She laughed. "I'm glad for more than one reason."

This easy admission and her wicked laugh rekindled his desire. If he hadn't been so hungry, he'd have dragged her back across the parking lot to the Hitching Post Motel. But instead he sliced off a wedge of tough beef and ruminated that Lila

132

took the Pill and was proud of it, unlike Dede, who when she'd started taking it acted as if she were about to give birth, rather than trying to prevent it. Her caresses and kisses had weighed on Walker like debts, and even her smile could chill his heart, for he knew it masked a love so deep and, in its way, demanding, it didn't dare speak. But honest, open Lila asked for little. No commitment, no marriage, not even love. Just respect. Hell, yes, he respected her. She was what he'd always wanted.

"Thank God, I went to a young gynecologist. People tell me the old ones, and especially the Catholics, won't give you a prescription unless you're married. But there was never any doubt about my doctor. First visit, he said, 'I'm at your cervix, madame.' And I answered, 'Dilated to meet you.' It's an old joke, but priceless."

Laughing, Walker bit his tongue. He'd raised an erection that was nudging the table. Maybe they could take the food to the room. Make love and eat at the same time. Lila could manage, he was certain. Intravenously, if need be.

"If I were a gynecologist, there's only one question I'd ask. Why did you . . .?"

Lila blushed. "I know what you're going to say. Why did I shave my . . . myself down there?"

"Exactly."

As she leaned forward to whisper, he leaned forward to listen, the two of them poised over the food that was getting cold.

"This summer I bought a new bikini." She couldn't suppress a giggle at the memory. "And no matter what I did, I couldn't seem to keep all of me covered. So I had to shave."

"You shouldn't have. Some things are like communists and should be exposed."

Her face darkened, but she was smiling. "When I came back to school this fall, I stopped. Or I tried to stop. But as it grew back, the itching drove me insane."

"Did you use lather and warm water? Soothing creams and ointments? Constant massage and jelly baths?"

"I used everything."

"Everything?"

She burst out laughing. "My God, what a horrible conversation to have over dinner."

133

"Not at all. But are you going to keep shaving?"

"What do you recommend, Dr. Hawley?"

"Wild, hairy abandonment to the course of nature. Let it grow. If it itches, scratch it. Let me scratch it."

"Shh. Everyone can hear you." But she didn't seem to mind.

"Why don't we finish dinner, go back to the room, and see if I can't offer a suitable prescription."

At once all talk ceased, and bending low over their plates, they ate with blinding speed and mechanical precision. The only sound was of stainless steel clinking against cheap crockery. Refusing dessert, Walker paid the bill, left an outrageously large tip, and sprinted with Lila across the parking lot, preceded by the divining rod of his cock. In the room, clothing flew in every direction, her flamboyant underwear sailing farthest and landing again on the bureau like a covey of exotic tropical birds.

Almost before he'd had a chance to kiss her, actually not long after he'd first touched her, she thrust him inside.

"Already?"

"I'm ready."

"No time to show my style."

"Style is personal. Do you have a quarter?"

"What?"

"Money for the machine."

"In my pants pocket. On the floor."

Coupled, they inched on hands and knees, elbows and ass-cheeks, to the edge of the bed, and Walker reached down.

"Ooh, that feels good."

"What?"

"What you're doing."

"Fumbling for my money. Got it. Coins for the loins."

"Now over to the slot."

"Not too fast. Conserve strength and bodily fluids. There."

The vibrator started.

"Does it have another speed, Walker?"

"Faster or slower?"

"Faster."

"No, slower."

"I itch."

"I'll scratch. Where?"

"Here."

"There?"

"Higher."

"There?"

"Now lower."

"There?"

"Over."

"There?"

"Back."

"There?"

"Up."

"There?"

"Down. Up again. Higher on the sides. Lower. Higher. Up. And . . . aah."

"There!"

Afterward, Lila switched on television, and lying in bed, the two of them watched a rerun of *Highway Patrol*, another of *M-Squad*, then *Hollywood Squares*, the *Beverly Hillbillies*, the late news and Johnny Carson. Any other time Walker would have been disgusted at spending six hours watching TV, but tonight he felt a drowsy, not altogether unpleasant, numbness. No thought. No regret. Lightly and absent-mindedly caressing one another, they leaned against the headboard, oblivious to specific images, but bathing in the light of the tube which filled the hollows of Lila's body with dusky purple. It made the mystery of her crotch unfathomable. Dark and shadowed with stubble.

At last his cock began to stir. His lone appendage capable of movement. And as Johnny Carson, dressed in a tank suit, leaped into a vat of jello, Walker's hand stumbled down the arid plain of her belly, over the mirage of invisible bush, and into a moist oasis.

Grinning at Johnny's antics, Lila sucked in her breath and held his wrist. "Careful. I feel a little tender down there."

"Sorry. What do you call it?"

As he moved more gently, faint red shadows feathered her cheeks. "Ramona."

"Seriously, what do you call it? You always say 'down there.' What would you say to a doctor? Vagina?"

"Ugh! Too clinical."

"Cunt?"

"Worse! What an ugly word," she said, still watching TV.

"Snatch?"

"Sounds aggressive. Predatory."

"Pussy."

"I like that. It's cute."

"But not really applicable to something that's not soft and furry. Poontang?"

"That's cute, too. I think I'm starting to itch."

"Are you going to let it grow?"

"If you want me to."

"I do."

"Will you scratch?"

"Always."

During a commercial Lila pressed her long, cool flesh over his, and sixty seconds later, when Walker was inside her and Johnny Carson brought on a guitarist to play a medley of country tunes—thunk-thunk-athunk . . . twang-twang-atwang— she was so caught up by the music or by some inner, self-induced urge, Walker knew he couldn't cope. Not at this late hour. So he lay back helplessly while what began as a lethargic attempt to drain the last drops of passion ended with a violent eruption that left them both flaccid as jellyfish, stranded between pleasure and pain. Only after Johnny Carson had signed off, the Chamber of Horrors had come on, and a massive pterodactyl had destroyed half of Japan, could he force himself to get up and turn off the set. Then, too exhausted for thought or doubt, he returned to bed, and nuzzling Lila, tumbled headlong into a ten-hour sleep.

In the morning Walker awoke and was surprised again to find a warm, naked body in bed beside him. "Lila. Lila, wake up." He nudged her, anxious to be moving, to avoid pay-ing another fifteen dollars, and to keep from thinking of Daddy Dick. "We've got to hurry."

"What for?"

"We just do." Getting up, he dressed quickly and started for the door. "I'll go pay the bill." Then, after hesitating to see

136

if she'd offer her share, he went outside, where a warm rain was falling. The snow had melted save for slushy piles, darkened by cinders and exhaust fumes, that lined the road. In the pasture across from the Hitching Post a herd of cows still huddled in the lee of the billboard, but now stood deep in pools of soft red clay.

In the office, the fellow with the crooked nose said, "I see you decided to stay and take advantage of the climate."

"My sister was sick and couldn't travel."

"That happens to a lot of girls every weekend. Must be the weather."

"Or your eager imagination."

He went back to the room, but Lila wasn't finished with her make-up. "Can't you do that in the car?"

"No, and I'd like to have a cup of coffee and something to eat before we leave."

So they ate another meal at the Wagon Wheel Inn, this one more subdued than the first. While Lila, who acted languid and, Walker presumed, fulfilled, chain-smoked Benson & Hedges, he fidgeted with the silverware, wondering whether they'd bury Daddy Dick today. Evil morning for a funeral. The lawn at Fort McHenry squelching underfoot. Not a chance they'd take him out of Cottage City. Horrible thought. To be planted there next to Bladensburg Road, across from the potato-chip factory, for eternity.

"I'm ready," she said at last.

Recklessly he drove the Pennsylvania Turnpike through the mountains, where the air was cooler and snow lay in larger mounds beside the highway. On the hills bare grey trees stood like iron posts in the frozen ground, while below in the valleys bleak hamlets clustered next to stagnant rivers, trapped and immobile, sucking for relief on slate stones and putrid water. He at least could move. Past slag heaps and abandoned tipples, through tunnels suffocating with carbon monoxide, and down dingy hollows speckled with coal dust. He drove as if at the crest of a storm, desperate to outrace the avalanche of ugliness. By-passing Pittsburgh, where the sky belched blue smoke as rank as week-old farts, he sloped toward the heartland, battling smog through Youngstown, and at last onto the sere winter plains of Ohio.

Another turnpike, flatter and faster, commenced, giving at first a thrilling experience of progress, but soon Lila and he paid dearly for this illusion, both at the tollbooths and in the fatigue of their eyes. After an hour Walker lost the slightest sense of speed and, panicking, felt motionless, suspended, lost on a sluggish green sea. Every time he passed a Hot Shoppe, each an exact replica of the last, he suspected he was having hallucinations. That he was sitting on an endless carpet that was slowly being dragged from beneath him. That the land was moving, but the TR-3 was not.

By late afternoon he could endure it no longer, and mumbled to Lila, "Do you have an itch you'd like me to scratch?"

"Yes, if it means getting off this goddamn road."

He took the next exit, turned down a narrowing country lane, and stopped at the Lone Star Motor Lodge, where for eleven dollars he found a place to hide his eyes, rest his heavy heart, bury his face between Lila's thighs, and kiss her hispidulous Venus hill.

For a week their days didn't vary. They rose late, made love, drove a few hundred miles, then stopped to make love again. Unable to bear going back to the Turnpike, they headed south toward Columbus and Route 40, but the countryside remained the same. Flat and featureless beneath an overcast sky, nacreous at high noon, black and burly by early evening. There were great red barns and white farmhouses imprisoned by rusty barbed wire. Fields of moldering compost, piles of steaming manure. Billboards advertising Allis-Chalmers tractors and Red Man Tobacco. Burma Shave doggerel which Lila read aloud. "Impeach Earl Warren" signs. "Register Communists, Not Guns!" signs. Interchangeable clapboard towns, where the state highway death count was toted on a grim scoreboard in front of the post office. Narrow streets canopied with the skeletons of summer, leafless and wet winter branches. Winding country roads blocked by puttering tractors, or hay wagons, or yellow school buses full of kids who gestured obscenely and spat out the windows at passing cars.

Strangely, in this bleak setting, every appetite—whether for food, sex, or sleep—pounced upon them with a brutal suddenness that grew worse each day. The moment one of them felt hungry, they both scanned the horizon for flashes of neon, for brilliant bold arrows, blinding pinwheels of color, or glittering gold parabolas—any hideous explosion of light that might rise above a diner or hamburger shack. Then while Lila waited in the TR-3, Walker would dash through the rain to place their order at the carry-out window and afterward would bear a bag of cheeseburgers, shoestring potatoes, and milkshakes back to the car, where, bathed in the odor of boiling grease, beneath a blinding sign, with the sound of the Beach Boys or the Rolling Stones booming from an amplifier, they'd gobble their dinner.

Memories of motels lodged in his mind as surely as the gummy taste of roadside meals remained in his mouth. The Yourstop Nightspot, Bideawee Cabins, Charlie's Courts, the Do Drop Inn—desperate extravagances of language and imagination to hide the essential sameness of every room. He couldn't forget the clean, antiseptic smell that clung to each as if it might have been sprayed like deodorant from a can. The cool contour sheets. Sani-strips across the toilet seats, guaranteeing that no buttock had touched them in at least an hour. Foam-rubber furniture. Plastic glasses wrapped in cellophane. The Magic Fingers pneumatic and lewd. They all acted as aphrodisiacs on Walker and Lila. Invitations to carnal indulgence. A plea for groans and moist smacks to soften the silence. Feeling of any kind, even lust or hate, to give life to these dead boxes stuffed with polished tile, chrome, and glass.

And much as the land, the season, and the rooms themselves seemed to conspire against them, Walker and Lila did their best, heightening passion with once-forbidden words, honest admissions of sexual fantasies, and awkward positions which produced new angles, pressures, and strains. With repetition, certain gestures, and banal actions, took on the aspect of ritual. Signing the motel register and carrying in the luggage were soon parts of foreplay. Sometimes, almost before he'd had a chance to put down the suitcases, Lila would force him onto the bed, then stand beside him and slowly undress, talking as she unzipped, unbuttoned, unhooked.

"Strippers must have trade secrets."

"You're doing fine."

"Special gowns and bras."

"Let me help."

"No, you watch. There's an art to this, I'm told. I wonder how they make their breasts spin in opposite directions."

Other times she'd tear off her clothing before the door was closed, fall back on the bed, and beckon to him with long grasping fingers.

"No time to take off your pants. Just unzip."

"Lila, wait."

"I can't. Catch up, if you can."

And they'd race for a climax. Usually Lila won, but Walker was never far behind.

Sleep came and went of its own accord. Twice Walker woke to find himself lying naked on top of Lila, inside her, in fact. But fortunately he slept without dreams. Or, at least, he remembered none. And even while he was awake he succeeded almost entirely in avoiding thought. Often they dozed in the car after eating, to waken minutes later with the taste of French fries still on their lips.

The only problem in those first few days was Lila herself, who continued to mystify Walker long after the image he'd had of her should have forged itself in cast iron, or crumbled. Instead, despite his familiarity with her body, she remained a shape-changer in his mind. Soft and vague as the bush that was blooming between her thighs. She forgot what she said, often contradicted herself, changed her mind, and seemed to believe she was whatever she claimed to be, but only for the time she claimed it. Surprisingly—at least Walker thought it so—she never mentioned vegetarianism, natural food, astrology, or marijuana again, seldom spoke of the theatre or acting, and although she promised daily to read "Drowning Voices," invariably left it on the floor beside the bed, where Walker would step on it in the morning. In less than a week her wardrobe changed completely, as the mod, improvised oddities she'd first worn were mixed with bell-bottom slacks from Bonwit Teller, Merimekko dresses, and Pappagallo shoes. While her make-up remained the same, Walker soon noticed how much time and effort she expended to create an illusion that she was wearing none at all. Just a dab of transparent lipstick. A bit of light flesh-colored powder. Artful brushstrokes of mascara. Cream to

140

preserve the tan on her arms and legs. Really nothing. But she wasted nearly an hour on it every morning.

Tuesday she insisted they stop to buy the new *Time* magazine, and when Walker hesitated, said, "I can't believe you don't read it. I think it's written in a masterful style."

As a matter of fact he did read it, but had never much cared to admit it.

"Besides, how else can you keep up with what's happening?" she asked. "Just look at this article on the military-industrial complex. If people don't keep themselves informed, those pigs from the Pentagon are going to force us into another Vietnam."

The next day, as they drove through western Illinois, after a morning of lovemaking in which he'd won the orgasm derby twice in a row, she said, "You know, Walker, you remind me of Howard Roark."

"Who?" he asked, although he knew the name.

"Howard Roark! My favorite literary character. A strong-willed architect who . . ."

"I thought *Siddhartha* was your favorite."

"Ah . . . that's my favorite book, but Howard Roark's my favorite character. Don't you believe in objectivism?"

"I don't think so." He tried to evade her.

"Well, I do. I'm an objectivist." Mistaking his diffidence for weakness, she sat up straighter, and a maddening self-confidence came to her voice. "I've read all of Ayn Rand's books, I've heard Nathaniel Branden lecture half a dozen times, and I'm convinced it's best to be selfish."

"A lot of people reach that conclusion without reading books or attending lectures."

"Well, if more people were like them, we'd have a better world. For one thing, nobody would let himself become a failure. Everyone would . . ."

"Don't you think objectivism conflicts even a little with your other interests and ideas?"

"Not at all. I want to see weakness destroyed."

"What would be left?"

"The strong!"

"All of them equal? Impossible."

"No, there'd, you know, be relative degrees of strength."

141

"Isn't weakness a relative degree of strength?"

"You're trying to trick me."

"Never."

"Yes, you are." She let out a brittle laugh. "But I'm not going to change my mind. I'm too strong. So there." She pinched his arm.

"How about weak subjectivists like me? What's to become of us?" he asked in a lighter voice.

"Come on, Walker. Don't try to fool me. You're not weak." She moved her hand down to his cock, but then drew it back and paused as if to decide whether he was or not. "Tell me your philosophy."

He smiled. No need to take things seriously. Tonight in a new motel room he'd strip her of floral underwear and fatuous ideas, and she'd be his sweet, naked Lila again. A girl with an itch. "I believe in the frangibility of the hymen, the tangibility of the clitoris, and the violability of the vulva," he said, squeezing her soft inner thigh until she squealed with laughter.

That night she evened the score and beat Walker two times running, talking incessantly as she used him to scratch her itch. This only added to his confusion. Why was bed the one place she seemed to think it served no purpose to act serious, intense, and sensitive?

The unanswered question left him unsure of himself, as well as of Lila, and filled him with a guilty revulsion he remembered from early adolescent dating. A distaste for mutual masturbation, which he found then, and still did, as depressing as the intersecting monologues he'd often had with his family. And so he wished just once they would come together, or if that was impossible, that Lila wouldn't come at all. Anything to put an end to the race they'd started, to slow their mindless speed with dissatisfaction, if with nothing else, and make human what they were doing.

The following night in Springfield, Missouri, he bought a bottle of bourbon and insisted they each drink two shots before undressing. Then they took a trial run. A sprint, to be exact. For the liquor, which had slowed him and inflamed her, failed miserably.

Still hoping the bourbon would bring them closer together

by slowing the beat of Lila's wild blood, he forced her to take another shot and suggested she sit astride him.

"Whee, it's like riding a horse. But what a funny saddle."

"Ride silently, please."

"No, I want you to be a bucking bronco."

He gave a stiff thrust—to keep her mouth shut.

"Ooh. Again."

"Look, Lila, just once . . ."

"Aah." Her body tensed, then sagged. A wilted flower on a sturdy stalk.

"Don't stop now," he said irritably. But the moment he spoke, he arched his back off the bed, lifting Lila in the saddle, and came.

This time she poured him a drink and whispered boozily, "You've got to slow down."

"No, it's you who's too fast. Have another shot."

"I'm always fast the first few times."

"Always?"

"Always with you." She grabbed his cock and squeezed. "It's so cute. I wish I had one of my own."

"It could probably be arranged." Then, feeling a quiver of life in it, he said, "Let's do it nice and easy this time. So slow it almost puts us to sleep."

The bourbon sloshed over the rim of her glass and onto her wrist. "Walker, I don't like it straight. Why don't you get us some ice and a mixer?"

"Now?"

"Sure. Let's have a party." Sipping the bourbon, she leaned over to kiss him and jet the liquor into his mouth. "There's ice and Pepsi down the corridor."

"I can't make it. I'm tired. Drunk." He flopped back on the bed, and when the room started spinning, closed his eyes.

"Hey, no sleeping." Pulling at his prick, she brought him to his feet.

"Careful!"

"I won't bruise it." Helping him into his raincoat, she handed him a Styrofoam ice bucket and pushed him out the door.

143

A dry cold wind was blowing and as he walked, his bare feet stuck to the freezing concrete. Frigid air rifled up his legs, cooling the heat of his groin. What had he come for? Pepsi. But he had no money in his pockets. In fact, he had no pants. Christ, it was cold! Almost as bad as the rec . . . Turning, he stubbed his toe and started back to the room with tears in his eyes. Wind. That was all. Throbbing toe. No sorrow. Not really. Not now. Please, not tonight. No thinking. With stiff legs he began to run.

Lila was in the bathroom when he fumbled through his pants for change, then went out again to let the wind buff his brain free of thought. The bourbon had betrayed him and let memory seep back. Leaning his forehead against the humming Pepsi machine, he tried to get a grip on himself, but there were few things he could safely think of. He was trapped between memories he couldn't suppress and a longing he couldn't satisfy. He didn't dare look back and yet couldn't imagine the future, because for all his determination to go there, California, except in the abstract, meant little to him. A land of sunshine and palm trees. The Golden State. But when he'd been there, it was chilly and damp, the summer nights filled with the foreboding of fall, sounds of the Bay and wind and foghorns in the darkness.

He shook his head. Forget that. Live for the moment. He bought three bottles of Pepsi and went over to the ice dispenser. But while ladling chunks into the bucket, he suddenly felt as if the slivers had shot like lethal pellets through his veins and into his heart. How long would the moment last? At his back curled that angry, high wave, heavy with everything he wanted to forget, while out there in the West another sea waited, blue, deep, and bitter with the emptiness of all his dead days. When they arrived, Lila would leave him to face alone what he'd done and what was to come.

The bucket slipped from his hands and crashed to the concrete, shooting splinters of ice like sparks. He had to slow down. Stop letting himself be chased. Of course he'd keep Lila with him. He couldn't make it without her. They'd continue from one motel to the next—but slowly, slowly—with the destiny of California always in the distance. Perhaps, absurd as it sounded, they should take a vacation from the trip. A detour—until his nerves healed and his memories dimmed.

Squatting barefoot on the sidewalk, with chunks of ice melting between his toes, Walker thought of warmth and sunshine, healing salt waters, a jungle of palm trees and wild flowers. Not California, but Mexico, clinging like a cornucopia to the underbelly of the States. Although he'd never been beyond the city limits of Juarez, he imagined *The Sun Also Rises* and Jake and Bill riding through Spain on the top of a bus, drinking wine from a goatskin. Villages like bleached bones beneath an implacable sun. Slow overhead fans trailing spools of flypaper in dark cantinas where straight tequila churned in the belly, thick and hot as the blood at a bull's neck. Fishing shacks next to motionless lagoons. Nets stretched on stakes to dry. The smell of hot peppers, spice, and cedar. Silence crystalline and complete. Jesus, he had to go there!

His frozen joints creaked as he stood up and ran with a thawed heart and a bucket of ice back to Lila.

"Where've you been?" she asked crossly, sitting in bed naked. The TV had been turned on.

"Lila, I've got to talk to you." Switching off the set, he shed his raincoat and, shivering, slid under the covers. "Keep me warm while I tell you what we're going to do."

"Eeyike! Your feet are like ice." She, too, started shivering.

"I'm sick of this. I need a change. The country's too cold and grey and ugly. Why don't we go to Mexico?"

"Mexico?" she mumbled. "Gosh, Walker, I don't know. I mean, Mexico? Just the two of us? Not that it matters, but what would people say?"

"They'd say it was great."

"Mexico?" she muttered again. The word itself bothered her, its strangeness filling her with a sense of foreboding. "Mexico?" She pronounced it like a moral judgment, as if traveling through the States with him was permissible, but leaving the country would be a debauch.

Bewildered, he asked, "What's wrong with Mexico?"

Chewing at a strand of hair, she shook her head.

"Suppose we had an accident or something and my parents found out I was in Mexico with you? It just sounds bad."

"Worse than if we were in Arkansas?"

"Much worse."

"That's why we have to go."

"Why?"

"Because it's different. I'd go for that reason alone." Her brown eyes blurred with confusion. Maybe with fear that she was being led farther than she wanted to go. He knew the embarrassment it'd cost her to mention her parents and ask what people would think. For the first time he realized how young she was. "Don't worry. I'll take care of you. But don't pass up a chance like this. Do you know what Mexico's like?"

She shook her head no.

"Border towns along the Rio Grande are like a strand of cheap Christmas lights. You can't say they're part of Mexico, but farther south it's different. The land . . ." Slowly he described this country he'd never seen.

Lila was soothed by his voice at first, but asked, "How about the food? I've heard it makes you sick."

"What's a stomach ache compared to mountains and jungles, palm trees and coconuts . . ."

Walker talked on until he'd put them both to sleep, then, lying awkwardly on his side, he dreamed for the first time in a week. Or rather, released by the liquor, he remembered with unnerving clarity what he'd done one Saturday when Mom was out and he was no older than three.

Daddy Dick had lifted him into the kitchen sink for his bath, and lathered his arms and legs, laughing and tickling as he scrubbed. "Looks like you got a potato patch growing behind your ears. A little bird must of built his nest in your belly button. God Almighty, how'd you get so dirty?"

After rinsing him with warm water, Daddy Dick dried Walker with a soft towel, stepped back, and whistled. "Clean as a hound's tooth." Then he reached out to set him on the floor. But as he moved closer, sight of that meaty red face caused a short fuse in Walker's synapses, and he balled up his tiny fist and drove it into Daddy Dick's jaw.

It couldn't have hurt much, but the florid cheeks sagged and the green eyes clouded. Were tears pooling? "That wasn't a very nice thing to do, was it?"

Walker shook his head, and flopping down on the cold drainboard, started to cry.

Daddy Dick pinched him. "Hey, boy, don't cry. I'm okay. It didn't hurt. Surprised me. That's all." Lifting him in his arms, he rocked him back and forth. "There, there. It's all right. Shh, before your mother comes home."

In the morning, waking with a buzzing head and a bad taste in his mouth, Walker was bothered by the dream and sorry for all he'd done to Daddy Dick. He even felt guilty for refusing to think of him. But what good would it do? He couldn't let his mind roam. Getting up, he drank one of the warm flat Pepsis, and while Lila put on her make-up, went out to a drugstore for a few postcards, a box of stationery, and some stamps.

At the counter, he made out a check to Nancy for five hundred dollars, scribbled, "Use this to pay for the funeral, or a tombstone, or whatever you think best," and sealed it in an envelope. Then on one of the cards, addressed to his father, he wrote, "I'm on the way, but have been delayed. Something has come up. Nothing serious, so don't worry. I'll be arriving a little later than expected. Look for me sometime before Christmas. Best to Tanya. Your son, Walker." But at once he tore this up, printed the same message, signing it, "Love, Walker," which somehow seemed less a commitment.

With minor variations, he copied the note onto a card for Grandmother Hawley in Boca Raton, and by this time the bourbon was oozing out of him. "Please forgive me. Will explain all someday. Love, Walker," he scrawled to his mother at Oak Knoll. Then to Dede, "Please forgive me. I'll explain everything in a long letter. I tried to call you, but you weren't home. I miss you and love you. Walker."

Seen in the mirror behind the counter, his face was luminous with sweat, guilt, and regret. It wasn't fair. He'd done only what he'd had to do to escape. But then he stared at the cards and the letter. Bonds with the past, like trembling hands reaching out through the darkness. Perhaps in a subconscious desire to hold himself back. Or to have it both ways. Go, and yet let part of him—at any rate, word from him—stay. Excuses, apologies, and pleas strung out like wire from coast to coast, with him dangling by the throat. Twitching. Death-rattling. Damn! He felt very weak.

147

Outside on the curb he ripped up the cards and watched the pieces float down a sewer. He preserved only the letter to Nancy, which he mailed on his way back to the motel.

Turning south, they followed Route 65 into Arkansas, and through the Ozark foothills he let the TR-3 coast down to Little Rock. A dizzying, rapid, and reckless descent.

"There must be a game somewhere today," said Lila, seeing the crowded highway.

Indeed today, the last Saturday of regular season, there was a game everywhere. The smell of football was in the air. Dead leaves. Moist sod. Wood smoke. Cigars. Manly after-shave lotion. Throughout the land, men and boys were pawing the turf, swatting each other on the fanny, or beating their gums, getting ready for the game.

Thousands headed for Little Rock to see the Hogs play, their car aerials streaming red and white crepe paper. "Go Big Red." From Pine Bluff to Fort Smith, Murfreesboro to McNab, New Neeley to Oppelo, Bigelow to Plainview, Conway to Forrest City, and most of all in Smackover the state was united—Oo-oo-o-Soo-oo-ie-Piggie-Soo—as Walker in the TR-3 dug out for the Southwest, a man in motion outracing everything, over flat swampy land, past Malvern and Arkadelphia, into and out of Texarkana, then gathering speed through Texas, cutting, faking, eluding. The countryside didn't change much, but he and Lila did. They were happier, livelier, and laughing as they plummeted toward Mexico.

In Greenville they stopped. Tomorrow they'd push on to Dallas and beyond. But now Walker needed a few hours to rest and luxuriate in the marvel of their progress. They'd come from the iron-grey North to the doorstep of a green world. Over five hundred miles. Lying on his back, he contemplated the future, while Lila, after plucking futilely at his groin, turned grumpily onto her side and fell asleep muttering. Soon Walker, too, dozed—rocked, swayed, and soothed by the motion of the open road.

Chapter *10*

Walker woke with Lila's hand on his cock. No doubt she'd had a hold on him for hours, and the instant his eyes opened, she started to guide him home. Still groggy and half asleep, he was frightened, like a man about to be thrust into a strange dark room, and so held back.

"Wait a minute. There's no rush." He wrestled away from her, then tenderly rubbed her breasts and belly to conceal his irritation.

"Are you always like this in the morning?" she asked. "Or is it because I'm here?"

"Like what?"

"Like this." She squeezed.

"It's because you're here," he lied, stroking her dark pubic hair, which was still short and straight. "Feels like a crew-cut."

She laughed and seemed to relax.

"Are *you* always like this in the morning?" he asked, dipping a finger into the moist crease.

"Always. Always when I'm with you." She pressed his hand against her.

"Easy. Let's play a game called peace and quiet. You be quiet, and I'll get a piece. Close your eyes. Open your legs. There!"

But as soon as he went inside her, she couldn't be kept still, and minutes later he withdrew, beaten and beleaguered.

Afterward, although he'd just told Lila there was no rush, he was anxious to be moving. To flee this room of beige walls and blond furniture. Escape the damp tangle of covers on the bed, which were knotted like his nerves. But the one thing Lila did with insistent slowness and maddening attention to detail was apply her make-up. For three quarters of an hour he sat on the bed, waiting, jangling his car keys, trying desperately not to think.

It wasn't until noon that, angry, agitated and far behind a schedule he hadn't known he was keeping, Walker goaded the TR-3 toward Dallas. The thump of the tires on the pavement kept count on the beat of his racing heart. He was so far behind. Getting farther every minute. Why in hell had Lila Caine begun to act on him like a threat rather than a wish fulfillment? Suddenly the easy and open opportunity she offered had twisted his head the wrong way and left him weak with doubt. So they burned at different speeds. What did it matter? In the end they were both satisfied. Weren't they?

Bent on making up lost time, he couldn't answer. Miles of time ahead. He'd think about it later. First he'd gain ground and get to Mexico.

"We're in Big D," said Lila. Yes, that was what she called it. "It looks like California."

In a way it did. A gauzy net of smog was draped like camouflage over the tallest buildings, and every breath of air burned the nasal membranes, as each automobile dribbled an almost solid spoor of exhaust fumes from its tailpipes. To Walker it seemed a blustering, landlocked Texan's idea of California. Los Angeles without Hollywood, without the ocean, a single hill or mountain. Immediately he detested it.

But Lila, who'd never been west of Pittsburgh, asked, "Aren't we going to stop and see it?"

"See what?"

"Dallas."

"Can't you see it from here?" How could they expect to make miles if she insisted? Already half the day was shot.

"This *is* where President Kennedy was killed, you know." Her voice sounded curiously sober. Her eyes were angry. "Or don't you even care?"

"Of course I do."

They saw everything—the grassy knoll, the Texas Book Depository, the underpass, the jail, Parkland Memorial Hospital, and Love Field—and it was as Walker had expected, drab,

cleared, he saw there was less than two inches of rusty water still bubbling in the radiator.

"What's wrong, Walker?"

"We've got to get to a garage."

Slamming the hood, he coasted toward the nearest town. Past the accident, traffic moved in a slow, single lane. Many people had stopped, no doubt to help, but now stood watching the Ranger, who duckwalked across the pavement measuring skid marks. The ambulance would take a while. But there was no hurry. Trapped in the green sedan, the driver was hunched forward, impaled on the steering column, face blue, probably dead, while passengers from the other cars and from the truck appeared to be all right except for cuts and scratches. In an air-conditioned Nash Ambassador five ladies wearing flowered dresses and floppy straw hats sat with the windows shut, chatting busily as if waiting for a long train to pass.

"Maybe if you stopped here, somebody could help," said Lila.

Walker didn't answer.

Minutes later the TR-3 limped into the town of Millett, where, since there was no garage, he filled the radiator with water carried in a leaking bucket from a diner.

"Been an accident up the road," said the waitress when he returned the pail.

"I just passed it."

Running a dishrag over the counter, she sighed. "People never learn, do they? Speed and sex is all they think of."

"Anybody hurt?" asked a small fellow who sat in a booth.

"One man looked like he was in bad shape. Maybe dead."

"Damn fools." Pulling on his Stetson, he headed for the door. "Better go see what I can do."

"A doctor?" Walker asked the girl.

"Him? Never."

"Sheriff?"

"Gawd, no! 'At's Tommy Jack Tinkum. State stock-car and demolition-derby champion."

With a loud shriek of tires, his Dodge Charger peeled onto the highway, headed north, making good time.

. . .

155

Turning her back, Lila stared stonily through the side curtain. More concerned with the TR-3 than with her, Walker was grateful for the silence, and tensely listened for the metallic ping of worn bearings or the thump of a thrown rod. Heat could ruin an engine, especially a finely tuned one like his. Pistons might lock. Valves blow. Gaskets split. And he was positive no mechanic out here would know how to fix a Triumph. What then?

Soon fear for the car reminded him of all that could go wrong. Mom, frantic and vindictive, might call the police. Might kill herself. No! It was more likely she'd kill someone else. Dede might find out about Lila. Lila might leave him. What if one of them died? Or worse yet, unnerved by the trip, constantly thinking about what could happen, he, like Mom, might go crazy. Maybe it was in his blood. Loose nuts, bolts, and wires from the Walkers. Jesus Christ, crazy here in Texas, far away from Dede, the only one who might help.

Of all the things that could go wrong, it seemed inevitable that at least one would, and as if to confirm his fears, the TR-3 started to overheat again. "How far to the next town?"

"How would I know?"

"Check the map."

Lila shook it open with a peevish snap. "Cotulla's a few miles ahead."

"How big is it?"

"I don't know. It's just a dot on here."

"Red or black?"

"What?"

"A red or a black dot. Are you deaf?"

"Black."

"Oh shit. Could that be it?" Emerging from a mirage, like a centerpiece on the broad table of land, were a few low buildings, a faint grid of dirt roads, and moving east to west, a railroad track. Bisecting it, north to south, ran the highway. At the junction, where the tracks and the road rubbed the earth a raw red, stood Cotulla.

Walker stopped at the lone gas station, and an old man in bib overalls came out of the shack. "Fill 'er up?"

"Yes, please." Then, getting out, "Is there a mechanic in town?"

"Yep. Me." Trailing the hose between his legs, he faced the open gas cap as if it were a urinal.

Walker ran a hand through his damp hair. "Have you ever worked on a foreign car?"

"Cain't say I have."

"I've got a leaky radiator. Do you think you can fix it?"

The man drew back. Looked at the TR-3. "This one of them new German jobs?"

"No. English."

"I reckon I can do it."

"How long will it take?"

"Have it for you by morning."

Walker glanced at his watch. Four-thirty. "Is there any chance you could do it earlier? Say, this evening?"

"Nope. Ah'm busy." Gasoline gushed from the tank, over his hands, and down the fender. "There's a wasted dime. Sorry." Twisting the cap tight, he dragged the hose to the pump, hung up the dripping nozzle, and said, "That'll be two-eighty-nine."

"Is there a motel in town?"

"Nope."

"Hotel?"

"Nope."

"Any place where . . . ?"

"Let's go," said Lila. "I'm burning up."

"The car has to be fixed. We're staying here tonight."

"You must be kidding. Where?"

"Y'all might try Phoebe Looney's place. She takes in roomers."

Reluctantly abandoning the TR-3, Walker staggered beneath their luggage down Main Street, the one paved road.

"You all might traa Phoebe Looney's place," Lila mimicked the man when they were a block away. "We must be crazy."

"Shut up."

"What's with you?"

"Nothing you'd understand."

"Don't yell at me. I didn't do anything. Take your foul mood out on someone else."

The suitcases crunched to the sidewalk. "Let's get one thing straight. I'm not taking anything out on anybody, but since you asked, you're what's bothering me."

"Me? What did I do? You've been mad all day. My God, you woke up mad. Don't you ever like to have fun?"

"It's hard to have fun waiting two hours every morning for you to get ready."

"So that's it. I thought something was wrong when you stood watching me like . . . like a vulture while I put on my make-up. If you hadn't gone out of the room, I'd have thrown something at you. Don't you like me to look my best?"

"Yes, but . . ." He faltered. Maybe it'd been his fault. "I wanted to get an early start."

"For what? Oh hell, don't answer. I have to get in out of this sun. I feel like the top of my head's been blown off."

They found Phoebe Looney, a buxom redhead in a pink sunsuit, sitting on her front porch drinking a can of Country Club Malt Liquor. Her skin had tanned and peeled so many times, it had lost its pigment and turned a pasty white in some spots, while in others it remained a deep, dry brown. Barefooted, sipping from the can, she led them around back, down an areaway, and flipping on an overhead fluorescent bulb, showed them the cellar which had been made into a spare room.

"It ain't much, but it's comfy and cool. Real private down here. You two married or something?"

"Something," Lila muttered.

Walker shivered. It reminded him of the recreation room. Dank, and musty as the inside of an old beach bag.

"Somebody just walked over your grave," laughed Mrs. Looney.

"I wouldn't doubt it."

The room contained two double beds set in opposite corners, and next to each bed stood a night light and a ladderback chair. The cinderblock walls were pink, and drawn curtains charcoal. "My favorite colors," explained Mrs. Looney. "The john and the shower's over there. Easy on the water, though. We ain't got much, and I have to sprinkle the yard. See you kids later," she said, backing out the door.

Walker dropped the luggage onto one bed, Lila put her hair dryer and overnight bag on the other. An ominous sign. Separate beds. Maybe the end. Gathering her cosmetics, she stalked into the bathroom, viciously whispering, "You all might traa Phoebe Looney's place." Blam! the door slammed behind her.

He thought she meant to defy him, that she intended to spend the rest of the day dawdling over her make-up, but then he heard a dyspeptic groan from the hot-water pipe. She was taking a shower. Not a bad idea.

But not for him. Troubled, he went to the chair, sat, and listened to the crackle of the fluorescent bulb, and as its gruesome light fell over him like disease, he wondered why, of a sudden, he was so displeased with Lila and, on further reflection, with himself. She was right. He'd been angry all day. For the last two days, in fact. And there was no reason for it, which should have relieved him, but strangely enough, had the opposite effect, convincing him that because he couldn't understand why he felt this way, there must have been a deep-seated and twisted reason.

Getting up, he prowled the room. Beneath his feet several puckered squares of tile snapped down, then popped up again. Why in hell should he be mad at Lila Caine, who was everything he wanted? At least everything he'd always thought he wanted. True, she took too long with her make-up, and tended at times to be as predictable in thought as she was outrageous in bed, but this shouldn't have made him want to get rid of her unless . . . unless there was something wrong with him.

At the bathroom door he paused with his hand on the knob. Lila was still in the shower. He could hear the water running and smell her perfumed soap. Each hollow of her body would be a trove of scent, the short hairs of her bush soft and white with lather, like fluffy dandelion gone to seed.

Quickly he shed his clothes, stepped into the small, steaming room, and shooting back the plastic curtain, squeezed into the stall beside her. "Look, I'm sorry. I . . . I didn't mean . . ." Mean what? He'd done nothing. ". . . to upset you. I guess the heat got to me."

"It's okay. I guess it got to me, too."

Pressing closer, Walker enfolded her soapy nude body, and before he knew it, had said he loved her. The words slid out as easily as her slippery hips eluded his hands when she drew back as if she didn't understand what he'd said. Seeing the puzzled look in her eyes, he wasn't sure he did either. But she let herself

159

be cornered, and on tiptoes, rubbed her groin against his. He forced her to the wall, kissed the cool crook of her neck, the hollows of her shoulders, lowered his mouth to her breasts, then in a straight line to her belly, her navel, and at last her cunt, so that when he stood up, she whispered, "Yes. Now. Right here," and he dipped forward and took her there in the shower against the wet tiles with warm water beating softly on his back.

After they had dried and dressed, Lila moved her hair dryer and overnight bag next to the luggage, but continued to act quiet, withdrawn. Sitting at the edge of the mattress, she gave it a bounce with her behind. "It doesn't feel too bad."

"Are you one of those girls whose mother warned her it would hurt?"

This coaxed a smile from her. "No, smarty. I mean the mattress. It's nice and firm."

"Not a bad room for Cotulla, Texas."

"If only it weren't so gloomy," she said, going over to the grey drapes. "Why don't we let in some light?" But pulling a cord, she parted the drapes to reveal more of the pink cinderblock wall. There were no windows. Sighing, she fell back onto the bed, shook her head, and said, "What a dump! This place, the drive today, the whole state, everything's starting to depress me. I feel, you know, stunted. I can't even relate to anything or to myself. I wish we could talk to a few people, just to make sure somebody else exists."

"Wait till we get to Mexico. Then things will . . ."

"What about now? Tonight?"

"There's no place else to stay."

"I don't care where we stay, but what are we going to do for the next ten hours—admire the view?"

"There must be a movie in town. Let's go look for it."

As they came around front, where Phoebe Looney was hosing down the dust in her yard, she said, "Look over yonder next to that oil can. Three horned toads. Gawd Almighty, they hate to get wet. Look at them hop." She flicked her wrist to make the spray fly farther.

"What's there to do around here at night?" asked Walker.

Winking at Lila, she said, "If you don't know, son, I ain't

going to tell you," then laughed and arched more water toward the toads. "Most people just honker down on the front porch and have a cold brew."

"Is there a movie?"

"Not any more. Used to be a drive-in, but the wetbacks and Indians started sneaking in and they had to close it down. In the dark nobody could tell them from the white folks, so the owner threw up his hands and left. Went to Corpus Christi and bought a Tastee-Freeze, they tell me."

"Isn't there anything?" whined Lila.

"Well, y'all might try Beegee's Roller Rink, if you like that kind of thing."

"The what?"

"Beegee's Roller Skating Rink. It's right up there past the feed store." She motioned with the hose, dousing Walker's shirt. "Sorry 'bout that."

Smiling, Lila gave his hand a squeeze. She didn't have to say a word. He knew what she was thinking. It'd been a miserable day. They'd gotten a late start, seen an accident, had their first argument, and the TR-3 had broken down. Now, trapped in this desolate town, wouldn't it be the crowning blow, the final turn of the screw, to spend a few hours roller-skating? A high camp experience in Cotulla, Texas, to top everything. Wouldn't that be hilarious?

The answer, of course, was no, and in normal circumstances he wouldn't have considered it, but in fact these weren't normal circumstances. They were in Texas, and dusk was settling on the wings of a low moaning breeze that spoke of loneliness and despair, of desperate men and dead souls. As the sun sank like half an orange on the horizon, the land turned a sickly fulvous yellow and the railroad tracks gleamed greasy black. Soon the roads would be reduced to dull scribbles in the sand. Snail tracks. Shriveled arteries. The world would recede. In the darkness Cotulla would disappear. If they hoped to survive, they had to be willing to take a risk.

So Walker smiled, nodded, and led her out the gate.

"You kids have fun, you heah."

At Beegee's Roller Rink, a huge grey Quonset hut, they rented skates and stored their shoes in a metal locker. From the lobby, where several weary skaters sat drinking Pepsi, eating

Zagnut Bars, and spinning their wheels idly on the threadbare carpet, they could hear organ music—"Heart of My Heart"—and the sound of ranchers, cowboys, counter girls, waitresses, and oil roughies circling the great wooden floor. When someone called over a crackle of static, "Couples only," the tune changed to "Spanish Eyes." Pulling on his skates, Walker thought Lila had been right again. This might be fun.

"Hurry." She'd finished lacing and was anxious to get out on the floor.

A tall young cowpoke in dungarees and flannel shirt wheeled up beside her. "How 'bout it, ma'am? Want to take a spin?" When he spoke, his Adam's apple, large and sharp as a knuckle, bobbed from beneath the knot in his checkered bandanna.

Lila looked down at Walker, who stared up at the cowpoke and since he assumed she wanted to refuse, said, "She's with me."

Working his lean jaw muscles, he swallowed and showed the Adam's apple again. "Maybe you should let the lady talk for herself."

"Not now, thank you." Lila smiled sweetly. "Maybe later."

"Don't forget." He skated off on slim bowlegs.

"A little possessive tonight, aren't you?" she asked as he stood up.

"You mean you wanted to skate with that hill-ape?"

"That doesn't matter. The point is, I like to make my own decisions. But forget it. I don't want to have another argument. I just want to skate."

She took his hand, and as they pushed off around the floor to "Moon River," it occurred to Walker that Lila might be experiencing doubts similar to his, might be reappraising, even as she held onto him with strong, dry fingers, her expectations of the trip and of him. The thought made him skate faster.

As they circled the rink the first time, the Texans stood aside and let them pass. Among that group of tanned, thick-wristed men and squat, powerful women in pedal pushers and hair curlers, there could have been no doubt they were strangers. Feeling pallid and powerless in his olive Dacron worsteds and black Banlon sweater, Walker pulled Lila closer.

"Hey, Leroy, who's the dude and that fine piece of poon?"

"Hot dawg, look at them tits."

"Too skinny. A decent-size cock would split her in half."

"Shit. She'd take twice what you got."

"That little old thing'll stretch a yard before it tears an inch, they say."

The dumpy women, silent on the arms of their men, sent Lila, who was dressed in blue slacks and a white cashmere sweater, withering stares.

Then, while they rounded a crowded bend near the snack bar, the tune switched to "Way Down Yonder in New Orleans" and the organist said, "Let's change directions, folks." But before Walker could turn, a young buckaroo barreling in the opposite direction lowered his shoulder and sent him into an ass-burning slide over the polished floor. Another cowboy collided with Lila, and to keep her from falling, took her in his arms. For an instant it looked as if they were dancing. He held her close, spun her around, and with insistent hands moved her away from Walker, who, flat on his back, watched the fellow slip one of his lean thighs between hers.

"Lila, wait for me," he cried, and as he struggled to get up, powerful hands seized him by the shoulders, yanking him to his feet.

"Say, pardner, you skate like old people fuck. Slow and creaky." His rescuer, a powerfully built Marine corporal with shaved head and jug ears, went off in pursuit of Lila, skating stiffly and slowly, dragging his heavy shadow like a cartload of stones.

Unsteady on his feet, Walker moved to the guard rail, and glancing back over his shoulder, spied Lila across the rink, rolling along with a radiant smile, surrounded by men, among whom the beefy Marine had gained control. While the others dodged and weaved, leaping and shouting for attention, the corporal, a persistent skater at best, held her hand, pumped his massive legs, and pulled her around the floor. Walker shouted as they passed, but she didn't seem to notice, for the whir of wooden wheels and the static of the amplifying system had garbled his weak words.

When the Marine finally brought her back—"Here's the little woman, safe and sound"—he held out a hand and said, "Lance Hoderbeck. Pleased to meet you."

163

"Walker Hawley."

"I don't know when I've had so much fun." Lifting the long ropes of blond hair, Lila let cool air touch the back of her neck. "I hope that little fall won't ruin your evening, Walker."

"Of course not," he said without enthusiasm.

"But, oh my, you do have a bump over your eye." Standing on her front wheels, she kissed it.

"You know, the simple things in life sure can be fun," said Lance, whose face, heavy with beard and muscle, looked like a braised slab of meat. "Specially for a fella like me who's going over to Veetnom next month and is liable to get hisself shot."

"Oh, I'm so sorry to hear that. It seems like such a shame when everybody else is beating the draft. But I'm glad to know there are still some patriotic Americans left."

Wha? Walker couldn't believe his ears. Where was that reader of *Time* magazine and *Siddhartha,* that archenemy of the military-industrial complex?

"Don't let that spoil the evening. I think we all ought to cut loose for a few hours and have a bang-up time. That'd be the best send-off I could ask for."

"Sounds like fun," said Lila.

"Want to duck over to the snack bar and get a few Dr Peppers? This skating really takes it out of a man." He smoothed the perspiration from his narrow brow with an index finger whose nail had been chewed to the nub.

"Great! I'm parched. Coming, Walker?"

He skated behind them, staring at the tapering triangle of sweat between Lance's shoulders. Big man. Even bigger than Daddy Dick. But what had gotten into Lila? Surely . . .

"You know, pardner," said Lance at the refreshment stand, "You're gonna have one hell of a shiner in the morning unless you take care of that eye. Why don't you go into the men's room and throw cold water on it?"

"I'll be okay." The man had to be a fool if he thought Walker would leave him alone with Lila.

"Won't take but a minute," he insisted, grabbing him by the arm. "Come on, I'll go with you."

"Cold water might help," said Lila.

"I'm all right, I tell you," said Walker, seized by a nightmarish suspicion they were working together against him.

"I learned about these things in First Aid. You don't look after them, they only get worse." He set out across the rink, pulling Walker like a toy wagon. "Be back in a jiffy," he called to Lila.

Laughing and applauding, the other skaters made way, forming a line of burned red faces and hard brown eyes.

"Atta boy, Lance. Whale tar out of him."

"Twist that long-legged, skinny prick into a pretzel."

"Kick shit out of him."

"Knock some respect into him."

"Beat his butt."

Powerless in Lance's grasp, he heard a hundred wheels spin off toward Lila. "Let me go, for Christ's sake. Lila, call the . . ." But it was useless.

A moment later he realized his fears were foolish. Stout-hearted lad, Lance simply wanted to help. As Walker leaned over the sink to bathe his eye, Lance steadied him with a firm hand so his skates wouldn't roll out from under him. Afterward his eye was red and his face slightly off center, but there was no real damage. Nothing to keep him from returning to Lila.

"Hold on a minute, old buddy," said Lance. "Lemme take a piss and I'll be right with you." Skating to the urinal, he fumbled with his fly.

Feeling a slight urgency in his own bladder, Walker joined him at the trough, above which ran an iron pipe worn smooth through the years by skaters who had held onto it to keep from rolling back or, worse yet, falling. But the moment he'd begun to make water, he glanced over and saw that Lance was making . . . sly bastard! . . . nothing at all. Fly still zipped, the marine spun away from the urinal and churned toward the door.

"You lousy son-of-a-bitch." Walker made a lunge for him, but in letting go of the pipe, rolled backward, urinating on the floor and down the front of his pants, hit the far wall, and falling, heard a loud crash. The doorknob sailed like a grenade across the room, rebounded off the plaster, and fell into the toilet. As the door slammed, a sound of wild cheering and laughter thundered from the wooden floor.

Leaping to his feet, he tucked himself back in, zipped up, and skated to the door, where Lance had shot the bolt before smashing off the knob. No way to open it. He rammed his shoulder into the oak panel once, twice, three times. Nothing. Except pain. He battered it with the toe of his skating boot. Still to no avail. Desperate and angry, he squatted down and peered through the key hole but could see only vague shadows and shapes. "Help! Let me out." But no one heard. No one came.

As the organist broke into "The Yellow Rose of Texas," he stood up and surveyed his cell, a windowless cubicle that smelled strongly of Lysol, which, he supposed, was better than he would have expected. Impatiently he skated from urinal to toilet, from sink to the prophylactic dispenser, from the toilet back to the door. Where was Lila? She wouldn't leave him here, would she? He'd go mad in this narrow room with its puerile graffiti. "Smile, you're on Candid Camera." "If you want a juicy piece, call . . ." "LBJ won't go all the way." A similar remark about JFK had been crossed out and "Have some respect, punk" written under it. Only two inscriptions had merit. "In 1814 Wellington tore Napoleon's bone apart." And "Lee Radziwill is a Polack."

Where the hell was she? Lila, not Lee. Out there with that cretin. To have Daddy Dick and Ben with him now. The three of them would clear out that whole crew of cowboys.

In the toilet bowl the doorknob lay at bottom like a fat turd with a fuse. He slapped down the lid, sat, and furiously spun his wheels. Damn! That made him madder. Wound his insides tighter. Tricked and trapped in a lavatory. "The bitch," he hissed through clenched teeth, sprang off the john, and building speed, smashed into the door. Crunch! Nothing. "Goddammit, Lila, let me out of here." Again, nothing.

Walker skated three fierce figure-eights and punched the prophylactic machine, jarring loose a cellophane package the size of a matchbook.

It wasn't a condom, but a strange potion with the brand name of Linger. "An ointment to aid in the control of premature ejaculation. Apply externally to male organ. Available from vending machines and drugstores everywhere. Taste every pleasure to the full. Prolong the marital act the safe, natural way. Use Linger."

Dropping the package into his pocket, Walker swore to do just that. Tonight he'd prolong the marital act with a vengeance, prolong it till Lila's itch was scratched bloody and she'd regretted all she'd done. Satisfy her until . . .

Satisfy her? What the hell was he thinking? Not after what she'd done. They were through, and he was leaving, this time with no neurotic fears or doubts. He crouched down on the toilet seat. He had to leave and not look back. Repeating this to himself, he began to spin his wheels again, until at last a heavy fist pounded the door.

"Open up. It's the law."

"I can't. There's no knob."

"Stand clear. I'm coming in."

The oak panels sustained one deafening wallop, then another and another before the wood snapped and the door opened on a burly Texas Ranger hefting a hatrack like a lance.

"What's going on in here, boy?" Hooking his thumbs through his cartridge belt, he waited for an answer with wary grey eyes.

"Nothing," said Walker, perched on the toilet. "Somebody locked me in."

"Don't say? Does that blond gal out at the Coke bar belong to you?"

He nodded and felt his resolve weaken.

"Well, you better hustle your butt after her or she ain't going to be yours for long."

Walker broke for the open door, crept through the lobby, and peeked from behind a pillar. There she was, still at the refreshment counter. A living advertisement for the age. Blond, beautiful, and young. The Pepsi girl or, judging by the way she filled the cashmere sweater, a model for lingerie, for the frothy confections of Frederick's of Hollywood.

Walker hesitated, torn between leaving and staying to claim what was his. Without a doubt she deserved to be punished. Even if he left her later, he had to tell her what she

167

was—a mindless misbegotten bitch—and he had to show this roller rink full of yokels that he didn't scare easily.

Unlacing the skates, he pulled on his street shoes and felt his confidence return as his feet took root on solid ground. He flexed his shoulders, sucked in his gut, thrust out his chest, and started across the floor. It was intermission. The organist was sipping an RC Cola. Thoughout the quiet Quonset hut, his footsteps echoed. Slap. Flap. Slap. Leather heels, lethal for stomping. He was tall and had a long stride. Maybe that would frighten a few of them. But his side began to ache. Had to let out his gut. Lila saw him first. Then Lance. The Marine's leathery face was immobile. Only the beady eyes moved. She was embarrassed, frightened. The cowboys, expecting a showdown, held the silence and made room.

"We're leaving," he said, and seized her arm.

The instant their eyes met, he knew she wouldn't say no. Large brown pupils swam like minnows in her tears. She held her head high, but her lower lip trembled as, with a hand at the small of her back, he rolled her toward the lobby.

"You gonna let that dude get away, Lance?"

"Poleaxe him."

"Whomp that mother 'longside the head."

They'd gone no more than twenty feet when the organist began playing "The Eyes of Texas Are upon You," and Lance skated around to confront them. Swaying unsteadily beneath the weight of his broad shoulders, he bulked large in their path like a side of beef, the Marine Corps anchor, globe, and eagle marking him as prime rib. Forcing a wooden lipless smile, he asked, "Where you going at, old buddy?"

Walker had one advantage. Lance was on skates. Even a feeble punch might topple him. No! That was insanity! The others would be sure to help him. And what about Lila, who was on skates herself? He couldn't drag her up Main Street to the safety of Phoebe Looney's place.

"Excuse me, Lance." Walker went to step around him, but Lance lifted one broad arm like a gate at a railroad crossing.

"I didn't hear nobody sneeze. Did you, fellas?"

"Not us, Lance."

"Hot damn."

"Let fly."

Lance folded his arms and drawled, "Pardner, I think you better ask the little lady what she wants."

Her eyes were still moist. About to cry? Strange. Was she sorry? Or simply frightened? "The little lady does what I tell her." With a flinch that must have been visible to everyone, he added, "She's my wife."

Lance looked at Lila, who, to Walker's surprise and relief, nodded yes.

"Well, if that don't beat all."

"Come on, Walker, let's go."

Stepping past Lance, they made for the lobby, she skating, he walking, half a hundred eyes drilling them between the shoulders. The organ music slowly died, as if the pipes had been strangled shut, and Lila removed her skates without a word, slipped on her red sandals, took his hand, and led him out the door, for Walker had lost initiative and could only wonder why, after playing up to that barn full of Oakies, she'd come away with him. Was there the slightest chance he'd been mistaken?

No, he hadn't, and so shook her hand away from his. "Look, Lila, we're through. I don't take the kind of shit you've been dishing out. Understand?"

Sobbing, she took his hand again, but didn't answer as they walked up the street through the warm black air, through the bristling, buzzing insects whose dry wings seemed to be sawing the night in half. "You can turn off the tears. We're finished."

Bawling most convincingly, she held on tighter. Maybe she'd been testing him, and now knew what a fool she'd been. He was dynamite on a short fuse.

"You're wasting those tears. You should've thought of this before you started flirting with that moron. Meaningful relationship. Productive experience. Situational ethics. Sensitivity. Shit!"

As they descended the steps to their room, she was still wailing. Why didn't she explain? Grabbing her by the shoulders, he gave her a good shake. "I said knock it off. I

169

don't want to hear it. I'm packing my bags and getting the hell out of here. You can do what you damn well please, but you're not coming with me."

Packing the few things he'd taken out that afternoon, he still couldn't understand what was happening. No matter what he said, he didn't want to leave, and it seemed she didn't want him to go. What the hell?

Then, as he started to shut the suitcase, she put a hand to the back of his neck. Was this her explanation? This hand that moved lightly over his body. He wanted more.

As if reading his thoughts, she undid his buckle, let his trousers fall to the floor, and reached a cool hand into his underwear. This really wasn't what he wanted either but he stood there, submitting to her caresses, until he was aware of two things—his own taut, aching cock, and the fact that he wasn't going to leave.

To justify the decision, he fell into bed with Lila, spilling his suitcase onto the floor, and made fierce, almost cruel, love to her. He didn't last long, but then neither did she. In their fury it was the closest they'd ever come to coming together, yet somehow it mattered less than he'd expected. Afterward, when the fluorescent light was out and the darkness hid them from the windowless room and each other, he was ashamed.

Chapter *11*

The shame persisted through the dreamless night
and was coiled on his chest like a snake when he woke next
morning—just as Lila, her arms tangled with his and one of
her long slender legs lassoed around his thighs, was coiled
beside him. The object of his shame. He should have left
her, but . . . He ran a hand down her cool naked flank, and
while in her sleep she moved closer, he pulled back to look
at the familiar face, the blond hair splayed against the pillow,
the petulant mouth, half open, showing strong white teeth.
Suddenly he felt he didn't know her.

Almost at once he corrected himself. Lila Caine was
alien, but not unknown, and his image of her had diffused
completely now, the final layer of that old identity having
laminated and fallen aside to reveal her for what she was.
Not a sensitive, artistic girl suffering in this white-bread
world from an insufficiency of opportunities, but a Tri-Delta—
the Sorority Belle—Rush Chairwoman—Homecoming Queen—
an archetypical Maryland coed like the ones he'd always
hated and considered the embodiment of evil. One who lived
by mottoes and misquoted aphorisms. A penny philosopher
who refused to think, and who hated anyone who did. This
sinister enemy curled beside him. Her head rested on his arm,
her saliva moistened his flesh. Had he defeated her? Or
had he given up the fight? It was too early to know, yet
already too late to turn back.

Shivering, he moved to the edge of the bed and stared at
the suitcase which had tumbled to the floor, disgorging
shirts, underwear, and socks. The two books—*Best Short
Stories on Campus* and *The Sign of Jonas*—lay next to one

171

another, twin symbols for what he was likely to lose if, indeed, he had given in to Lila and what he believed she repesented. Religion and art, soul and mind would be obliterated. He'd be left hollow and alone, with no defense. Nothing to sustain him. Without them he'd . . .

But what had sustained him until now? he wondered. Certainly not those two slender volumes, or anything they stood for. If he'd depended on them, he'd have fallen long ago. Instead it'd been the hope for escape to someplace like Mexico, with someone like Lila, that had allowed him to endure Cottage City and the humiliation of his solitary abortion, "Drowning Voices." Religion and art, God, what cruel jokes! Although he had nothing with which to replace them, except Lila and her body, he wasn't sorry to lose them. What had they ever done but leave him sad and lonely? While Lila, for all she lacked—maybe he'd been too demanding—was at least warm and living, altogether palpable, not a cold and futile notion.

So after teetering on the edge a moment longer, he went back, and lifting her head onto his shoulder, said, "Lila. Time to wake up."

She murmured and looped a leg over his thighs again. He could feel her bush against his hip. Reaching down, he found it moist. Ever ready. Then he massaged her back and her buttocks. Slowly, slowly. No call for anger or haste with Mexico less than seventy miles to the south. There was time to dally, time to reinforce the bond welded by last night's passion.

In tune with this change of pace, he applied a pinch of New Formula, Double Strength Linger Ointment to his penis. A single dab worked miracles, just as promised. For five minutes, ten, fifteen, he was a flawless machine with easy action and fluid drive. Plunging about like a porpoise in shallow water, he never felt a hitch or hesitation. One minute he'd race, next he'd glide, then sprint again, safe and in control.

Lila started at her normal rate, about sixty strokes a second, but soon the ointment slowed her too, and when, after five minutes, she hadn't had a climax, she closed her eyes and steadily pumped. For once they moved as one. No more aching asymmetrical agony. No contrapuntal coitus. With her arms and legs wrapped around him, they were locked at the lips and loins. The metal bedstead lurched loudly, but was muted by the sound of heavy breathing in his ears.

172

At the twenty-minute mark, Walker's nerves began to fray, and finally, although he kept working, he felt nothing. He was as big and hard, but also as insensitive, as the Rock of Gibraltar. Opening his eyes, he saw that Lila's lids had also rolled back to reveal pupils dazed and distant as chipped marbles.

He glanced away and gave a wiggle. Impossible, but he felt . . . No. He still felt nothing. Solid wood. A petrified pecker. Drawing a deep breath, he tried again, trusting momentum to carry him to the finish line, but as he turned and churned to bring it off, although the spirit was willing, almost frantic, the body was dead. Desperately he ransacked the corners of his brain for sordid images of naked female flesh. Fondling adolescent memories, he milked them for the last driblets of desire. Shamefully he even thought of Dede, her miniature breasts and luxuriant bush, but it was no use. Nothing worked.

At last, since Lila had lost interest and seemed to be holding only the most precarious grip on consciousness, he did them both a favor, and groaning as if in ecstasy, shuddered once, twice, three times, faked a tremendous orgasm, and weary and woebegone, withdrew his lingering organ.

Still gorged with blood, the cock was an incandescent purple, glowing and throbbing like a neon tube. What could be done? He gave it a stinging flick with his fingernail, but it wouldn't deflate. Maybe he'd have to use a leech. While Lila curled into a fetal position, he went into the bathroom, let it fall like a blue-gilled monster into the sink, and doused it with cold water. Yeeow! But that was better. Still amazingly cucumiform in girth, the cock lost its rigidity and could be folded—even if painfully—into his underwear.

It should have come as no surprise that early that afternoon, when they crossed the border, Walker found himself in a sense still lingering, waiting. For one thing, his turgid penis had begun to ache again, reminding him of unfinished business. For another, Mexico wasn't at all as he'd imagined. Or perhaps it was so exactly what he'd imagined, it forced him to admit it wasn't what he wanted. There was no dramatic change. After rattling across a crowded bridge from which the Río Grande was visible as a slimy green intestine far below, they quickly obtained tourist cards, changed some money, and were waved on. The impression he carried away from Nuevo Lareda was one

173

of donkeys, dust, automobile insurance offices, and young boys who ran up to the TR-3 pinwheeling their arms and shouting, "Parking!" "I am your guide." "She is my sister." At each traffic light one of them threw mud on the windshield, and another demanded two pesos to clean it. When this had happened the fourth time, he started to drive away without paying, but then noticed a boy on the sidewalk, hefting a brick. He paid.

Out of town the road narrowed and crumbled to potholes, the land looked like little more than Texas without hot-dog stands and Holiday Inns, and heat ricocheted off crushed white rock. An acetylene sky arched overhead, blowtorched a brittle blue, the clouds burnished like brass. The roadside was dotted with dead animals. Glittering, rotund armadillos. Squashed desert mice. Disemboweled dogs. One steer, belly blown big with gas and its hoofs held straight up, like a bronze statue that had been turned upside down. And feasting on the carrion were hunchbacked, slewfoot buzzards which waddled from carcass to carcass, sampling, pecking daintily, then burying their beaks deep in rotten flesh.

Driving through this cactus-studded desolation, Walker couldn't suppress a gnawing sense of expectancy. Around a last bend in the road, beyond the highest mountain, he was certain he'd discover the true Mexico, that Mexico of the mind where he and Lila could forget last night and make a new beginning. But, of course, he did neither. He didn't find the Mexico he wanted—not that day, anyway—and he couldn't forget Lila's behavior or his own weakness. Although he attempted to act as though nothing had happened, his studied efforts at affection seemed to set greater distance between them.

Lila held a very obvious and unnerving silence until that evening, when, as they approached the slums of Monterrey, she said, "I wonder if this is what the song's about."

"The song?"

" 'It Happened in Monterrey.' "

"It'll get better. These are just the . . . the suburbs."

"What a dump! I'll have to send Frank Sinatra a postcard."

The TR-3 clattered over a railroad crossing, down two miles of unpaved alley, and past a warren of miserable shacks made from Coke cartons, packing crates, and old billboards. While rickety dogs, so thin each cartilage in their tails showed through the fur, and dirty children with distended bellies chased each other in the suddenly cool air, old women drew tattered shawls about their stooped shoulders and foraged in the vacant lots for scraps of paper and rare pieces of wood for the kitchen fire. From the mountains beyond the town strong gusts of wind blew down the streets, raising dust to smother the smell of smoke and hot peppers.

Back on the macadam again, they'd gone a few blocks when Lila grabbed his arm. "My God, look at that." She was pointing to a chrome-plated diner, Chuck's Chicken Shack. *Hamburguesas. Hamburguesas con Queso. Pollo Frito. Shakes de Leche.* "Let's stop and see what it's like."

"You know what it's like."

"No, it'll be different, I'm sure."

"I'll bet." But, feeling hungry, he stopped.

Inside, they could have been anywhere in the States. The Jersey Shore. U.S. 40. Panama City, Florida. Long Beach, California. In the background, grease sizzled and popped, and Mitch Ryder and the Detroit Wheels belted out "Sock It to Me, Baby." They sat in orange plastic chairs and were staring at each other over a gleaming slab of formica which looked as if it had been drip-painted by Jackson Pollock, when the owner, an immense, pockmarked American named Chuck Gilhooley, came from behind the deep-fat fryer to say hello.

"Gee, this is a great place you've got," said Lila. "How long have you been here?"

"Opened up last June." Wiping his hands on an apron, he sat down. "The niggers and Yids chased me out of Rahway, so I decided to try my luck here."

"How's business?"

"Real good," he leaned closer to whisper. With a face lost to red cheeks and jowls, his nose alone held its shape—small, sharp, almost fragile—and beneath bushy white eyebrows his blue eyes were slightly out of focus, like a con man's or those of the drunken clowns who play Santa Claus for the Elks' Club Christmas party. "These people love grease, and it's good for them. Cheap and filling."

"Do you use special ingredients?"

"You bet. Nothing but secret recipes. Come on. Lemme show you around."

"No, thanks. We really . . ." Walker tried to stop him.

"You gotta see my new milk-shake machine." Leading them behind the counter, he rapped his knuckles against a polished aluminum box. "There it is. Five thousand bucks, and worth every penny. Three flavors. Fully automatic. And guaranteed for five years. Made in Sweden. But the best thing is, it doesn't even need milk. You just drop a fistful of this special powder in it every morning, add water, and forget it. These people love it. Most of them don't know what real milk is anyhow."

"Amazing." Lila shook her head. "I mean, this is the last spot in the world I'd expect to find a place like this."

They went back to the table, and while Lila continued to marvel—How curious! How bizarre! And what a coincidence that on their first day in Mexico they should eat Maryland fried chicken in a restaurant run by Chuck Gilhooley from Rahway, New Jersey—Walker silently picked at the unidentifiable chunks of meat that had been breaded, scorched, and served to him on a paper plate. The experience seemed more grotesque and confusing than bizarre, and as he gagged on the stringy fowl, he was filled with a great sense of dislocation and not a little disappointment. He'd come to Mexico because he thought it would be different, but so far everything that was different, foreign, and strange—the fetid streets, dirty children, and ancient women staggering beneath cords of firewood—left him feeling guilty and depressed. He knew already that the poor natives, not the tourists, paid a blood price to keep the country picturesque, exotic. But on the other hand, those areas where America had made inroads seemed to him even more offensive, for they brought out and blended the worst in each country. Given a choice, he preferred that Mexico be one thing or the other— the dream he'd imagined, or the familiar nightmare he thought he'd left behind—not a shotgun marriage of sad possibilities. South of the border he didn't believe he should have to compromise.

That first night, after leaving Chuck's Chicken Shack, because he couldn't locate a spot that vaguely approximated his dream, or perhaps out of habit or fear, he returned to the familiar nightmare, to the place where, if one couldn't find a trace of Mexico, he could at least find comfort and reassurance. Out of town, atop Topo Chico Hill, stood the new one-hundred-

and-forty-five-room Ramada Inn. A mighty fortress overlooking Monterrey, a home away from home for fastidious Americans who, after a night in gamy old Mexico, wanted to return to a carpeted room, bathe their privates in purified water, take two aspirins, and throw themselves on the Magic Fingers. It had central heat, a pet kennel, two tennis courts, a heated pool, a restaurant, gift shop, curio shop, coffee shop, a cocktail lounge, and Muzak that couldn't be silenced.

Walker registered as Mr. Lumin Perry and Wife, Muncie, Indiana, and followed the porter to the room with every intention of spreading Lila out on the double bed and shaking himself free of the goddamn Linger Ointment, but in the bathroom, lowering his trousers for an inspection, he saw his cock was still swollen twice its normal size. A delight for her, but not for him. It looked livid and diseased. Dousing it this time in warm water, he read a sign over the john. "Please do not throw foreign objects in the toilet. Thank you. The Management." Funny. The people who ran the place were the only foreign objects he'd seen in the Ramada Inn.

"Are you coming?" called Lila.

"Not tonight."

"Why?"

"I have a war injury," he said, going over to the bed.

"My God, you do."

"Nothing that a little silver nitrate wouldn't cure."

"Walker, what is it?" She touched it gingerly.

"Merely a masculine member that has been skinned down to the subcutaneous level."

"What can we do for it?"

"Rest it."

"How much?"

"Every inch of it."

"I mean, when will it be better?"

"Soon. Meanwhile we can get to know each other."

Within ten minutes Lila was asleep, her back turned to Walker, who lay awake, still lingering, waiting for he didn't know what. He'd have liked to find another night of dreamless sleep, safe from memories of home or recollections of the last few days, but his stomach stirred uneasily, keeping him awake well past midnight. No matter what position he assumed, he couldn't keep his belly from bubbling, caterwauling, shifting its weight. Finally, when a long, almost liquid, fart slipped out, he started for the bathroom, got halfway there, then realizing he wouldn't make it unless he hurried, dashed to the toilet, where he spent the remaining hours until dawn. Laid low by an order of Chuck Gilhooley's Maryland fried chicken. As if to mock him, his intestines shuddered with Montezuma's Revenge, and the room reeked with the effluvium of his innermost pouches, with the smell of a putrefying animal that had crawled out of its dark cave and died. Hunched over in misery, he leaned his head into a sweaty palm, waiting for the next attack. Soon his aching anus began to bleed, for when the toilet tissue ran out, he took to using the harsh pages from *The Sign of Jonas*, then from *Best Short Stories on Campus*, careful, of course, to preserve his own story. What would he do when this, too, was exhausted? Ask Lila to . . .

Oh, God, she'd soon be awake, and he'd have to tell her he couldn't leave the Ramada Inn. The mere thought of travel—of bouncing over the potholed road to Saltillo—started a loose rumbling in his descending bowel, heralding another seizure. And yet, to remain all day in the room, hoping she wouldn't notice the smell—Lila wishing to hell that she didn't—would be even worse. He preferred to suffer alone.

When through the frosty distortion of the bathroom window Walker saw the sun rising, he decided to spare them both, took a bottle of Mennen Skin Bracer in one hand, a can of Right Guard in the other, and fumigated first the bathroom, then the other room. As the mist of deodorant settled, he woke Lila. "Up you go. On your feet. Step lively." Fearing another spasm, he didn't dare waste time. When she hesitated, still half asleep, he dragged her to the side of the bed and peeled off her nightgown. "Hurry."

"Wha?"

"Time to get up."

"What's wrong?" she asked, frightened.

"Nothing. It's a beautiful day. I don't want you to miss it."

"It's six-thirty in the morning."

His stomach lurched. Walker folded his buttocks tightly together and pranced from one foot to the other. Catastrophe if he wasn't careful. "You have to leave the room. I've come down with a contagious disease."

178

"It's not . . ." Reaching a hand halfway to his crotch, she quickly drew it back. "What's that smell?"

"I broke a bottle of after-shave lotion. Now will you get out of that goddamn bed?"

Scrambling to her feet, she stepped into her panties. "You're scaring me."

"Nothing to be scared about. Just a virus or something. Be over it by evening." He nudged her toward the door.

"Okay, okay. Give me a chance to dress and go to the bathroom and . . ."

"No. Not here! Stop at a gas station."

"Walker, you're acting insane. What's the matter?"

"If you must know, I'm about to shit my brains out." He opened the door. "Hurry."

"Isn't there anything I can do?" she asked, dressing quickly for fear someone would see her.

"Nothing. Here are the car keys. Enjoy yourself. Stay all day. Just go!"

When he'd forced her outside and closed the door, she called, "Are you sure you'll be all right?"

From the toilet, where he was once again enthroned, he hollered he'd be fine by evening.

The most recent attack ended, he ripped the cover from *Best Short Stories on Campus.* Only "Drowning Voices" remained, and it looked so paltry lying there on the floor, he was tempted to ball it up and flush it away. Rid himself at last of this reminder of his failure. But he couldn't bring himself to do it. Instead he tucked it into the pocket of his raincoat, then called room service, reserved a separate room tonight for Lila, and asked that three Cokes, a bucket of ice, a box of Saltines, a bottle of paregoric, and two rolls of toilet paper be sent up to him. He had to ready himself for a siege.

The bellboy, dressed in bright red, appeared with a tray and stood at attention next to the bureau, admiring his uniform in the mirror while Walker rifled his pockets for change. Suddenly the boy's dark proud face lifted, his nostrils flared as if he were about to take the Dristan nasograph test, and he sniffed.

"Señor, are you seek?"

The deodorant had failed him. Walker admitted he was.

"I mean mucho bad seek?"

"Yes, plenty bad sick."

"I bring something," the boy said, returning a moment later with a bottle of Diodoquin pills. "These fix," he said, and made a motion with his hands as if tying Walker's intestines in a knot.

Perhaps because he was dehydrated and had no more to yield, or because the pills were more effective than any unprescribed drug should have been, Walker didn't go to the bathroom again that day. Sipping a Coke cooled with chipped ice, he stretched out on the bed, switched on the Magic Fingers, and listened as the loud gurgle in his belly diminished and finally died. Motionless, calm, and solid, he felt like a stone and soon fell asleep, to dream in his weakened and drugged state of Dede. They were at her apartment in Beltsville. That was all. No sound, little movement. Sitting on the bed, leaning against the headboard, she held a book, but was smiling at him rather than reading. He was at the desk and he was happy. Such a strange sensation could come to him only in a dream. Was he writing? The soothing pulse of his body made him think he might be. He'd felt this way a few times while working. An easy sense of confidence, wholeness, and control as the words slipped effortlessly as a silk thread from his pen. He looked down. No, he wasn't writing, but it didn't matter. To be there was enough. To see Dede holding that heavy book with a child's hands and smiling at him over its edge.

He woke wishing Dede were with him, so he could take her in his arms and lift her easily into bed. Where was she? In class? Tonight a long-distance call could . . .

No! He moved to the side of the bed, nibbled a few crackers, and drank a bottle of Coke. His stomach ached with its fullness. The thought of a normal meal—chunks of meat, mounds of vegetables, and rich desserts—nearly made him vomit.

Getting up to take another pill, he heard a frantic knock at the door. "Oh, God, let me in. Hurry." It was Lila. Moaning, she pushed by him and into the bathroom to begin paying her debt for the order of fried chicken.

Leaving behind a few Diodoquin pills, he spent that night in the room he'd originally reserved for her, and sleeping alone for the first time in more than a week, he enjoyed the freedom and sprawling comfort of the double bed. Maybe it was the thought of her ravaged by Montezuma's Revenge, or the memory of his dream about Dede, but Walker had had enough of Lila Caine

180

for a while. Strategic detachment seemed advisable. A course of action that corresponded to his frame of mind, a new slimmed-down attitude of mental and physical vigor. Cleaned from the inside out, he was back on his feet, lean, tough, ready for whatever lay ahead. Adventure in Mexico and a new life later on in San Francisco. Now that he'd recovered, he intended to be detached, cautious, temperate. This way he'd be happy.

      The next day, driving west, he was miserable again, for the Diodoquin pills, which had succeeded in staunching his dysentery, had brought on severe stomach cramps and an agonized feeling that his entrails had been case-hardened in cement. Every few minutes a sharp, gripping pain doubled him over, and Lila had to steady the steering wheel. Then, a moment later, she'd clutch her own belly and slump against the door. Never have any two people wished so fervently to break wind.

      The countryside offered little to distract them from their misery. If anything, the arid, desolate land increased it, and as they climbed the mountain roads beyond Saltillo, although the air cooled, and lush green grass sprouted in the valleys, Mexico still seemed forbidding, isolated, barren. In one small town an Indian woman with a baby waved her hand to beg for pesos, and as Walker continued slowly up the steep grade, she ran beside the TR-3, holding out her child, who had a scarlet boil on his cheek. For an instant Walker gunned the accelerator, desperate to get away, but hearing her deep hoarse breathing, paused long enough to drop ten pesos into her brown leathery palm, then sped off to escape the other people who'd come out of their huts when they'd seen him stop.

      All day it was like this, with Walker massaging his belly and slowing down every few miles to throw pesos out the window.

      "You can't help them all," said Lila.

      He didn't answer. There were more of them ahead. Peasants huddled next to the road, selling cactus flowers and glittering slivers of quartz. Who ever stopped? Old men in colorful serapes led burros piled high with firewood. That was picturesque. But where were they going? For miles in every direction the land showed nothing but sagebrush and Spanish dagger. Where, he wondered, were the jungle flowers and warm beaches? The green world of his imagination? Farther west on the shores of the Pacific, he realized, but because it was so inaccessible to these people who scratched for a living on the high windy plateau, so insignificant compared to the lifeless inner reaches of the country, he began to question his whole concept of Mexico.

But that night in Torreón neither doubt nor feelings of guilt could prevent him from fleeing past the native quarter once again and registering at the Calvete, a modern five-story hotel. How fine it was there! Like home, or as he wished home had been. In the large, brightly lit dining room, it filled Walker with something like nostalgia to see the polished stainless steel and porcelain. If it hadn't been for an occasional word of Spanish on the menu, he might have assumed they were in the Howard Johnson on Baltimore Boulevard in College Park.

For some reason, that thought alone brought on a mammoth appetite, leading him to renege on his recent resolution. He ordered the house specialty, Chicken à la Parisienne, followed by pecan pie and two cups of black coffee. Then stuffed, even if not satisfied, he led Lila upstairs, planning to ransack some rare hidden pleasure from her already too familiar body, but once they were in the room and she'd stepped out of her clothing, he lost his desire. Going into the bathroom, he sat on the side of the tub for half an hour before calling out to her that he was sick again, and that she should go on to bed.

Walker was even more surprised than Lila by this sudden lapse of his libido. But there was nothing he could do. Not even the next night in Durango when she stood beside the bed and went through her stripping routine. She'd become quite good at it, yet had lost her spontaneity, after three loveless days, a bit of her confidence. Maybe she was still lingering from that time in Cotulla. Dangling from a thin thread of desire. Eagerly she flipped down the straps of her slip, let the pink rayon pile up at her feet, then kicked it high into the air so it landed on the bed beside him. Flexing her arms behind her, she unhooked the bra—one he'd never seen before, blue transparent mesh with green flowers at the nipple—and pressed her breasts together to form a deep, suggestive cleavage. The panties were also new, the same color as the bra, but with only one flower and a faint shadow of pubic hair like decorative foliage fanning out behind it.

"I still don't feel well," Walker mumbled as she removed the panties.

"Oh, no!" But then pulling back the covers, she saw he had an erection. "What do you mean? You're big as . . ."

"Yes, but it hurts. See how rough and red it is. Looks like alligator hide."

"Oh, Walker, we've got to do something." Sliding into bed beside him, she kissed his belly, his chest, his face. "I've been going crazy without you. I itch."

"You've probably got the same thing I do."

"I doubt it. Why don't you look?" When she'd forced his face between her legs, he brought her to a climax with his mouth. She offered to do the same for him, but he said he didn't think she should, and went into the bathroom, brushed his teeth a second time, and while picking her short hairs from the bristles, wondered what was wrong with him.

That night he dreamed of Dede again. She was standing beside the bed and slowly undressing as Lila had done, but blushing and fumbling with her buttons. "Walker, do you really want me to?" She asked, removing a blue sweater.

"Yes."

Letting her skirt fall, she folded it neatly and laid it on a chair.

"Faster, Dede."

"I'm not good at this." Now she was folding her slip.

"You're wonderful. But don't bother folding your clothes."

Thumbs under the elastic of her panties, she paused. "Oh, Walker, please. I can't. I feel so silly."

"You're going about it all wrong. The bra first."

A pear-shaped tear shimmered on her cheek. "I'm sorry, but . . ."

"Baby, come here." He reached up, and the moment his fingers touched her breast, he came.

In the morning he found a dry wafer of semen pasting him to the sheets. The first wet dream he'd had in ten years. Something was definitely wrong.

Chapter 12

For the first time Lila was ready before Walker, who remained in bed, weak, disconsolate, and worried. The seed of life—that's what the Brothers who taught him in high school had called it—had spilled out of him, and although it had happened while he was sleeping, he was ashamed, as if the wet dream had involved a pollution of Dede, or his memory of her. With great effort he moved to the edge of the bed, stared at the wall, and felt himself running down badly like a cheap plastic clock. He needed to think things through, but couldn't, for Lila fidgeted noisily in packing, then stalked out to wait in the car. The bustling departure an obvious reproach. Wasn't she ever satisfied? After all, although he hadn't scratched her itch in several days, he'd at least salved it with a kiss, whereas his own desires— which for the moment had nothing to do with sex—continued unrelieved.

In the bathroom mirror, confronted with haggard eyes, he saw he needed a shave, but decided not to bother. He wasn't in a hurry. He just didn't care. After splashing cold water over his face and brushing his teeth, he left.

The morning was bright and brittle, and people moved through it with a stiff precision that left one thinking the day would never soften and slide toward noon. A cock's crowing or the angry asthmatic hee-haw of a donkey sprayed against the sky like shards of piercing metal and were suspended a long time in the thin air before dissolving. West of Durango the high plateau ended with dramatic abruptness at a series of deep, dry arroyos, too wide for bridges. An unbanked road zigzagged like a great path down one side, ran straight across the dusty canyon floor, and rose in the same tight, traversing pattern on the other side before lunging precipitously into the next canyon. Balanced

He walked home slowly through the chill spring sunrise, seeing Johnny Mason and his two sisters already in their front yard searching for the hard-boiled eggs their parents had hidden. Lucky Protestants. They had no worries. Colored eggs and chocolate bunnies were what Easter meant to them. Just once why couldn't things be that easy for him?

Mom met him at the back door with a slap to the face which set his ear ringing. "Where've you been?"

"Mass," he whimpered.

"Why?"

"It's Easter."

"Don't sass me, you little devil. What have you done?"

"I . . ."

"What?" She shook him.

"I went to Communion."

"What?" Her voice rattled the silverware on the kitchen table. "What did you say?" But the voice had lost its volume as she sank back into a chair. "What have you done?" She sounded heartsick.

"I'm sorry," he sobbed, crying more from regret than fear. "I didn't want to wear short pants."

"Do you know what you've done? You've missed your First Communion. The biggest day of your life."

"I didn't miss it. I took it early."

"It's not the same."

Remembering the emptiness he'd felt as he knelt in the vestibule, Walker couldn't deny what she said.

"What will people say? Jesus, Mary, and Joseph, I invited your grandmother and your father to the church." Immediately she was flustered, angry again, and her fingers plucked nervously at her chin. "What if they come?"

"They won't."

"How do you know? He might have flown in last night." She stood up and clutched her neck. "Oh, God, what if they come but you don't show up?"

"Mom, he won't. I know it."

"But his mother might. She could have that nigger drive her. Oh, why did you do this to me, Walker?"

"I'm sorry," he repeated.

187

"That's not enough." She raised her voice again. "Go put on your white suit."

"Why?"

"To receive First Communion."

"I already did."

"That's what you think, mister."

"You want me to do it again?"

"Yes." The word came out like the hiss of a snake.

"But it's a sin," he pleaded.

"I don't care what it is. I'm not going to have your father and grandmother laughing at me."

"But, Mom . . ."

"Do what I said."

Another slap, this one to the opposite cheek, balanced the buzzing in his ears.

An hour later, when he took Communion for the sacrilegious second time and returned to his pew feeling he'd drunk his own damnation, Walker disobeyed Sister Philippa's instructions—yet another sin—and glanced toward his family. Smiling broadly, holding Ben in one arm and Nancy in the other, Daddy Dick, in a maroon gabardine suit, iridescent with age, nodded and winked, while Mom stood beside him, crying and darting anxious looks over her shoulder. But neither his father nor Grandmother Hawley had come. He'd sinned for nothing. Was that why she cried?

Seeing her, Walker felt he might cry himself, or might be sick, or might die there in the aisle, consumed by guilt and sorrow not so much for his offense against God, who was All-Powerful anyway, but against Mom, whose tears washed away her make-up, leaving her looking old, worn, and vulnerable.

By now they were high in the mountains, winding dizzily back and forth through a lush jungle full of soft spreading ferns, eucalyptus trees that smelled sharp and medicinal, and banana plants which put forth green, finger-sized fruit. The sun had spun a hazy web over the sky, which was heavy with a premonition of the sea still a hundred miles away.

This was what he'd waited for, and also was, for once, exactly what he'd expected, but Walker felt horrible. Guilt, having stewed deep in his chest, began to ferment and squeeze out on his cheeks as an angry blush. It was Lila, as much as the past, that bothered him. How in hell had he thought he could escape with her hanging around his neck? Hanging, rather, as a dead weight from his cock. Was this what his longing for freedom had been reduced to? A chance to pump away until his penis peeled off in scaly strips of dead skin? Now, as he agonized about the state of his soul, she stared blankly out the window, probably hating what she saw.

"What's with you?" he demanded.

She didn't answer. Didn't move.

"What's the matter?" he asked louder.

She shook her head.

"Maybe you didn't hear me." This time he roared. "I asked what's wrong?"

"And I told you, nothing," she said, eyes still avoiding his.

"No, you didn't tell me nothing."

"Ah ha! The famous writer gets caught in a double negative."

"Don't be a smart-ass."

"Don't be a garbage mouth."

"I'll be anything I damn well please. And if I am a garbage mouth, it's because I've been eating your pussy."

"Don't you dare . . ." She whirled on him.

"Dare what?"

Folding her arms, she turned and stared out the window again.

"Don't give me the silent treatment. I won't . . ."

"I happen to be thinking, if that's all right with you. Meditation and silence are crucial to the cultivation of love. Maybe that's what's wrong with you."

"What?" He stomped the brakes, bringing them to a stop at the brink of a sheer precipice. "Look, if you don't like . . ."

"Like what? There's been nothing to like or dislike for so long, I forgot what the word love means."

"Let me assure you, it means a hell of a lot more than what we've been doing."

"That wouldn't take much, since we've been doing exactly nothing."

"Why, you . . ." Walker lurched out of the car, around to her side, and opened the door. "Out! Get out. I've had enough."

"Like I said, that apparently doesn't take much." Sliding off the bucket seat, she stalked up the road, arms folded, red sandals flapping, as if she planned to walk to Mazatlán.

"Where are you going? Come and get your goddamn luggage. Did you hear me?" Angrily he ran after her.

When he was almost upon her, Lila spun around and shouted, "I don't think I have ever . . ." Then, eyes widening with fear, looked beyond him and screamed, "Oh my God, the car."

He turned to see the TR-3 rolling backward toward the cliff, the wheels turning slowly as if to mill the loose gravel to powder, and he heard himself groan, an animal sound of anguish that came from deep inside. Feebly he reached out a hand that fell a good thirty feet short.

"Stop it," she yelled and pushed him roughly from behind. "Don't just stand there. Go get it, dumb ass. My luggage!"

Fists clinched, he started to smack her in the mouth—no one called him dumb ass—when he heard a crash which doubled him over at the waist as if he'd been punched in the belly. At once the fight, the anger, everything but the despair, bled out of him. Groaning again, he raced to the cliff, and staring down, saw a pinwheel of grainy dots spin before his eyes, and thought, Oh God, no! Not again. Daddy Dick!

Far below, on a clump of mesquite bushes at the bottom of the *barranca,* the TR-3 was smashed on its back, the Dunlop tires still whirling, and from the front end drained a steady stream of . . . no, of course it wasn't blood . . . water, or oil, or gasoline. It might catch fire at any moment. Incinerate. Cremate. Weak in the knee and in the will, he almost plunged after it, but Lila shouted again, "My luggage," and he recovered his senses.

On hands and knees, he eased over the edge, groping for a foothold. Maybe he could help. Could save. Maybe. Jesus, please help. The loss was more than he could bear. He had nothing left. Clinging like a lizard to the crumbling shale, suspended in the mellow Mexican air between a dead past and a dying future, he looked up to Lila, who folded her arms and turned her back to the abyss. A gust of wind snapped at her bright orange shift, twirled about her bare knees, and seeking warmth, whistled up

190

her thighs, so that her buttocks, panty-clad pink, tightened, shooting an icy pang through Walker's heart. Lost.

"Don't worry," he said. "I'll get it."

Gazing at the jagged green mountains, he tried to collect his wits, but it was useless. Everything was ruined. Shattered. A judgment against him. At last he truly felt Daddy Dick's death. Felt it in the corrosion of his powers of endurance. There was nothing to do but slither down the rock wall and salvage what he could of the luggage.

It took him an hour to make four terrifying, fingernail-breaking, knee-and-elbow-skinning scrambles down into the *barranca* and back again with their suitcases. He expected to fall and skewer himself on a century plant. He was certain the gas tank would explode, swathing him in flames, studding him with shrapnel. He feared his heart would fail. Death seemed inevitable, reasonable, the perfect escape. But nothing happened. He saved the luggage, and Lila didn't even say thanks.

Afterward he sat on his suitcase beside the road in the cruel heat and trembled, as all the emotions he'd suppressed at Daddy Dick's death swept over him. Sadness, deep and ineffable, penetrated his heart, and yet left him feeling empty. Desolated. A mixture of tears and sweat, and maybe some blood from a scratch over his eye, fell in persistent plops to the ground. Doom, guilt, despair. Drops like grains of sand in a depthless hourglass.

For a moment he struggled to concentrate very hard on nothing, complete nothingness. The state of stillness Lila always talked about. Forget ego and imagine himself a nail driven into a board. A mere pinhead. A flyspeck. A monad. And then, when this failed, he tried every time-worn consolation he knew. He had so much left. Plenty of money for a new car. Mexico itself. With an eye, he followed the road downhill to the village of Los Negros, only to have sunlight off the tile rooftops painfully blind him.

Eyes watering, he turned to Lila. She, too, sat on a suitcase, arms knotted across her breasts, legs locked together like a vise that would never open again. Groping for her, as he had for the TR-3 as it rolled off the cliff, Walker asked, "What's the name of this place?"

She nodded to a sign. El Espinaza del Diablo. The Devil's Backbone. Gruesome, but accurate.

"Very appropriate," he chuckled. "It's hotter than . . ." But he couldn't finish. Too late for words. Too late to extend a good-natured paw and pinch her inner thigh.

Rising unsteadily, the imprint of the suitcase handle stamped on his asscheek, he stumbled to the *barranca*. A trip here would end it. A cool free fall, then thud! Darkness and . . . No, that wasn't all. He believed in the afterlife. The afterbirth, as Ben had called it until he was twelve. A bloody mess. And yet there was always hope, wasn't there, Sister Philippa?

Its blue doors flung wide like wings, the TR-3 looked like a butterfly impaled on the thorny mesquite bush. Yet although the convertible top was crushed, little damage had been done to the body. There had to be a way to save it. Haul it up and set it running. A medium-sized crane could do it. But where would he find one?

Swooping like the downward arc of his despair, two buzzards glided on soundless wings into the canyon, and landing on the car's underbelly, pecked once at the sturdy Dunlops, then jabbed at the fuel line, with no success. The TR-3 was holding fast. Waiting for rescue.

"A car!" squealed Lila, jumping to her feet.

"Where?"

Seeing him, she sat down, face drained of expression.

In the distance the car was little more than a black, beady heat molecule swirling out of Los Negros. Maybe a mote of dust driven by parched wind. But as it drew closer, Walker returned to his suitcase and watched it grow large and assume its true proportions. Long, low, American. It looked the size of a freight train, trailing exhaust rather than smoke. Its grille glinted like a mouthful of teeth. A convertible with the top down. Maybe a Chevrolet. Yes, a Chevy with two riders. Men. They leaned against either door, arms on the window ledge, wearing identical blue jackets. Then, when the car was nearly upon them, Walker noticed the gleaming red license plate—" 'Bama No. 1" —and lowering his eyes, prayed that it would pass.

But it was not to be. Lila was back on her feet, yelling and waving and swishing her lovely ass. The black Chevy swerved, its tires screeching for their lost purchase, and throwing a spray of sand and gravel, skidded to a halt.

"Howdy! Anythin' wrong?" The two boys spoke as one.

192

"Oh, thank God," she said. "I thought we'd be stranded here forever."

Dread in his heart, Walker forced himself off the suitcase. "Hello, fellows. We've had an accident. My car rolled over the cliff." He spoke carefully to keep his voice from cracking. Even squeezed out a thin smile, but the good old boys were unamused. The instant they saw Walker, they assumed he and Lila were married, and so slumped down in their seats, peeved at the delay. "I'm afraid we're going to have to ask a favor of you." He tried to stir in them a sense of duty, a reminder of their Southern heritage.

The dark-haired driver looked over at his friend, raised his eyebrows, and shrugged, before the two of them reluctantly climbed out of the car. Good-sized boys, wearing Weejuns, wheat jeans, madras sport shirts, and blue windbreakers with a fraternity insignia on the left breast. Sigma Chi's from Alabama.

"Hi. Ah'm Jim Guy Barker," said the dark-haired fellow. "This here's Al Ballard."

"Walker Hawley." He shook with Jim Guy, then with Al, who said, "Pleased to meet you," and used both hands, one to squeeze Walker's palm, the other to grasp his forearm as if testing its strength.

He introduced Lila as . . . well, as Lila. No last name. Let the chips fall where they might.

"She sure would make a fine traffic officer," said Jim Guy. "Brought me to a stop on a button. Now what seems to be the trouble?"

"Over here."

Leaving Lila by the Chevy, the three of them went to the cliff. Yes, they were lean, hard, and healthy studs. They looked like football players, or, that is, what Madison Avenue might think a football player should look like. But on close inspection they seemed to have all their teeth, their noses were straight, their faces unmarked, and although big, they didn't have the mastodonic size of true ballplayers.

Jim Guy was an inch shy of six feet, but appeared shorter, for he was stocky and powerful in the shoulders. With shiny hair that lay like patent leather across his skull, his face had a square, firm-chinned openness, innocent and expressionless brown eyes, and jaw muscles that flexed when he spoke. Walker saw him as the perfect left halfback for an after-shave lotion commercial.

Al Ballard would have been a credible tackle—big, rough, and ruddy—but he wore his auburn hair too long, combing the front locks over his forehead like the wing of a cardinal. This made his face, with its full lips and grey eyes, look delicate, almost pretty. Yet, in the long shots, he would come across as a brute, for at six-three and two hundred pounds he had a massive neck, ham-sized fists, and long flat feet.

Seeing the TR-3, Jim Guy shook his head, "'At's a crying shame. None of you-all got hurt, did you?"

"No, we weren't in it when it went over."

"Danged lucky," said Al.

"Yeah, danged," said Walker.

Making sure Lila wasn't looking, Jim Guy hocked deep in his throat and spat out a spinning oyster which put the buzzards to flight. "That mother's way down there, isn't she? I tell you one thing, I cain't haul it out. My car's got a 'Vette engine, but you need even more pulling power than that."

"I understand. Actually, I was hoping you might give me a ride into town, so I could hire a tow truck. I think I . . ."

"How'll you get down there to put a line on it?"

"I crawled down to fetch our luggage. I guess I can do it again."

Al whistled through his widely spaced front teeth. "That must of been some climb."

Both of them turned to check him over. Walker stood a little straighter.

"'At took real balls," said Jim Guy. "But where are you going to find a tow truck out here?"

"Durango."

"Hmm." He stuck his hands in his back pockets, shifted his weight, turned and stared back to the Chevy. "Tell you what, me and Al are headed for Mazatlán. 'At's about a hundred and twenty miles up the road. Durango's ninety-five in the other direction. Way I see it, it's six of one, half dozen of another. So if you want to ride to Mazatlán, you're welcome."

To Walker, who desperately didn't want to arrive in Mazatlán and have the balm of the Pacific made bitter by two rednecks in a '66 Chevy, it definitely wasn't six of one, half

194

dozen of another. "Do you think they'll have a tow truck in Mazatlán?"

"Sure. Why not?" asked Al. "It's a big town. Over sixty thousand people."

Walker was speechless with disbelief. How could any paradise be that large?

"And lemme tell you somethin,'" said Jim Guy. "I know a little somethin' about cars, and I'd say even if you got a tow truck to come out here—which isn't likely—and you dragged your automobile out of that ravine, it never would run right again. The frame would be bent all to hell. 'Scuse my language," he said to Lila.

"I guess you're right," mumbled Walker, feeling low and lost.

"You have insurance, don't you?"

"Of course," he said, and gave a brave shrug. "I'll have to contact my agent. Send a wire from Mazatlán."

"I hope to high heaven you got Mexican insurance," said Al. "Otherwise you aren't going to get a cent. A stateside policy is no good down here. 'At's what it said on all the signs and billboards at the border."

He'd seen the signs, too, but convinced he wouldn't have an accident, anxious to push on, he'd ignored them. Now his right knee buckled. The hollowness in his belly swelled. Things were coming too fast.

"Yes, I've got it," he lied, not wanting to appear more foolish than he already did.

"Well, I reckon you can take care of things in Mazatlán," said Jim Guy. "Let's load up and start rolling before we bake our brains out."

He and Al piled the luggage into the back seat before it occurred to them this left no room for Walker and Lila.

"Why don't we get in first, then you stack the suitcases on our laps," suggested Walker.

"I won't hear of it," said Al. "I'll stay in back with you, Walker. Lila can sit up front."

Now that they knew they weren't going to be dragged out of their way, Jim Guy and Al relaxed and warmed to the encounter. Perhaps to them it seemed an adventure. Next semester in Tuscaloosa in the game room of the Sigma Chi house, between

195

Ping-Pong matches and the perennial talk about Joe Willie Namath, they'd tell of their trip to Mexico and of the young couple they'd rescued.

Walker craned his neck for a last look toward the *barranca*. He couldn't see the TR-3, but the buzzards were still circling overhead. How long would it last? Worms would bore into the upholstery, a puma might puncture its tires, lizards lodge in the headlights, and years of sun glaze and crack the enamel. Jesus, the thought made him ill.

His head snapped back as the Chevy dug out with a throaty roar from its glass-pack mufflers, but for once motion didn't unravel the dry bolt of loneliness in his belly. Yet Lila looked happy. To be like her. She left the past behind the way a snake sheds its skin. Face flushed with sunlight, eyes sparkling with laughter, her long hair sustained on the wind. Walker wanted to touch the soft down at the nape of her neck, but thought no. He felt small and cold, divested of hope. Alone. Could passion be rekindled from the twigs and shavings that remained? Another conflagration might burn him out.

"Isn't this somethin'?" said Al. "Seems like every place we go in old Mexico we meet someone interesting."

"'At's a fact," Jim Guy agreed. "Tell them who we met back in Durango."

"John Wayne." Al grinned proudly. "Met him in a restaurant near the plaza."

"You're kidding," said Lila.

"No, indeed."

"How lucky!" She curled sideways on the seat, and the hem of her shift hiked up to mid-thigh. Darting a quick look, Jim Guy tightened his grip on the wheel.

"He's a fine man. Really, just a super human being. Big as a house and friendly as you'd like. He was a Sigma Chi at Southern Cal, you know?"

"Is that right?" As she squirmed, the hem rode higher.

"Yep." Jim Guy stole another look. "Quite a man. He must be over sixty, but he's kept his body ready, lemme tell you. He invited us out to the movie set, but we had to push on for Mazatlán. We got a lot of ground to cover before we go back to Tuscaloosa."

"Oh, do you go to the University of Alabama?" asked Lila,

as if it'd just dawned on her. "You must know Ashleigh Fenton. She's a Kappa."

"No. But I once dated Lolly Head Beckham, another Kappa."

"How about Trudy Cavener?"

For an hour the three of them plucked names from their brains like feathers from a chicken and tossed them into the air. Names of people they might know, people they'd once met but didn't really know, people who'd dated distant friends, or people who'd been in Panama City the same year for Easter vacation. As far as Walker could tell, they knew no one in common, but they continued till they'd exhausted the possibilities, and then began to take turns praising the Greek way of life.

Friendlier by the minute, Jim Guy took a bottle of Southern Comfort from the glove compartment and passed it around. To lead off, Lila swallowed a healthy gulp. "Ummm. I just love that stuff. When I dated at UVA, we drank it all the time."

"So you went to Virginia?" Al asked Walker.

He nodded, not bothering to admit he wasn't the date she meant, and the boys were impressed, for although weak on the ball field, UVA held a high place in the hearts of Southerners who fancied themselves gentlemen. But Lila, knowing he never had fit in there, maliciously giggled.

Walker cared, but didn't protest, for the sweet thickness of Southern Comfort had burned out the last of his resistance and turned his tongue the consistency of bubble gum. When the boys asked him about fraternity life in Charlottesville, he could barely slur out an answer. Yet they didn't seem to notice, since their own mouths had gone dry as burlap, and their words emerged lightly downed with lint.

Later Jim Guy stopped at a cantina to buy cooling drinks, and Walker, clinging weakly to the bar, stared at the stuffed heads of four mountain lions which had been nailed to a plank. The waiter told him brave hunters had killed the cats in the mountains nearby, but one of them bore a black smudge on its skull that looked suspiciously like a tire track. No doubt a car full of drunken tourists, like them, had run it down.

Higher into the mountains the road to Mazatlán looped and curved, then snapped straight as a bullwhip, cracking the Chevy at its end, while prickly, smothering heat wrapped itself around Walker like a wool sweater he'd been caught in and couldn't get free of. Thin air came to his lips lightly powdered with dust, and at each bump in the road his stomach shuddered and threatened to rip free of its mooring. Once a gush of bile came to his mouth, but swallowing quickly, he paralyzed his digestive muscles at the brink of reverse peristalsis. When Jim Guy produced a second bottle of Southern Comfort, he refused with a dizzying shake of his head.

Yet Lila, who had a stronger constitution, drank deeply and sang, along with the good old boys, a few throaty choruses of "The Sweetheart of Sigma Chi."

"So you were a Tri-Delt," said Jim Guy after the song. "I was always pretty thick with the Chi O's, but the Tri-Delts are a fine group, I can swear to that." Nodding for emphasis, he caught a glimpse of her bare brown thighs. Did her pink panties show? Suddenly the right front tire slipped off the pavement, kicking up a spray of gravel, before he brought it under control. He took another drink and spoke gravely to Al. "You know, buddy, every morning, I thank God you talked me into this trip. If I hadn't of got out of Tuscaloosa, I wouldn't of lasted another week."

Al gripped Jim Guy's shoulder with an awkward paw. "Don't waste time thinking about it. Pass the whiskey and sing a song. Tonight we'll have the pick of Mazatlán." In a hoarse voice he chanted.

> "Oh, there'll never be a nigger Sigma Chi
> No, there'll never be a nigger Sigma Chi.
> There'll be nigger SAE's and nigger Zeta Psi's,
> But there'll never be a nigger Sigma Chi."

As if afraid this had broken his continuity, Jim Guy repeated, "Yeah, it's sure a good thing I got out of Tuscaloosa. A man can only stand so much." Grimacing, he fought the car around an unbanked turn.

"Don't make it hard on yourself. Forget, even if you can't forgive."

They worked together like pros, two good old boys stringing a line to see what they'd catch. Ignoring them, Walker stared off at the wickerwork of jungle. But, of course, they weren't fishing for him.

"Is something wrong?" Lila took the bait. "Are you in trouble?"

"It's nothing. Forget it. I should of kept my big mouth shut." After a savage gulp at the bottle, he stomped the accelerator.

"Easy there, Jim Guy. That won't help anything."

The Chevy slowed, snorted, backfired.

"It's a girl, isn't it?" asked Lila.

Jesus Christ! Walker's skin crawled.

"Let's forget it," said Jim Guy. "It isn't right to talk behind someone's back. It was as much my fault as it was hers."

Touched by Jim Guy's sense of honor, Lila had another drink.

"Pass the whiskey when you're done," he said. "I got a terrible taste in my mouth. I should never of said anything."

"Better ease up on the booze a spell," said Al.

Jim Guy finished the bottle and heaved it at a road sign. Now he was overdoing it, but Lila didn't seem to mind.

"Lemme tell you somethin'," he said to Walker with sudden and solemn lucidity. "I hope you're thankful for what you've got. Lila's a sweet and wonderful and beautiful woman. Not everyone's lucky like you." Then, squinting quizzically, he asked, "You two are married, aren't you?"

Walker glanced at Lila, whose eyes, dark and merry with liquor, moved from him to Jim Guy and back again, as if trying to choose between them. Although he shouldn't have, Walker cared, and, surprisingly after all that had happened, experienced a strange emotion, part hope, part anger. Like a trapped rat, he was ready to fight for what was his. He had so little left.

"What do you think?" she asked Jim Guy with a wicked little laugh.

"Well, 'course, I thought you-all were married." But seen in the rear-view mirror, his eyes were alert to new possibilities.

"I did too, but I notice neither of you is wearing a ring. Back home even niggers wear wedding bands."

"Maybe we're not traditionalists. Or . . . or maybe we're living in sin." Giggling, Lila tickled Jim Guy's ribs.

This sent a shiver up Walker's spine, and he could well imagine what it had done to Jim Guy.

With these unanswered questions hanging in precarious balance like the buzzards that drifted high overhead, a deep silence fell over the car, and the sun passed behind a cloud, filtering a silver sheen over the jungle. Above the hum of the tires they could hear the harsh cry of brilliantly colored birds that flashed red, blue, and yellow through the highest trees, reminding Walker of Lila's underwear. How many times had he seen it dazzle a dull motel room, exotic and erotic in the careen of its flight? Would he ever again?

There were more palm trees now, distilling the essence of wild green everywhere, save on those cliffs where magenta scrolls of bougainvillaea unfurled. Walker kept watch for mountain lions, but saw only iguanas, armadillos, and blue dragonflies that hovered above the road, to part like a curtain of gossamer when the Chevy approached. Tonight, he thought, the savage cats will come, and in Mazatlán he'd leap on Lila and set her straight. What in hell was she doing, leading on this pimply punk, a Sigma Chi from, of all places, Alabama?

In the small village of El Refugio, Jim Guy stopped again and said, "We're all out of Southern Comfort. Let's get a bottle of the local mash."

At the edge of a precipice, as sheer and high as the one the TR-3 had rolled over, a thatch-roofed cantina was poised like a great shaggy bird about to plunge into the canyon. While the others stepped inside to buy tequila, Walker went to the toilet, a drafty bamboo privy, dark and narrow as a coffin, canted out over the brink on rotten lumber. It creaked as he came in, but he wasn't frightened. Didn't really care. Through a hole in the floor he made water which fell in a yellow stream two hundred feet. Giddy and weak with his bladder relieved, he wondered what it would be like to follow the flow. Float in the stream of your desires, Lenny Cohen had said.

He shivered. Bullshit! He preferred to fight, even for something as worthless as Lila. Zipping up, he went to join the others.

The three of them sat at a table, a bottle of tequila and four empty glasses in its center. They seemed to be waiting for Walker, but when Jim Guy saw him coming, he poured himself a double shot and tossed it down with no mixer, salt, lime, or chaser. His eyes clenched and puckered, his jaw unhinged, and shaking his head in agony at the mistake, he tried to pretend it's been a joke. "Smooth! Yeah man, 'at's some kinda smooth liquor."

As several Mexicans gathered at the bar to watch, Walker said as condescendingly as he dared without risking open warfare, "Let me show you how it's done."

Sprinkling salt onto the back of his hand, he chucked it into his mouth, took a shot of tequila, and bit into a lime. The Mexicans nodded their approval. A clean job. He hadn't even blinked.

Jim Guy's eyes narrowed and his drawl thickened, as this challenge roused in him that redneck obstinacy of which neither the University of Alabama nor the noble brothers of Sigma Chi could ever divest him. "I reckon there are some who don't mind ruining the taste of good liquor, but my daddy always told me a real man does his drinking straight." Taking a belt at the bottle, he blinked twice, flexed his jaw muscles, and pushed the tequila back to Walker.

"Careful, boys. This isn't Southern Comfort. And it's not Tennessee sipping whiskey." Without drinking, Walker passed the bottle to Al.

He followed his friend's example, forced down a gulp, choked back a sob, and handed the bottle to Lila, who paused. Once again, just as she had in the car, she glanced from Walker to Jim Guy and back again, trying to make up her mind. At first Walker thought he didn't care to have her hurt, no matter what she decided, but then deep down in the asshole of his soul he suddenly wanted very much to see her face twisted with pain.

He didn't have to wait long. Lifting the bottle, she chugged a shot, and immediately her face did a frightening contortion, draining of color and pulling tight as if someone had yanked it together with a drawstring. "Oh God, water! Walker, please help! Water!"

"No, not water," he said, going to her. "Stick out your tongue." He put a hand under her chin. "Farther." Then sprinkled salt on it. "Swish it around and let it melt."

As Lila sagged in the chair, defeated, the boys stiffened in their resolve. Back and forth they passed the tequila, drinking with dogged, almost maniacal, determination until their lips turned purple and began to tremble. A sound of exquisite agony, as of silk being torn by the yard, rose from inside them after each shot, and stinging tears popped out at the corners of their eyes, so that no amount of blinking could clear them. Sweating,

201

shaking, and beset by nervous tics, they refused to yield, or even to slow down. Finally, when less than an inch of filmy liquid lay at the bottom, Jim Guy handed Walker the bottle and whispered in a tortured voice, "Kill it, Ace."

With salt and lime he finished the tequila, wiped his mouth with the back of his hand, and stood up. "Well, I guess it's time to get on our way."

A hush fell over the bar as the Mexicans watched and waited. From the ceiling a spider that had been weaving a web suspended its operation and dropped on an invisible thread as if to get a better view, and three geckoes on the window ledge raised their spade-shaped heads, flicked their tails, and also appeared to look on.

The good old boys got up with no trouble, but shifted their weight unsteadily and soon started to waver. Their eyes went blank, like retractable headlights that had turned inward, and they pinched their arms and legs, amazed that there should be no feeling in them. Al, who had nothing at stake except his balance, crumpled first, but Jim Guy, who had something to prove, struggled mightily, giving that fine second effort Bear Bryant expects of all his players. He took one step, staggered another, pitched forward, and crawling for first-down yardage, collapsed on his face. For a second his legs thrashed, then grew deathly still.

The Mexicans applauded, and as Walker turned to acknowledge them with a bow, there was another crash. Lila had fainted and fallen between the boys.

Collecting Lila first, he carried her to the car and deposited her in the front seat. Back inside, the good old boys were still out cold, and a Mexican, who'd already stolen their watches, was turning their pockets inside out. Standing up, he expanded his chest. "For the health. So they can breathe."

Walker got the man to return their belongings, but gave him five dollars from Jim Guy's wallet to carry the boys outside, which he did with delight, dumping them like sacks of maize at the base of a palm tree, where they vomited.

"Walker, what happened?" Lila was mumbling. "My head hurts. I feel sick."

"You fainted," he said, fighting back a rush of tenderness. Why was it only when she was semi-conscious that he could care for her? "Lie down. I'll get something for your head."

He fetched a chunk of ice from the bar, wrapped it in tissue paper, and pressed it to her forehead.

"That's better," she whispered, and tightened her arms around his waist. "I don't know what got into me."

"Try to sleep," he said, wondering whether she was speaking of this afternoon or the last few days. Did it even matter? He pried loose her arms and got out.

Jim Guy and Al had struggled to their feet and were stamping about in the dust, snorting like wounded animals.

"Ready to go?" asked Walker.

They didn't answer.

"Why don't you two get into the back seat and let me drive. You'll feel better once we're moving."

Jim Guy yielded the keys and stumbled with Al to the car. Two beaten men, they buried themselves beneath the luggage and slept.

The drive to Mazatlán was quiet, lonely, and beautiful, but, of course, because of the TR-3, because he'd left so much behind, because, in addition to it, he'd lost in the last few weeks a stepfather, a home, family, girl, and somewhere en-route, all sense of direction, Walker couldn't enjoy it, even though Lila, who was sleeping with her head in his lap, now had her thighs bared for him alone. If Mazatlán had an airport, he thought, he could fly to San Francisco. But what about Lila? Having sworn to leave her so many times, and having suffered an equal number of humiliating failures, he wanted to avoid more melodramatic resolutions. It wasn't the time to think of being alone or, despite his paltry conquest of the boys, to swear what he would or wouldn't do. From the neck down he was weak. Only his mind worked, and that in weary, narrowing circles, which the long shadows at dusk further reduced and clouded.

Slowly the jungle crept closer to the road, until the tallest trees intertwined to form a dark tunnel, an echo chamber for the call of wild birds seeking a perch for the night. Overhead a single grey cloud, drifting east, squeezed free a few drops of rain, and having cooled the air and settled the dust, sailed toward the mountains. In Chupaderos, fording a small stream, the Río Rosario, he entered a palm grove where shards of coconuts had been spread on the ground to dry into copra. In the fading light men with machetes could be seen hacking at hard green husks, spilling milk into vats, and peeling loose the soft white meat. The air smelled of cocoa butter, reminding Walker at first of suntan lotion and the endless beaches of the Pacific, but then of cracked nuts, wasted semen, and empty vessels.

In Concordia, a tiny whitewashed village, a soldier on a motorcycle blocked the road. Thinking he wanted to check their tourist cards, Walker stopped and got out of the Chevy, but the officer stayed where he was, impassive behind wraparound sunglasses, the polished leather seat creaking beneath his fat butt.

"*Qué pasa aquí?*" asked Walker. He nodded to a procession that was swaying down a side street. The men still wore white cotton work trousers, and the women, as usual, were in black, all of them following a tiny wooden casket carried by two altar boys. A few people bore lighted candles, some sang, others laughed and rattled rosary beads. Many appeared to be drunk. "Is it a festival?"

Peeling away the wraparounds, the soldier revealed dark malarial eyes. "No, señor. It is a funeral, as you can see by the coffin."

"But why are they laughing?"

Spinning his sunglasses by the earpiece, weary at Walker's ignorance, he said, "They are happy. It is a joyous funeral. A baby has died and is now a saint in heaven praying for her family and the village."

"How lucky."

Walker returned to the car, and forgetting himself for a moment, lifted Lila's head back onto his lap, stroked her cheek, and quietly repeated that she was alive, as if this guaranteed that he was too.

Beyond Concordia the darkness was complete. Fording two more rivers, he descended from the mountains and gathered speed through flat sweet fields of sugar cane. He encountered no other cars, but blinking yellow eyes dotted the roadside, and every few minutes a pathetic little animal would dart onto the asphalt, then seeing it wouldn't make it to the other side, would turn in terror and try to outrun the Chevy, which, despite all

Walker's efforts at mercy, always caught up and killed them. Like shredded shoe leather their flattened bodies flapped beneath the tires.

At last, when they came to a fork in the road, although he saw nothing, he thought he could hear the sea, feel it through every pore in his body. A warm breeze riffling the palms was heavy with brine. Wind moaning through saw grass unnerved him. Here at the land's end, no longer wanting to be alone, he stroked Lila's cheek again, and lightly tugged at a strand of her damp hair. "Lila, wake up."

Groaning, she rolled her mouth against his leg, so that he felt the wetness of her lips through his pants.

"Sit up and look."

But at what? Emptiness everywhere. It was as if they'd slipped anchor and drifted off on a waveless sea. Far ahead, the Chevy's high beams sought vainly for a landmark, a sign, anything. Then an old man appeared. Simply stepped out of one side of the darkness, crossed the road, and started to enter it again at the other side when Walker called, "Which way to Mazatlán?"

Shielding his eyes from the light, the man pointed right.

"And the sea, where is it?"

"Six feet ahead, señor, and you are in it."

Once he'd made the turn, the smell of the ocean was stronger, and the waves against the shore shook the road.

"How much farther?" murmured Lila, sitting up.

"I don't know, but we've reached the sea. It's off to our left. Hear it?"

"Dark. Frightening." She shivered.

Minutes later, spying a faint dome of light, they crested a hill and saw Mazatlán strewn like a necklace along the beach. Walker braked the car for an instant, but when Lila said, "Oh, isn't it lovely," he let it coast down into the town. At the first hotel, a tall modern place, the Freeman, he stopped and said, "Thanks for the ride, fellows. This is where we get out."

The good old boys didn't revive until he'd lifted the luggage from their laps. "Here, lemme help," Jim Guy insisted, and carried one of Lila's suitcases into the lobby, where the night manager and the bellboy stood at either side of the front desk playing dominoes.

"Are you staying here too?" Lila asked them.

"No, indeed," said Jim Guy. "Al and me sleep in the car under the stars. So I reckon this is goodbye."

"We'll see you on the beach tomorrow."

"No, you won't." His words were short and hard, and he looked at Lila as if she'd let him down. "Come morning, we'll be moving on. I guess we're just wanderers. We got a lot of ground to cover."

"But, Jim Guy, I . . ." Al started, then just as suddenly stopped.

"Sorry to hear that," Walker forced himself to say now that he was sure they were leaving. "I wanted to buy you a drink at least."

"Don't mention it," said Al. "It was all . . ."

"Just meeting you, even for this short time, is all the thanks I want," said Jim Guy to Lila, and as they would have wished it, Al and he vanished into the throbbing tropical night.

Although the hotel appeared to be empty, they were given a small, poorly lit room on the seventh floor which had no view of the sea. Walker didn't care. He was only half conscious of where he was anyway, and the one thought that did manage to eat its way through the haze of his fatigue was that, after this long day, after all that had happened, he was alone again with Lila in a strange room with an untried bed. The idea disturbed him. Frightened him. Was there no place else to go? Nothing else to do? Talk. But of what? Remain silent. But how? The bare brown walls begged to be softened. The quiet to be broken. The sagging bed to be boarded. The fathomless night itself to be somehow drawn together, to be made small and manageable.

Lila flopped on the bed and lit a cigarette. Keeping his distance, Walker wasn't sure he could bring himself to touch her.

"Hot, isn't it?"

"Yes. Very," she said.

"How do you feel?"

"Crummy."

"Your head?"

"Yes, and I think I'm about to have a visit from my bitchy little friend."

"Your what?"

"My period." She exhaled a stream of smoke, and extended an

arm toward the end table. "Hand me the ashtray, will you?" After crushing out her cigarette, she let Walker put the tray back on the table.

"I'm sorry," he said for no reason. And yet there must have been some reason, for at the moment he did feel very sorry.

"What about?" she asked, sitting up.

"About your period, I guess."

"No kidding?" She smiled.

Walker leaned against the wall. Was this the answer? She'd acted strange and ill-tempered because of her period? Nothing wrong. Simply nature. A tide inside her, rising and receding with the moon.

Lila stood up, slid out of the shift, and wearing bra and panties, sat down again.

"A shower might make you feel better. I mean, it might . . ."

She looked at Walker as though seeing him for the first time in a long, long while. "Not now." And after a pause, smiled and said, "Honey."

The word "Pardon?" escaped his lips, a feeble, confused question that both of them ignored.

Leaning forward, she unhooked her bra, and as it fell toward the floor, he reached out on impulse to catch it, but wound up with her breast in his hand instead. The pale flesh was curiously cool. In a way, that was its greatest attraction, and was perhaps why he pressed it to his lips as if to drink.

What followed frightened him. He'd done it all before. Of course. He'd ridden her body before as if it were a greased rail leading to a familiar and uninteresting destination—the same net of twitching ganglia—but this time it was worse, for her uncalled-for, unprovoked, and even unwanted ardor left him feeling he'd jerked off in the dark with a soft machine, or buggered a thrashing animal. Afterward they pushed away from each other like snakes that had coupled and oozed apart to let the air cool their bellies and dry the sweat.

Chapter *13*

Next morning the sky was Gulf Stream—blue, warm, and flowing through the window from which Walker could see a steep hill with pastel houses strewn like cubes of sugar down its sides. Above them, set in a palm grove, a large hotel raised its walls of white stucco. The air held in delicate suspension the scent of cocoa butter, drying mortar, fresh sea water, and frangipani, and rising with the smells from somewhere far below was the sound of a marimba band. Music in stray tatters stirred his blood, dispelling almost completely the evil mood of the night before. In a place like this, his senses alone might sustain him until he decided what to do.

Then a door opened, and Lila, looking pale and dour, emerged from the bathroom with a white string nestled in the short hairs of her bush.

"It's a beautiful day," he said, as if to remind himself even as he looked out the window.

"I'm sick."

"You'll feel better after breakfast."

"Ugh!"

"A cup of coffee won't hurt you," he said, turning. "Why don't you get dressed?" But when she slipped on a blue bikini instead of underwear, he asked, "Why are you wearing that?"

"In case we go swimming."

"I thought you were sick."

"I'll recover."

"But aren't you supposed to stay out of the water during your period?"

"Man, you really are living in the Dark Ages. Don't you read the ads? 'Feel fresh, free, cool, clean, and unencumbered every day of the month.' " Singing, she danced a little jig as she pulled up the bikini pants.

"I'd like to feel that way myself. So if you have a spare tampon . . ."

"Where would you put it?"

"I'd find a place." Pulling on his clothes—an outfit he'd purchased the day before Thanksgiving: red trunks, mustard Bermudas, and a green knit sweater with a yellow alligator on the pocket—he repeated the jingle to himself. "Feel fresh, free, cool, clean, and unencumbered every day of the month."

Christ, what was the secret? he asked himself as they descended in the elevator and stepped out of the Freeman to see that first day in Mazatlán, not a white sand beach, or an endless expanse of cobalt sea, but Jim Guy and Al, still in their Sigma Chi jackets, sitting on the seawall across the street. Not a chance to escape. The jingle died on his lips, and suddenly he felt stale, trapped, hot, dirty, and very much encumbered, in need of a tampon for the mind.

"Oh, wonderful! You didn't leave. Fabulous!" gushed Lila.

"We decided we couldn't abandon you-all without a car," said Jim Guy, crossing the street to join them.

"How sweet of you."

"Very sweet," mumbled Walker.

"And besides wanting to help you-all," said Al, "we found out this is a pretty good old town. Really a super place. So I said to Jim Guy, 'Wouldn't it be a gas if you and me, and Walker and Lila stuck together and had a groovy time?' "

"Very groovy," whispered Walker weakly.

"This place is out of sight. Miles of deserted beach, lots of good cheap beer, and great seafood. Me and Jim Guy might stay on forever."

"Look, Lila doesn't feel well. We're on our way to get something to eat. Why don't you meet us later?" Walker tried to lose them for a few minutes. Enough time to switch hotels. Hell, switch towns! Countries!

But big Al slung an arm around his shoulder. "Heck, we ate breakfast hours ago, but we'll tag along anyway. 'At's a slick-looking outfit you got there. Come on. We know a nice diner up the road a piece."

Jim Guy fell back with Lila. "Still feeling bad from yesterday?"

"No, I'm better now." As they crossed the street, she took his arm.

At a sidewalk café on the Avenida del Mar, she and the two boys began debating, for some unknown reason, the concept of fraternity service in the university community, leaving Walker to do little more than pass the cream and sugar and stare at the sea. Then, without transition—or perhaps he'd been lost in daydreams when the leap came—Lila, that avatar of the Old Immorality, led an intense discussion of the New Morality. "I think it's had an important liberating effect on women."

"Oh, heck yeah," agreed Jim Guy. "I mean, a girl doesn't have to turn a boy down just because she's scared. She can make a mature and productive decision."

Walker's mind boggled. Even good old boys from Alabama had learned the right lines.

"What do you think, Walker?" asked Lila archly.

"I want to go swimming."

"I go along with Hugh Hefner," said Al. "As long as an act involves consenting adults, there's nothing wrong with it."

" 'At's my philosophy," said Jim Guy.

"How about you, Walker?" Lila asked again.

"Why don't we . . . ?"

"Do you know what we're talking about?"

"Yes. Between consenting adults, everything is permissible. Even rape."

"Huh?"

"Hot dawg, 'at's somethin' I didn't think of."

"For Christ's sake, let's go swimming."

Jim Guy insisted on driving them out to Playa Gaviotas, where the sand was smooth and hard and curved on for miles till it disappeared in a mist of high rushing waves. At first Lila refused to go into the water, but finally, after the boys had taunted and begged, she waded in up to her knees, and standing there at the edge of the sea, scooping water onto her face and neck, she looked to Walker, who had swum far out, like a goddess returning home. Her greased body dazzled in the sunlight. A breeze lifted her hair and swung it like a pendulum over her left shoulder, then back and forth against her loosely cradled breasts.

Walker felt he should keep swimming. Paddle secretly back to town and disappear. Leave her, as he'd often thought he should, but now not in anger, fear, or guilt, but simply because she seemed so beautiful and complete in herself. He wanted to remember her that way. Real, of course, but distant. Too far away for him to tell her beauty was as depthless as a mirror which would yield up from the sleek flesh nothing but a shimmering distortion of whoever approached her. Too far away to realize that although she appeared to offer everything at once, for nothing, he would come away with empty hands and bruised knuckles if he tried to reach out for her.

And yet, he didn't leave. He turned toward shore and swam back to fend off Jim Guy and Al. For he and Lila were still linked by guilt, if nothing else. She was what he'd gotten in exchange for leaving Daddy Dick. Without her there was no justification—not even a way of understanding—what he had done.

For this reason or another—he could always think of one—he continued coming back to her. Like a fox to its hole. A lemming to the sea. A dog to its vomit. He lacerated himself with cruel analogies, but neither they nor the maddening presence of the good old boys could crack the yoke that bound him. The longer he stayed, the less he felt capable of going, for no matter how grotesque the situation, he couldn't bring himself to leave Mazatlán alone and empty-handed, without the TR-3 and without Lila. This, he knew, would be running from disappointment to certain despair, with no hope, no dream, no fiction to hide behind. Thought of it led him to imagine himself strapped to the prow of a ship, headed north, plunging through a dark sea full of icebergs. Such a return could only be fatal.

Always in the past he'd managed, even in disaster, to retain on some misty horizon of his brain a sustaining illusion or hope—freedom, at last, from Cottage City, success in his writing, the possibility of love, and after he had Dede, the possibility of passion undiluted by love, the thought of money, happiness, or, if nothing else, the consoling assurance that everything, no matter how painful and frightening, came to an end. Yet now, in Mazatlán, he no longer retained this meager assurance. Each night he thought he couldn't go on, but the next morning found himself on the beach with Lila and the boys, and although his growing anxiety deluded him into believing things had gotten worse, they remained agonizingly the same, as for the first time in his life Walker was totally immobile.

Mexico, itself, had failed him, inducing a fearful sense of dislocation. Sometimes at night, having heard Spanish in the hallway, he'd whisper, This is Mexico, but was never convinced or reassured, perhaps because, at Lila's request, the bellboy had installed in the room a rusty electric fan whose metallic clatter reminded Walker of melted snow gurgling down drainpipes. A babbling mockery of his vain delusions. As the whining blades stirred the slow air and sprayed it like lukewarm dishwater over the two of them, Walker would shiver in bed and try to recapture a memory of the TR-3's cozy warmth. The firm security of its bucket seats. The smell of well-worn leather. The dashboard indicators that glowed in the dark like a tray of jewels. Back then his one desire had been to drive so far and so fast he'd never find his way home, but now that he'd done it, he couldn't stand it, for here in a strange place it seemed he'd outdistanced himself instead of the past.

His rare moments of lucidity—those times when he could admit that, yes, he was Walker Hawley, down in Mexico for a vacation—were worse, for then, although perfectly aware of his surroundings, and of Jim Guy, Al, and Lila, he realized he was losing her as well as himself. Her loss shouldn't have mattered. He didn't love her, didn't care, but he had nothing else. This, he thought, must have been how Mom felt when his father left her. Each time, in fact, that he, himself, left her alone in the emptiness of her life, helpless and stricken.

Gradually, as his skin tanned, his blood thickened, and his mind turned to jelly, he found himself repeating, The air is liquid. Is fire. Is solid and unyielding as earth. Unremitting in its cruelty, this mixture of the four elements crushed all hope out of him. Everything he'd wanted or struggled for oozed away. Nothing remained—nothing except a recognition of flight, change, and loss.

The sea pitched forward and rolled back, and the sun beat upon it, as it did upon Walker. In the morning at Playa Gaviotas, large buzzards perched atop the cabanas and spread their wings to let the breeze blow their feathers free of lice. Then during the stillness at noon, when the breeze which had been trapped for hours in the jungle seeped back toward the ocean, raking with it the smell of muck, of rotten fruit, and distant dark lagoons, they clattered off in search of what was dead. Usually they circled Walker at least three times before deciding he wasn't ready.

Often it seemed that Jim Guy and Al circled and eyed Lila in the same predatory way, waiting for him to leave, or let down his guard, so they could pounce upon her. An attack she was about as likely to resist as a chunk of carrion would a buzzard's beak. But he clung on gracelessly to frustrate them. And maybe her. He stayed at her side every hour of the day, and at night, when he could, made love to her, even though his mortal flesh, already flayed by tropical heat, soon weakened and deteriorated. Now there was never any doubt who would win the orgasm derby. Walker did, with unnerving regularity. While Lila laughed and called him her Super Man. Faster than a speeding bullet.

In at least one way the good old boys possessed greater staying power. They were patient, consistent, and single-minded. Every morning they met Lila and Walker in front of the Freeman, drove them out to Playa Gaviotas, swam with them, ate with them under the cabana where a waiter named Rigoberto served club sandwiches and cold Carta Blanca beer, drove them back to Mazatlán, ate dinner with them at the Belmar beneath a thin rind of moon, talked drowsily with them over snifters of Kahlua while the breeze cooled their sunburns, and finally walked them back to the hotel, along Avenida del Mar, where silvery waves crunched against the bulkhead. At times Walker suspected they might come inside, accompany them in the elevator, and climb into bed with them. And in a way, it was as if they already had, for he and Lila slept at the far edges of the mattress and took pains not to touch each other unless they were making love. Most nights there was ample space between them for Jim Guy, Al, and even Rigoberto and the bellboy.

If, preparatory to concocting yet another reason, Walker often asked himself why he went on this way, he wondered just as frequently why Lila did. Simple inertia? Or was she, too, afraid to change? It pleased him to imagine this might be the case, for it gave him some small hope he might leave her before she dumped him.

But this chance was slight. One day, after swimming, he came back to the cabana, and standing at the bar where no one could see him, heard her say to Jim Guy, "You know, square and irrelevant as it sounds, I don't know a thing about you. I mean, I don't even know what your major is."

Tearing the label from his beer bottle, Jim Guy chuckled. "You're not going to believe this, but Ah'm a religion major. Al and me both are."

"Why, that's . . . that's wonderful. Are you going to become ministers?"

"No, indeed. I only went into it because when I was in Recreation and Health, I kept flunking comparative anatomy. You see, I didn't want to go on probation, or lose standing in the fraternity and all."

"What's your favorite book in the Bible?"

"Leviticus. You know, where the Lord tells the Jews not to do it with animals or with women during their periods."

"Yes, that's always fatal." She laughed.

"And how 'bout you? What was your major?"

"Drama. I've got my heart set on show business. Soon as I get to California I'm going to audition for the Playboy Club and try to raise money for voice and acting lessons."

"Hey, you can't be a Bunny."

Her chin lifted proudly. "Why not? Don't you think I could qualify?"

"They don't take married women."

"Er . . . I'll see if they won't make an exception for me." Smiling, she combed a hand through her hair, which had been bleached even brighter by the sun and the salt water.

The next day Walker woke early, and his fears seemed confirmed. Lila was gone. He sat up, sorry she'd beat him to the punch and that there hadn't been one last fight. A few well-chosen words of advice, and a boot in the ass is what he'd have given her. The bitch!

But then he noticed her suitcases still in the closet, her underwear and cosmetics on the bureau, and her nightgown on the floor of the bathroom, from which came a dull scraping sound. Climbing out of bed, he crept to the door and peeked in.

Legs spread wide, Lila sat naked on the side of the tub, and holding a mirror in front of her crotch, was awkwardly shaving her unlathered cunt. Walker drew a sharp silent breath. One slip, one wrong move, and she'd lop off her labia. Why in hell was she doing it? There could be no good reason. Hadn't he told her to let it grow? With each stroke she severed the slender threads that bound them.

"Preparing for your audition with Hugh Hefner?" he asked, going to the sink to brush his teeth.

Lila lurched, dropped the razor, and nearly fell into the tub. "Don't sneak up on me like that. I almost cut myself."

"What a pity. It would have ruined your lovely smile. I thought I told you to let it grow."

"Told me? Who are you to tell me what I can or can't do with my own pubic hair?"

"Okay, do it with that nitwit hick's razor. Not mine."

"Maybe I'll let him do it for me."

"You do, and I'll whip both . . ."

"My God, who are you kidding? You don't have the strength to get it up, much less . . ."

"Watch it!" he said, and with a nudge sent her thumping into the tub, where she lay sprawled at the bottom, eyes blurred in fear, one side of her bush cleanly shaved, the other dark and shaggy.

Rage drove him into the other room, but the small drab cubicle provided no scope for his anger. Going to the window, he faced the same sense of frustrating limitation, for the skein of hot brassy days had ended and the sky was dark with clouds. A perfect reflection of the grey cobblestoned plaza below. A storm seemed imminent. As a cool breeze blew over his shoulders, Walker shivered, and suddenly was afraid he might kill Lila.

She seemed to know this. Coming out of the bathroom, she kept her distance while she dressed, and with difficulty succeeded in avoiding his eyes. Then they walked silently to the elevator, and waiting for the lift, folded their arms and turned in opposite directions. Lila toward a mirror, Walker toward a potted palm. On the ride down, closer to each other than either of them would have liked, they were careful not to touch. One mistake might have driven him to murder.

Fighting to control himself, Walker was without thought until he saw Jim Guy and Al in the Chevy, waiting to drive them

those pants off. Everybody into the water. I don't want anybody to chicken out. Last man in has to let me sit in his lap all the way back to Mazatlán."

Leaving Walker behind at the table, the four of them raced down the beach, Jim Guy, Al, and Lila tossing off their clothes as they ran, while Harry, with short lumbering strides that shook white fat out from under his trunks, pursued them, bellowing, into the ocean. Walker waited and watched for him to make his first move for Lila. Then that tub of guts would see someone sprint with real speed. One punch to the paunch would double up the lecher for life. As Harry dived underwater, Walker craned his neck and squinted. Where would he come up? Between her legs, his bald, greased head like a massive hard-on?

No! Strange. He'd gone after Al, and gotten him in a bear-hug, romping and roughhousing with the good old boy. But Lila and Jim Guy swam out to stand in shoulder-deep waves. How about them? Were they touching underwater, his fingers wriggling like cool fish in her cunt?

A loud shout from Al broke his concentration. Harry was still at it. In fact, at . . . no, it couldn't be! Al wouldn't stand for it. Would break every bone in a fag's brittle body. After all, he was from Alabama. A Sigma Chi. And yet . . .

Minutes later Harry staggered up the beach alone, panting and sputtering water from his face. "Whew! I cain't take too much of this grab-assing around at my age. That boy's strong as a bull. Just look at him." Al was chopping his way through the waves with heavy, awkward strokes. "What do you reckon he goes?" asked Harry, falling into the chair next to Walker. "I'd say two-ten and not an ounce of fat. I bet the girls in Tuscaloosa just eat him alive with no salt. The boy must be hung like a stallion."

Walker chewed his lip and hoped it wasn't wishful thinking. No, after a last look, he realized he wasn't wrong. Although the good old boys didn't know it, Harry would be no help in abducting Lila, for he was after Al, the brawny, beautiful Madison Avenue tackle from Tuscaloosa. Suppressing a laugh, Walker felt a touch of joy for the first time since arriving in Mexico.

Lips purple and teeth chattering, the others soon came back to the cabana.

" 'At water's freezing," said Al.

"The great scrotum-tightening sea," laughed Harry, and tossed him a towel.

"Is 'at what the Mexicans call it?"

"No, but I do." Harry laughed again. "Come on over here, Sport, and tell me about Alabama's football team. I hear they play a pretty mean brand of ball."

"I'll say they do. They haven't lost a . . ."

As the five of them sat beneath the dark clouds, letting the dreary light spread like corrosion over their tans, Al rambled on for hours about the Crimson Tide, the toughest little guys ever to take the gridiron. There was that time Joe Willie Namath played against Mississippi with his knee in a cast, or the time a never-to-be-forgotten hero—whose name eluded Al—had kicked a field goal to beat Tennessee in the last four seconds.

At one point, eying Al's thick thighs and flat, washboard stomach, Harry interrupted to say, "Hell, boy, you look like you might of played a little ball yourself. You sure are big enough." Then, his hairy belly rumbling with laughter, added, "Or did you save yourself for mattress polo?"

"Heck, Harry, I'm not that big, but one time in high school I . . ."

The stories went on all afternoon, punctuated by Harry's ribald and taunting remarks, which he reemphasized by squeezing Al's thigh or rumpling his auburn hair. Al didn't seem to mind, maybe because Harry insisted on paying for lunch, and he kept them laughing. Or, at least, he kept Al laughing.

Lila and Jim Guy sat together, coupled by a solemn unspoken colloquy which excluded everyone else, while Walker, feeling very much alone, sank lower in the chair and held himself absolutely still, hoping the acorn-sized goose bumps on his chest would disappear. But he could neither stop shivering, nor rid himself of the gooseflesh which was brought on by anxiety as much as by the cold.

And so as the shadowless day, which had appeared crepuscular at noon, moved imperceptibly toward evening, his mind continued the search for warmth which his body had given up. Soon, since Al had paired off with Harry, and Jim Guy's chunky back shut him off from Lila, since misty clouds hid the sky, discolored the sea, and obscured the jungle, and, finally, since they had nowhere else to turn, his thoughts regressed to Cottage City, to the house on Whittier Street, to Daddy Dick, Dede, and even Mom, all of which he associated for the first time with warmth, security, comfort, and brightness. He knew it was dangerous to indulge himself this way, but consumed with a desire to be far away from these people, snug in the TR-3, and moving toward home, he couldn't help it.

The thoughts enveloped him in a faint glow, as if he'd wrapped himself in a warm, familiar blanket or settled into a soft lap. Gradually he remembered a spring two years ago when Dede had found a litter of rabbits in a pile of lint beneath the exhaust fan of the laundry room at Ashtree Townhouses. Most probably the mother had been flattened on U.S. 1 by a Mack truck.

So Dede sorted out the live lumps of fluff, which were dark brown and no larger than her thumb, and put them in a shoe box on top of her old slip. Every four hours she fed them warm Sealtest milk from an eyedropper, and for a week they seemed to flourish, nuzzling next to a radiator, rarely moving or making a sound, as Walker and Dede sat whispering nearby.

"For Christ's sake, it's like having a baby." But Walker really didn't mind.

"They'll be grown soon."

"Yes, and then what? They'll overrun the place, doing all the things bunnies are famous for."

"Such as?"

"Such as reproducing at the rate of thirty an hour."

"That many?"

"At least."

"How do they do it?"

"I'll show you."

Lying beside her on the couch, he put a hand between her legs, and whispered, "Bunny." That was warmth. Softness.

But then the bunnies began to die. Weeping frantically, Dede called a veterinarian, who explained gently that Sealtest Dairy didn't produce even a vague facsimile of rabbit's milk. He gave her a formula she might try, but told her frankly they weren't likely to survive even if they got the nourishment they needed.

"But why?" Walker had heard her wail as he wrapped

another tiny corpse in a napkin. There were only two left.

"What's wrong?" he asked when she hung up.

"The poor little things can't go to the bathroom. They need their mother."

"What do you mean?"

"Well"—she grimaced—"the mother rabbit licks their . . . their behinds to relieve constipation."

"Now look, Dede, I'll do almost anything, but . . ."

"The doctor said we could use very soft wet rags."

"But, Dede . . ."

"You don't have to, but I am."

For a week they took turns swabbing and massaging the convoluted pink anuses of the remaining bunnies, but finally they, too, died. After the last one had been buried, Dede cried for an hour, while Walker crooned and rocked her in his arms. Weary and depressed, they found it hard to . . .

"Hey, what's with you? Cat got your tongue?" It was Harry. "I just asked why don't we go back to my place and have a few drinks? I got a girl working for me who can whip up a mean guacamole."

"Sounds great," said Jim Guy, helping Lila to her feet.

"You hungry, Sport?"

"I can always eat."

Walking to the car, Lila glanced once over her shoulder at Walker, but said nothing. Would she leave without him? He didn't have the strength to test her or himself. At last he followed them to the Chevy.

In the open car on the way to town the cold air cleansed his stinging skin of gooseflesh, but after he and Lila had left the others in the lobby and were alone in the elevator, the prickly bumps reappeared. Nervous, he felt as if the rash had spread down his throat and into his stomach.

In the room, dense grey air streamed through the window, leaving it dank, forlorn, and cold. Walker fell heavily onto the bed and stared first at the ceiling, then at Lila, who'd taken off her bikini and now stood nude in front of a mirror, drawing a brush through the tangles of her hair. Front and back she carried almost identical globes of white flesh—her breasts and buttocks, which looked soft and vulnerable in contrast to the varnished skin stretched thinly across her back and belly. At this angle her cunt was an optical illusion, for on the left, where she'd shaved, one saw a smooth pink purse of flesh, and on the right, a triangle of tufted brown hair. Little girl and woman at one and the same time. Her greatest—would it be unkind to say, her only—attribute.

As she pulled the brush, her breasts made startled little leaps, stirring in Walker what seemed like an ancient memory. Yet it had happened only three weeks ago in that motel room in Breezewood. What a fine start it had been. Filled with promise for what lay ahead. He'd thought a limitless opportunity was open to him. Wasn't there any way to recapture the brilliance of that illusion? Or, failing this, to salvage a few chips of glass from the heaped ashes of his hopes?

Sitting up, Walker extended a hand toward Lila, reaching out for what might have been tenderness, love, an escape from loneliness—but encountered a buttock, smooth and cold as ivory. She stopped brushing, and stood motionless, apprehensive, watchful, as he moved behind her, encircling her with his arms, cupping the left breast in his right hand and the right breast in his left. As he could see in the mirror, her brown eyes wandered uncertainly before closing. This wasn't what he wanted. Not if it meant passion.

"Lila, open your eyes," he whispered.

"I like it this way."

"I've got to talk to you." He shook her gently. "Of course I like making love to you, but . . ."

With a dexterous turn of the wrist, she unzipped his fly and had her hand inside his pants.

"Listen," he said, "why don't we stay up here tonight and talk? I'll tell the others you don't feel well. Tomorrow we can decide . . ." But when her fingers tightened, he felt a strange despair, along with the more predictable desire, and a malicious inner voice whispered, Fuck her and get it over with. Even after all that had happened, she'd fall easy as ripe fruit. With her, it was always the first time. The new beginning. Promise without fulfillment. Finally he knew—no, that was wrong, for he'd known it a long time, but only now could admit it—that although they might come together, they would come to nothing. Although they might go hand in hand, they'd arrive nowhere. In bed, of course, but really nowhere.

Yet he tried once more. "Lila, we have to talk."

"Not now."

He shook her harder. "Yes, now! For your own good, you've got to understand . . ."

"Same old story." Her eyelids rolled open. "I should have known better. You have the sex drive of a turtle."

"Maybe it's the company I keep." He released her with a shove, and in the grey room the only sound was of their angry breathing and of wet swimsuits being thrown into the bathroom sink.

       At the Balboa Club, Harry had a suite of rooms overlooking the south beach, the wharves, and Belvedere Island, which curved from the foggy sea like an ominous dorsal fin. While Harry helped the maid mix margaritas for Lila and the boys, Walker poured himself a tumbler of straight tequila and went out to the balcony, where the air was now much cooler. A steady wind off the water sent low clouds scudding inland, plunging and rolling, like the shrimp boats which were returning to the harbor, and in the west, where the sky had cleared in ragged patches, the darkness of night showed through. Tomorrow the sun would return, but to Walker it didn't matter. He'd be gone. Where, he didn't know. How, he didn't care. But he was leaving, he swore, and forced down a mouthful of tequila, which tasted like a spiny chunk of cactus. Bristling with strength and self-confidence, he went back inside, drunk from one shot.

Harry and Al sat on the sofa, bare feet propped on a marble-topped table, while Jim Guy and Lila, lounging in a love seat opposite them, had their feet on the other side. Lila's panties showed, Walker noticed as he flopped into a chair and took another swallow.

"Don't you want some salt and lime with that?" asked Harry, who looked as if he'd put on, along with his brightly flowered shirt, a new application of cream. His bald dome dazzled.

"Don't need it," said Walker, and at once, as the white fire forked like heat lightning through his chest, regretted that he had. He was acting like a fool, just as Jim Guy and Al had that day in El Refugio. Yet Jim Guy had gotten what he wanted.

Maybe a little drunken lucidity would help him, too. He had to make plans. There was an airport in Mazatlán. Tomorrow he'd buy a ticket to . . . Why not tonight?

Gagging down another mouthful, he felt the tequila work at him. Already his right leg was numb. It was really moving now, needling through his veins and into the marrow of his bones, claiming him a limb at a time, buffeting his brain and blurring his thoughts. Looking at Jim Guy and Lila on the love seat, he toyed with a fantasy he was Bogart-strong, Bogart-tough and independent. No strings on him. He'd shucked the blood-sucker. Better alone. No room for . . . Anyway, no car. Tomorrow he'd fly to . . . His mind slipped a cog.

"Well, I just don't believe that," said Harry. "You'll have to prove it to me. I know you're big, but . . ."

At the tattered edges of his brain Walker thought he heard mice gnawing.

" 'At's the truth," said Al. "I never lost one yet. You can ask Jim Guy." Blushing, he patted his auburn forelock into place.

Walker found a brimming tumbler of tequila on the arm of the chair. Jim Guy's work? And in his hand a bowl half filled with green mush. Had he vomited? He raised it to his nostrils. No, thank God. Guacamole. To coat his quaking belly, he spooned down a mouthful.

"I'm not going to let that claim go unchallenged," said Harry. "Let's step over to the table and see how strong you are."

At the dining table they sat opposite each other and clasped hands to arm-wrestle, but Harry appeared more interested in contact than competition. "Lemme get set." He wriggled his shoulders. "Okay, let her rip."

In a milli-second his hand hit the table.

"Whoa there! You didn't gimme a chance to get set. Let's try it again."

This time his arm went down even quicker, and when they switched to the left hand, he did no better. His knuckles thudded against the board with a resounding smack. "Damned if that don't beat all." He ran a hand over Al's shoulder and down his arm. "My Gawd, where'd you get all that gear? There must be some way to make money with it."

Al gave a modest shrug. "Heck, Harry, I . . ."

"Jim Guy, get over here and see what you can do."

"It'd be a waste of time. I've been trying for years, but never once come close to beating him."

Lila tested the strength of his bicep. "I bet you'd give him a good fight."

Setting aside the guacamole, Walker squared his shoulders, convinced in his drunkenness this was the moment he'd waited for.

"How about you?" Harry asked him. "Want to give it a try?"

"Don't mind if I do."

Lila laughed out loud, her scorn too great for words. But she had good reason to be bitter. Nobody had ever dumped her before. Yes, this was another delusion the tequila had wrought. That he'd put her down, and she was chewing her guts out.

Wearing a smile tight as a rubber mask, Walker pushed out of the chair and walked to the table with the stiffness of an automaton.

"Why don't you take off your shirts?" said Harry, anxious to see bare straining flesh.

"Don't reckon I need to," drawled Al, narrowing his grey eyes. He hadn't forgotten that day in El Refugio when the vortex of tequila had dragged him under, then spat him up smelling of vomit.

Walker pinched at his biceps. No feeling. Lost to liquor. A good sign. From what he'd seen, he knew that sober he stood no chance against Al. His hope rested on the power of a muddled mind over simian matter.

"Hope this won't cause a problem, but I'm a southpaw," he lied. "A time judge will have to declare the winner."

"Huh?" Already Al was befuddled. "What's he saying? Quit stalling."

"It's this way. First we'll use our right hands, and see how long it takes you to put me down. Then we'll go at it lefthanded, and see how long it takes me to beat you. After . . ."

"We'll see 'bout that!"

"After that we'll add up the total time of each man, and subtract the lower from the higher to find . . ."

"Okay, for Christ's sake, let's go."

"Don't rush me. I've got to prepare," said Walker, as Jim Guy and Lila came over to watch and Harry unbuckled his wristwatch and held it in the fat palm of his hand. In his loose-fitting sport shirt, with lamplight glittering on his greased skull, the man looked like a perverted Buddha. A deviate Dalai Lama.

Walker spat on his palms, vigorously rubbed it in, then, searching for any small advantage, took a shot of tequila which coiled like rigor mortis around his joints. To put him down, Al would have to break his arm.

"What is this crap?"

"I'm ready."

" 'Bout time."

The instant Harry said "Go!" he knew he'd lost with his right arm. Al bent it at once to a forty-five-degree angle, and Walker could do little more than play for precious time. The tequila had failed him miserably. The pain was intense, jutting like a hot wire from elbow to shoulder, then scooping down into his chest. As his arm was forced lower, it felt as if it were being used as a handle to pump up his guts.

Walker glanced up at Jim Guy, Lila, and Harry, all of whom were amazed. "The old right wing isn't what it used to be," he mumbled.

Enraged by this play to the grandstand, Al growled and bore down. Walker could feel the seat of his pants lifting off the chair, until, after a last wrenching pain, it ended.

"Fifty-one seconds," said Harry. "Not bad there, Walker."

"Did my best," he sighed, shaking his head as if he'd expected to do better. But, sipping the tequila, he hoped to soothe the pain that engulfed his whole right side.

Shaken, Al ripped off his shirt. The coppery hairs on his chest sparkled with perspiration.

"Anythin' wrong?" asked Jim Guy, rubbing his friend's neck.

"Ah'm awright. He surprised me. 'At's all."

Desperate for encouragement, Walker looked again to Lila, but found her face devoid of pity, love, or even surprise. Instead, her eyes were aflame with something like passion. A bright, hollow stare. Maybe in a twisted pride, a belief that they—not just Al and Walker, or Jim Guy and Harry, but all the men she'd met, or was ever likely to—were fighting for her.

Without a friend or ally, he belted down more tequila and settled in for his last stand.

When Al and he remained at ninety degrees for what felt like an hour, Walker knew he'd failed. Time was running out, but what was worse, when his arm had been forced to the painful pump-handle position, it seemed a ragged claw was dipping down into his rib cage. Cartilage popped, bones creaked, and muscles were strung so tight they almost hummed as Walker strained to hold his hand up and keep his stomach down. Something had to give.

"Fifty-three seconds," said Harry. "Al wins, but Walker gave him a rough battle."

"I don't play by no damned clock," hissed Al. "I always put my man down."

"Aaah rrraghh!" Walker begged for mercy. He wanted to quit, but couldn't. His arm wouldn't budge. Instead his stomach started to give way, bringing the taste of tequila, only slightly diluted by guacamole, to his lips.

Face red with anger, Al muttered, "Ah'm goin' to clean your plow, old buddy."

"Oooaahmmh." Suddenly—already beaten and three inches from total defeat—Walker lost everything. Breakfast, lunch, guacamole, and tequila exploded onto Al, Harry, Jim Guy, and Lila. Then like a curtain of doom the vomit fell over Walker, too, and he blacked out.

He woke to a vision of whiteness, as if his eyes had been iced over with falling snow. Flakes like stars stung his face. The pain, too, seemed white, and he wore it wrapped like brocade around his body. When he tried to rise, he slipped, and clunked his head against something hard and white. But it was porcelain, not ice. He was lying at the bottom of a bathtub, with pellets of shower water beating in his face.

Seizing the soap dish for support, he stood up and twisted the faucet shut. Silence throughout the apartment. Now that he was standing, the pain clung heavily to his flesh, and he felt he'd been pulled inside out like a threadbare pocket. All his raw nerves were shooting sparks. Where was Lila? That drove electricity through his veins. But vaulting out of the tub, he weakened and fell onto the toilet. What did it matter? Burying his head in his hands, he asked himself again, What did it matter where she was? Desperate to move, all he wanted was to get out of this apartment, out of the city, out of this country.

The hallway parquet squelched like a marsh under his soaked shoes, and rivulets of water spilled out of his hair, over his forehead, and into his eyes, but from where he stood behind the heart-shaped leaves of a potted philodendron, he could see both the living room and bedroom.

In the bedroom Al and Harry sat on a king-size mattress in their underwear—trim jockey shorts for Al, baggy boxers for Harry. Vomit-spattered clothing was piled in the corner. But neither of them seemed to mind the odor. By the gathering moisture in Harry's eyes, Walker judged it was about five minutes to blast-off. Yet who could say what Al might do. Bed down with, or tee off on, Harry. Strange desires lurked even in the hearts of good old boys.

In the living room Lila lay on the couch with her head in Jim Guy's lap. He wore only his undershorts, while she had on a yellow silk robe—Harry's, no doubt—which lent her body an oily sheen, sleek and lethal as a long bar of soap with old razor blades embedded in it.

Jim Guy ran his hand over her shoulders, down to where it was no longer her shoulder, and farther along the medial line of her belly to a point where one could safely say her belly ended. Having seen enough, Walker crept on seeping soles out the door and stumbled with slow, aching steps down the stairs.

Although the air was still cool, the clouds had cleared and the wind had died, creating the kind of dizzying, upside-down night seen only in the tropics. Mazatlán, despite its garlands of neon light, seemed ominously dark, a prisoner of impenetrable jungle, but overhead the sky spread out bright as a peacock's tail with pinpoint stars showing as eyes. The sea had worn itself smooth and flat as a silver tray, and the darkness was given over to insects and animals, to anything that crawled or scuttled, crept or squirmed, hooted or chirped. As Walker stumbled over the sidewalk, cockroaches and palmetto bugs, sand crabs and lizards skittered away from his feet and into their holes, and giant moths brushed his cheeks with powdered wings, sprinkling white dust.

At first he headed for the Freeman to pack his suitcase and catch a taxi to the airport. Tomorrow he'd be . . . But then, convinced there would be no planes leaving tonight, he wandered aimlessly through the deserted streets, searching for sobriety and a destination. Where would he be tomorrow? Somehow his mind couldn't make the leap from Mexico to San Francisco, but persisted, instead, in regressing, as it had that afternoon, to Cottage City. As he shivered, his feet continued to squeak on the cobblestones. The sound of footsteps on the boggy grass of a graveyard.

"Fucky-fucky, señor?" A wraithlike woman, shawled in shadows, plucked once at his crotch, then was gone down a narrow street, fluttering and insubstantial as one of the giant moths.

When the pain lost its grip and fell behind, Walker missed it, for it had protected him from thought. Now as he blundered on, teeth chattering and bath water sprinkling from his tangled hair as if from his own personal rain cloud, there was no way to escape memories of home and of warmth, which again seemed synonymous. He thought longingly of his room in the attic, sultry as the tropics, and the lampshade that spun off a gauzy green light, weaving for him there on Whittier Street a bamboo hut. The real Mexico.

"Fucky, fucky?" The woman stepped from the shadows again, probed with expert fingers, and drifted down an alley. Had she followed him? No. After all his walking, he'd circled back to the Balboa Club, where Jim Guy's black Chevy stood at the curb. Leaning against the rear fender, Walker was tired, but knew that on a night like this, sleep would elude him like the dollar bills which in nightmares slip as quicksilver through one's fingers. First he had to straighten the kinks in his brain, a slow process in the best of times, now made more difficult by atmospheric conditions—broad, empty skies outside, a corresponding emptiness within. He had to get in out of this endless night.

The top of the Chevy was up, but the doors had been left unlocked to save curious Mexicans the trouble of slicing through the canvas to see what might be under the seats. Dragging himself to the driver's side, Walker crawled in and lay down on the cold plastic seat. Just for a moment, to rest and decide what to do before Lila and the boys came out. Closing his eyes and holding his breath, he imagined himself a skater racing over thin ice. Gingerly, for reference, he thought of Cottage City, then dodged away from it to the days that had passed since he left, and finally tried to compel his mind into the future, toward California, San Francisco, his father. But his brain caught in a rut and pitched him headlong.

Why would he want to see his father? There was so little between them. The weak bond of a common last name. The hastily scrawled postcards which he sent every few months. What else? Tanya. But after a month with Lila, he couldn't bear to think about her, or art, mind expansion, or beauty.

Groaning, he sat up. Since he'd stopped moving, the pain had caught up with him, and along with a virulent tension, had sunk like rabid, mad dog teeth into his flesh. God, he knew this feeling, which had always taken hold of him when he couldn't make up his mind, or when there was nothing about which to make up his mind. When one narrow path opened before him. He had to go . . .

He let his head fall against the steering wheel. He couldn't go home. He was mad to consider it. After what he'd done—abandoned Daddy Dick to molder in the permanent midnight murk of the recreation room—Mom would . . .

Groaning again, he raised his head and recognized what a base delusion, what a sickening, self-serving, melodramatic lie this was. If he went back, his mother would take him in her arms and kiss him. He could always go back. Even if he'd murdered Daddy Dick with his own hands, mercilessly choking the life from his thick neck, she'd forgive him.

Home! It was the one place he could return, no matter how great his guilt or self-digust. He could always go back, because he could never really leave without carrying it around wherever he went.

Slowly the yoke of an unmade decision cracked and fell from his shoulders, and he knew he had to move. Not on foot over the winding, bug-littered street, but faster and much, much farther. Lifting a scrap of tin foil from the ashtray, he pressed it to the ignition wires and coaxed the engine to life. He was leaving. Going home—not because it was a better place, but because for him it was the only place. The spot where, even if the past was waiting to haunt him, a future was at least possible.

When the motor purred smoothly, he switched on the high beams and raced the cockroaches and sand crabs down Olas Atlas Street to the Freeman, then, after packing and checking out, quickly outdistanced them, leaving paradise and heading toward the States in Jim Guy Barker's mile-long Chevy.

230

Chapter *14*

Walker drove all night and half the next day, keeping himself awake with lukewarm Coca-Colas and cups of black coffee. But in Quaymas, afraid Jim Guy and Al—perhaps in Harry's coral-pink Cadillac—would overtake him, or that they had alerted the border patrol, or, even more, that he might talk himself out of going home if he didn't hurry, he abandoned the Chevy in the marketplace and took a taxi to the airport, where he reluctantly boarded a fat, ungainly craft with scorched silver wings and two small engines. When it had completed its ascent, Walker stared out at the barren waste of Mexico on one side, and the blue waste of the Bay of California on the other. Each gust of wind battered the fuselage and set his belly quaking, but he knew he wouldn't throw up again. He had no more to give. He'd been cleaned out, reduced to a hard essence.

Leaning back in the seat, he listened to the uneven drumming of the engines, which pounded on the dry pan of his brain a litany of insults to which, in his weariness, he could only nod in agreement. Son-of-a-bitch. Son-of-a-bitch. Stupid bastard. Stupid bastard. They jarred and throbbed, and seemed to grasp him by the collar and give him an impatient shake. Yes, he was a son-of-a-bitch and a bastard for wasting time on Lila Caine when a girl like Dede Clinton cared for him. Or used to. He hoped it wasn't too late.

Five hours later, from the airport in Phoenix, he dialed her number, and almost ill with tension, stood in the stifling phone booth waiting for her voice to inchworm its way through the circuit.

"Hello."

231

For an instant he couldn't speak. The word somehow brought to his mind the sight of her lips, full and smiling, and he thought if he were silent, he might feel them against his.

"Hello," she repeated.

"Dede, it's me. Walker."

Another silence, as her mind tried to shape itself around the words she hadn't expected to hear. "Oh, Walker, I . . . Oh, thank God. Where are you?"

"Phoenix."

"Walker, I . . ." She started to cry. "I thought you were dead. I thought I'd never hear from you again. I thought . . . I don't know what I thought. I've been so worried."

"I'm sorry. I didn't want you to worry."

"It's been horrible. You know, don't you, that your step-father is dead?"

"Yes, I know. I tried to call you before I left, but you weren't home. I got scared, and ran. But I'm coming back. Will you . . .?"

"Walker, wait a minute." She brought her voice under control. "I have to know something. Please don't lie. I love you and trust you. Did you . . .?"

She'd found out about Lila, Walker thought as her voice cracked.

"Did you kill him?" Dede blurted.

"What?" He nearly dropped the phone.

"Your stepfather. Did you do it? I have to know."

"Of course I didn't." He was trembling. "Does anyone think I did? Did Mom call the police?"

"No one called the police. No one has dared say anything. Nancy told everyone that you left Cottage City early to keep from being snowed in. Chip claimed he called the funeral parlor. But a few nights ago your mother admitted to me that she thought you'd done it—killed him—because of all the pain and suffering he'd caused her."

"That's absurd. I loved him. He . . ."

"Do you promise?"

"Yes. Look, I'll be home tomorrow and explain everything. Will you meet me at National Airport?"

"Of course, I'll . . ."

"But don't tell anyone I'm coming. I want to see you first."

"Can't I tell your mother? She's sick with worry."

"All right, tell her I called, but nothing else. I'll see you tomorrow morning at six-thirty A.M. TWA flight 213. And, Dede . . . I love you."

"I love you, too, Walker."

Flying to Dallas, he repeated what she'd said, trying to recapture Dede by remembering her words, but when darkness was drawn like a black shade over the thermopane window, the stewardess interrupted to serve him dinner on a plastic tray and ask him if he wanted a drink. He didn't dare. Shambling, weary, and derelict in dress, stained with sweat and dust, carrying the pungent spice of Mexico on his clothing, he staggered down the aisle to the lavatory, barely able to stand up. In the tiny bathroom he had to sit down to keep from weaving and missing the bowl. Ah, better. He leaned his head against the door. Would a flush fling urine onto the clouds? Maybe suck him out by the buttocks and tumble him bare-ass-over-end through space? God, he was tired. It seemed to him he had attained at last that state of complete stillness in body, mind, and soul which Lila had often spoken of. But he'd gained it through exhaustion rather than contemplation, by motion rather than meditation. After much travel, he was at peace and never wanted to move again.

Rap! Rap! Rap!

"Sir, are you all right?" asked the stewardess. "Shall I send someone in to help?"

Pulling up his pants, he opened the door and stumbled back to his seat.

On the jet from Dallas to Washington, Walker finally managed to sleep, but as they were landing the next morning, woke to that same vision of whiteness he'd had the last night in Mazatlán. Except this time the snow was real. As the plane dropped out of the clouds, he gripped the arm of his seat in fear at what he saw. The whole city, save for the slick brown river, was white. Piled deep in snow. Hadn't it melted since Thanksgiving? Or had it stayed to prick his conscience with frozen slivers? Beautiful, though. And in a higher sense, a type of poetic justice. No matter how much had happened to him, things here were the same.

In the terminal, seeing bright red and green decorations, he remembered it was nearly Christmas. The full catastrophe for his homecoming. Well, he'd bear that, too. Flowing passively in the noisy stream of people who jockeyed closer to the luggage counter, he avoided the sprigs of holly that had sprouted on everyone's lapel. Even at this early hour seasonal clichés dribbled out to compete with a weak Muzak background of carols, while college kids, home for the holidays, slung skis across their shoulders like lethal loads of lumber and shoved toward the conveyor belt to grapple for luggage. As he searched for his own suitcase, the butt of a ski cracked Walker in the head, and for a moment he saw stars before spying Dede in a navy-blue raincoat on the other side of the belt. She was in a state of mild panic, as if she might cry out, or even run.

"Dede, over here!" he called.

She gave a small wave of the hand.

Ducking under the conveyor belt, he carried her away from the crowd and leaned her against a marble pillar, but when he went to kiss her, he found her lips cold and unyielding as the stone.

"Walker, put me down," she whispered sternly.

He set her down, but kept his arms around her. "I'm so happy to see you. I . . ."

"Please, Walker, let me go." She wouldn't look him in the eye.

"I don't understand." His hands fell weakly from her shoulders. "Last night on the phone . . ."

"That was different. I was too excited to think."

Cupping her chin, he tried to raise her head. "Don't be this way. Dede. I feel bad enough already. I've missed you and I . . ."

"You say that every time."

"But you don't understand, I . . ."

She shook her head. "I don't want to talk about it. Not here."

Aching and empty, Walker retrieved his suitcase, and as they walked through the terminal that had become frighteningly quiet, the sound of their footsteps preceded them. Outside, there was the dry crunch of snow. The sound of the suitcase slapping his knee. The firm thump of a closing car door. "Dede, I . . ." he started, but his words were whipped away on the wind.

The Corvair coughed to life while Walker leaned over the hood to clear the windshield. Dede was slumped behind the wheel, her eyes still down. Then Walker got in, and as they waited for the feeble defroster to clear the inside of the windshield, he asked again, "What's wrong?"

"I'm tired."

"I am, too," he said quietly. "I haven't had much sleep in the last few nights, but . . ."

"After you called, I couldn't sleep, I was so excited you were coming back. For a minute I forgot how much it hurt when you left, and how much I worried when you didn't write. No one knew where you were or what had happened." At last she turned to him, her dark eyes full of pain and sorrow, but for once no tears. "Can't you understand how horrible it was? Your stepfather was dead and your mother was frantic with grief and worry, but you didn't even call. So it didn't take very long for my excitement to turn to anger. I kept asking myself how you could be so sure everyone would be waiting with open arms when you came back. I resent you for that. I . . ."

"When I left, I honestly didn't think I was ever coming back. I'm the one who found Daddy Dick at the bottom of the basement stairs, his skull crushed. He'd already turned cold. I . . . I fell apart. I know it's hard for you to understand, but I was afraid I'd be stuck. Trapped."

"Why did you come back? Just once, why in the hell don't you go away and stay?" Her voice was still flat, devoid of anger, or of any emotion, but it made the hair on the back of his head bristle.

"Look, if that's the way you feel, I can do it," he said angrily. "I'll get on the next plane out of here and I'll . . . I'll . . ."

"You'll what?" She refused to yield.

"Nothing." He shook his head. "I won't do anything. I'm tired, Dede." He took her hand, and this time she didn't draw it back. "I can't go on this way."

"Why not?" Her voice was dry, even if her hand wasn't.

"There's no place to go."

"That's silly. There . . ."

"No, not for me. I've run out of ground, out of energy, and out of desire, all at the same time. But I don't care. I . . ."

"So you came back to reliable little Dede?"

"No, goddammit! That's not the way it is."

"That's the way it sounds."

"What do you want me to say? That I love you? Okay, I do. You've always known that. That I've changed? Even if I said it, you wouldn't believe me. But I have. And it hasn't been easy. Not that I did it myself. It was done to me."

"What do you mean? What happened?"

"Everything."

"Where did you go?"

"Everywhere. I wound up in Mexico."

"Where's your car?"

"Wrecked. Gone. It rolled off a cliff."

"Oh no! I'm sorry, Walker."

"It doesn't matter. I'm through running. Now will you please take me home?"

"Is that where you want to go?"

"Yes."

Sliding closer, she said, "I'm sorry," and kissed him lightly on the lips. "We'd better go before we're snowbound."

"Do you want me to drive?"

"No, it'll give me something to do with my hands. They're shaking." Over roads sprinkled with sand and rock salt, she crossed the Potomac and made her way into Washington.

"Not much traffic," he said, once his pulse was quiet.

"It's Sunday."

"I haven't been keeping track."

Turning to him, she smiled. "You look awful, Walker, but you do have a suntan."

"I guess it wasn't a wasted trip after all."

"I told your mother you called. She's very excited, but worried. She really thinks you killed him."

"Please don't say that again. What I did to him is bad enough. How's Mom otherwise? Still at Oak Knoll?"

"No. She came out for the funeral and refused to go back. She's living with Nancy and Chip."

"Oh Jesus."

"They don't seem to mind. She's much better now. Quieter. More subdued. The funeral took a lot out of her. That, and your leaving. It was like shock treatment. Anyway, Doctor Wolter didn't think there'd be any harm in letting her stay with Nancy."

"And the house? What's become of it?"

"Nothing. It's empty. Nancy goes over once a week to clean,

but your mother seems afraid of it. She hasn't been back."

"I think I may be afraid of it, too."

They drove in silence then, as Dede kept the Corvair under careful control, leaning forward in the seat, both hands on the wheel. But she was so short her feet barely touched the pedals.

"How tall are you?" he asked, smiling.

"I tell everyone five-two, but don't ask me to prove it."

"Okay, I won't." He reached for her thigh, paused, but after hesitating, went ahead and squeezed it. "I have missed you."

On Rhode Island Avenue, as the day grew a shade brighter, snow continued falling. Falling on the rubble of vacant lots, on the charred ruins of last year's riot, and on the Negroes, some still red-eyed and half-bombed from the night before, who shaped up on street corners just as they did every working day. In the windows of houses hung plastic holly wreaths, strands of lights, and clusters of Dixie cups covered in aluminum foil to look like bells. At Shaw Junior High, a cardboard Santa Claus, warped by the snow and wind, swung like a corpse from the highest window.

Walker put a hand to the back of her neck.

"That feels good," she said.

"When we get out of town, why don't we stop at a motel?"

In a nervous spasm, she touched the brake, then the accelerator, rattling their teeth with the sudden change of speed. "You don't bother with small talk any more, do you?" But she didn't appear to be angry.

"I want to be alone with you."

"You are alone with me."

"Not alone enough."

At a red light, she took his gloved hand in her lap and wistfully asked, "What are we going to do about us, Walker?"

"We're going to get us into bed."

"Do you think that's the answer? Maybe it is. We always wind up there." Removing the glove, she kissed his palm.

"It may not be the answer, but it's a start."

"A start?"

He didn't mention the motel again.

When they got to Cottage City, the snow was coming down in breadlike chunks that spun, crisscrossed, and sometimes collided to shatter into smaller flakes. Not one was lost; not one failed to find a tree branch, or rooftop, or space of frozen earth to cling to. Only the high iron bars fencing Fort McHenry Cemetery retained their true color and shape—black, sharp, and spearlike. Beyond them the clock of flowers was covered, and the tombstones, set in unerring rows, looked like loaves of high-rising bread.

"Is he there?" Walker asked.

"Yes. But way in the back, off the road."

"Is there a stone?"

"They ordered one with the money you sent." Then, after a pause, "Because of all the whining I did, I never told you how sorry I am. I didn't know you were so close to him."

"He was like a father to me."

"Father? It's funny. No one mentioned that word at the funeral. Not even Nancy or Ben. And what's even stranger, everybody talked about you instead of him. I had a long talk with the parish priest. He told me you'll go far as soon as you find yourself."

"Well, I went as far as I could, but as for finding myself, I don't guess I was really lost. Here I am, right where I've always been, home in Cottage City. It doesn't look different."

But it did. Over the potato-chip factory, fastened to the highest chimney, was a picture of Santa pulling a sled full of chips and Fritos. Farther on, in front of the firehouse, stood a life-size Nativity tableau jigsawed out of plywood, and although someone had crayoned red nipples on the Blessed Mother, the scene reminded Walker of his childhood, of the time before he knew, or thought he knew, how bad Cottage City was. Back then, he had stared with wondering eyes at the silver star which capped the Peace Cross monument and thought how beautiful the town was. Now, despite the warehouses, billboards, gas stations, and bars, it looked that way again. Whittier Street, buried beneath seven inches of snow, could have been the setting for a Christmas card.

But sight of the asbestos-shingled house sent a frozen stab, like an icicle, through his heart. With the venetian blinds closed and no wreaths or lights in the windows, the place looked sad and abandoned, ghostly. The pickup truck in the driveway carried on its bed a hill of snow.

"Will you come in with me?"

Dede glanced warily at the front door. "I don't know whether I should. I've never been in your house before, and it doesn't seem right to . . ."

"Please, come in and have a cup of coffee. I don't want you driving to Beltsville in this weather."

"Are you going to stay here tonight?" she asked, getting out of the Corvair.

"I'd planned to," he said matter-of-factly, even though thought of it unnerved him.

"Wouldn't you rather stay in Beltsville?"

"Well, let me at least go in and get some clean clothes. Come with me. Hold my hand." He tried to make a joke of it.

"Walker, I'm scared."

"That's silly. Daddy Dick was never frightening in life and he shouldn't be now." After staggering through ankle-deep snow, they stopped on the porch, and he whispered, "Listen."

Her tiny hand squeezed tighter. "What?"

Moaning through the bare treetops, the wind sent flakes of snow hissing against the blind windows.

"Nothing. Absolute nothing. This is the best time in Cottage City."

Once he'd unlocked it, the door swung open, releasing from the hallway a warm, odorless sigh.

"The heat's on," he said heartily, and listened to a faint echo. "Let's get inside."

As they stamped their feet loudly on a mat in the hall, Walker said, "That should scare away the ghosts."

"You've been lying to me all these years," said Dede, going into the living room, where the furniture had been draped in old sheets. "It's not so bad. As a matter of fact, with a little work, it could be quite homey."

"You must be kidding."

"Well, it is a little dingy. It would need paint."

"The kitchen's this way." He nudged her ahead of him, giving the recreation-room door wide berth. "There should be instant coffee in the cabinet. Yes, here it is."

"I'll do it."

"I wonder what happened to the roaches while I was gone? They must have starved."

"They probably moved next door to your neighbors."

"Let's hope so. They deserve each other."

Laughing, she took off her raincoat to show the red knit dress she was wearing.

"New?"

"Yes. A Christmas present to myself." She laughed again for no reason, and he joined her, as if to fill the hollow corners of the house and put an end to the echoes.

While folding his coat over a chair, he noticed on the table a postcard and a letter addressed to him. The card, from his father, pictured the Golden Gate Bridge, strung like a web across the sunset with the beautiful fixity of a child's dream. But the message was nightmarishly gruff.

Matt,

Where are you? Your grandmother is very upset and irritated, and Tanya and I have been unable to make any plans, because we're unsure when you'll be arriving—if you're still coming. I send this to Cottage City on the slim chance someone will have the courtesy to forward it to you. Actually it wouldn't surprise me to hear you never left home, or have gone back. By this time nothing would surprise me, except maybe if you started to act like a man. Have the decency to let me and your grandmother know what you're doing. Tanya joins me in Season's Greetings.

M & T

Seeing torn scraps of the card drift like snowflakes into the wastebasket, Dede, who was bringing a pot of water to boil, asked, "What's that?"

"A bit of paternal advice."

The letter, postmarked Boca Raton, was from Grandmother Hawley, or to be more exact, Jordan Oliver.

Dear Matt:

Since we have not heard from you in a month, nor have you arrived yet in San Francisco, we can only conjecture as to your intentions, but it seems clear that you have broken the promise you made to your grandmother. Therefore, she has asked me to make you the following proposal, which should be considered firm, final, and beyond the possibility of future change. Although, to repeat, you have ignored the terms of the verbal contract made with your grandmother in my presence on November 23, 1968, you may keep the five thousand dollars given to you on that date. An additional sum in the amount of five thousand dollars will be deposited in an account opened in your name in Washington, if you will agree in a written statement, witnessed and sealed by a notary public, to change your surname. There is no stipulation as to the name you must assume, so long as Hawley is no longer used by you, or by your future progeny. My colleague in Washington, John White Scarbutt, will assist you, *gratis,* with any legal difficulties which may arise.

If you choose not to acept the offer, that is, of course, your prerogative, but you should be advised that I have recently helped your grandmother write a new will in which, dear Matt, you are not mentioned. It should be understood that this will not change, no matter what you decide to do. I would encourage you, therefore, to make a mature and reasonable decision. Please reply as . . .

Slowly he tore the letter to confetti, let it, too, fall into the wastebasket, and went over to the table where Dede had set his coffee.

"Are you sure nothing's wrong? You look troubled."

Stirring, and watching cream lace the cup, he quietly asked, "Would you marry me if it meant your name would be Murdock?"

"What?" Choking on a mouthful of coffee, she dropped her spoon.

He patted her on the back as she coughed to clear her throat. "My grandmother wants me to change my name. I've never much liked Hawley anyway, so I thought . . ."

"The first part, Walker. I want to hear it again."

"Would you marry me?"

Suddenly she shook her head. "Don't say it again. Not now. Not until you've had some sleep and have been at home at least a week. And have seen your mother," she added.

"I mean it. Why are you crying? Aren't you happy?" With his thumb he blotted a tear from her cheek.

"It's not fair. You caught me with my guard down." She blinked back the tears. "But I've changed my mind. You can ask again if you want."

"Would you marry me if it meant your name would be Murdock?"

"Yes. Yes, I would." She kissed him. "But why does your grandmother want you to change your name?"

"She's disgusted with me and doesn't think I deserve to be a Hawley."

"She'll change her mind."

"Not when she finds out I've come back to Cottage City."

"Do you care?"

"Not a bit."

"In that case I'd gladly be a Murdock."

Pushing back from the table, she finished her coffee and asked, "Would you like to show me the rest of the house? I want to see your room."

"I don't think you'd . . ."

"Yes, I would." She took his hand.

At the top of the creaking steps, she turned, threw her arms around his neck, and pulling herself off the ground with surprising strength, ran her tongue lightly around his lips. Leaning against the newel post, he cupped her buttocks and pressed against her.

"Oh, Walker," the words brushed like feathers against his neck, "I'm so happy you came back. I didn't think I'd ever see you again, but I swore this time I wouldn't chase you."

"You don't have to chase. Here I am."

She kissed him again.

"Why don't we skip the rest of the tour and go up to my room?"

With Dede in the lead, and Walker's hands on her hips, they mounted the narrow stairwell to the attic.

"I like it. It's warm and cozy," she said, looking out the window.

Walker turned on the lamp. "Actually, it's a thatched hut beside the water. Mexico."

Together they fell onto the cot, Dede's small body molding itself to his touch like the contours of a dream. But then she pulled away from him and stood up. "Wait. I want to show you the rest of the Christmas gift I got myself."

Stepping out of her shoes, she unzipped the dress, let it and the slip fall to the floor, and stood before him in a red bra and matching panties. Shivering, she asked, "Do you like them?"

"I love them." Reaching out, he brought her close and kissed her navel. "Now, if you were going to take them off, which would you do first?"

Hesitantly she slipped her thumbs under the elastic waistband.

"You'll never learn," he said, and lifting her onto the cot, removed her underwear. "Here's another present."

But she was so small, so fragile, he hesitated until she said, "I won't break," and pulled him toward her.

"I may myself."

He didn't. Despite his fatigue, he coaxed her along, the two of them working as one, while outside snow fell on Cottage City and on the past. At last the tender force of Dede's climax brought Walker to an orgasm which carried him off to sleep.

When they woke late that afternoon, Dede leaned close to his ear, and of all the things she might have said, whispered, "Are you going to church?"

"It's Sunday, isn't it? I'd forgotten." He rolled onto his back. "I guess I'll go to evening Mass."

Propped on an elbow, she somehow managed to look very serious even as she tickled his ear with her finger. "Will you take Communion?"

Since he knew what was coming—they'd been through this so many times before—he tried to avoid her unblinking brown eyes, yet felt compelled to tell her the truth. "No."

"Do you think what we did was wrong? Was it a sin?"

"Yes, it was an evil, foul sin." Laughing, he pulled her face to his chest. "And that's why I did it. To corrupt you."

Dede raised her head. "Be serious, Walker. I want to understand this. You never seem to like going to church, but you always go."

"Not always."

"Almost always. And I bet you think it's wrong to sleep with me, and yet you always do it."

"As often as I can."

Climbing onto his chest, she gave a bounce to it and the creaking cot. "Don't put me off with flip answers. I'm not going to let you up until you tell me why you act the way you do."

"We may be here forever—which wouldn't bother me—since I don't know myself. I guess I never liked church because it reminded me of frightening things. Death and punishment when I was a kid, then, later on, boredom and being trapped in a place like Cottage City. I believed in God, but religion seemed like another thing that would hold me back. I was afraid I'd wind up like Mom and Daddy Dick."

"Aren't you afraid any more?"

"Oh yes. More than ever."

"Walker, that sounds so crazy and depressing. Religion is supposed to make you happy. If it doesn't, why bother? Why not forget it and . . . ?"

"Because it's there, whether it makes you happy or not. Telling me to forget it is like telling Mom to forget she's crazy. In the end, forgetting it doesn't change things, and it doesn't make you happy either. I know, I've tried. So I go to church." He patted her bare flank. "Let me get up and dress."

Leaning down to give him a kiss, she said, "I think I'll go with you. The pastor won't mind having a wicked Methodist in the congregation, will he?"

"Not at all."

When they'd dressed and gone outside, snow was still falling, but in small, fine flakes that had drifted up and over the fenders of the Corvair.

"Do you think we'll make it?" she asked. "I don't even have snow tires."

"We can walk. It's not far."

"That sounds like fun." She took his hand, and they started up Whittier, walking in the middle of the street where the snow had been packed down. It was easily as quiet as it had been that morning. Perhaps more so, for the wind had died, leaving its scalloped traces to fill slowly with tiny transparent flakes. Somewhere behind them a rotten limb broke and fell with a whoosh!, a sound soft and muted as the rustle of silk. Then silence enveloped them again.

Even Bladensburg Road was empty of traffic, and its deep ruts ran like furrows of plowed earth toward Washington. Ears on the alert, expecting to hear a tractor trailer bear down on them with a loud blast from its horn, Walker and Dede stepped into the widest rut and stumbled on, still hand in hand, too breathless and light-headed to talk. Through stinging eyes squinted against the snow, they saw the Christmas lights of Cottage City come on at five o'clock to compete with the perennial neon of Pincus' Tavern, the Dixie Pig, Jerry's Hot Dog Stand, and the Rustic Cabins. Although in the past he'd often laughed at this gaudy seasonal stand-off, comparing it to the Cancer Society's anti-cigarette ads set back to back with Salem commercials, tonight, maybe because he couldn't see clearly to start with, or because Dede was beside him, Walker thought it looked almost beautiful.

They got to St. James after Mass had started, and slipped into the fourth row from the rear, but since in front of them there was only one old couple who knelt in the first pew, Walker felt uneasy and exposed, as if he and Dede stood in the vanguard of some unstated but sullen effrontery to Father Relihan. Behind them, in crowded, nervous ranks, more than a hundred people withdrew as far from the altar as they could go and still be in church. The last pew was crowded, and so was the aisle behind it, and even the distant reaches of the vestibule. Farthest back, leaning against the wall, was a weary brigade of men whose assignment or punishment was to support with their slumped shoulders the cold concrete stones. During the sermon, when Father Relihan exhorted them to come forward to join the Mystical Body, raise their voices in song, and participate in the bloodless Calvary, they didn't budge, and at Communion only the old couple in the first pew received.

It was five-fifteen Mass, the Alka-Seltzer Mass, as the priests called it among themselves. But to Walker it was a perfect emblem of his own ambivalent religious feelings, and he thought the other people, in reluctant attendance like him, were the best Catholics. True, even if weak and confused, believers. For the first time he felt with them a sense of kinship, of community. Perhaps they weren't parts of the Spiritual Body, but they were limb, and shank, and torso of a very tangible force Walker could respond to. For them, nothing was easy. No prayer was sufficient to calm their fears, doubts, and guilt. No threat of perdition was worse than the strange forces that drove them. And yet they returned every week, shuffled back into church, mumbled along with the priest, coughed, sniffed, wiggled the toes in their wet shoes, and after making a last, hasty sign of the cross, slunk out the same way they'd come. Weary, hesitant, bewildered.

Seeing them, Walker recognized himself for what he might be. The necessary witness of their endurance. The one person among them gifted with just enough perception to see them and this place, and know them for what they were. To act as a silent advocate for these people and for all those like them, for the motherless and misbegotten, for the fearful, the fuck-ups, the failures, for those who measured their lives in terms of things missed, things lost—wallets, bus tokens, opportunities, youth, love, but never that last spark of hope.

As Father Relihan said in his sermon, faith is a paradox, a blind leap into darkness. It's God taking on a human form, the King of Kings born in a stable, or a Virgin giving birth. In his own way, everyone in St. James would have agreed. For the people backed against the wall, the paradox was that, half-convinced religion had nothing to do with their lives, they kept coming to church.

To Walker, he was his own paradox, standing there next to Dede, steeped in mortal sin, yet feeling a sudden upsurge of devotion, love, and understanding at the very moment he should have been consumed with guilt.

When Mass was over, and they'd filed outside, the snow had stopped, but the wind had picked up again and was driving dry powder in great white puffs down Bladensburg Road.

"Brrr," said Dede as they set out toward home, and hunching her shoulders, she put a hand in the pocket of Walker's raincoat. "Hey, what's this?"

"What?"

From the pocket she pulled a dozen sheets of paper. "They look like pages from a book, but I can't read them in this light. Wait till we get under a streetlamp."

"Let me have them," he said, realizing what they were, and took them from her, rather roughly, then set the pages loose on the wind. They flew out like moths toward the light, but were crumpled before they reached it. Tumbling wildly with the drifting snow, they finally dispersed into the white haze which

246

glowed like cold cosmic dust around the immense star on top of the Peace Cross.

"What was it?"

"My story. A copy of 'Drowning Voices.'"

"Why did you throw it away?"

"I wanted to see how far it would fly."

Dede didn't speak again until they were on Whittier Street, within sight of the house. "Will we stay here tonight?"

He nodded.

"Walker, what's wrong? You're crying."

"It's the wind," he lied as a few tears fell from his face onto her hand.

"No, it's not. I can tell."

"It's Daddy Dick," he said, and with Dede holding his hand, started again for the house.

ABOUT THE AUTHOR

*Michael Mewshaw was born in Washington, D. C., in 1943,
and raised in the suburbs of that city. After graduating
from the University of Maryland, Mr. Mewshaw spent a year
and a half in France and England on a Fulbright Fellowship
in creative writing. He returned to the United States
to earn his Ph.D. at the University of Virginia and
now lives with his wife in Massachusetts, where he
teaches English at the University of Massachusetts.*